A FAR COUNTRY

DANIEL MASON is the author of *The Piano Tuner*.
This is his second novel. He currently lives in California.

Praise for A FAR COUNTRY

'Mason is a superb storyteller. He inhabits Isabel's mind with
fine sensitivity, and cleverly uses his imaginary setting to write
dauntless, timeless love and loyalty'   *— The Times*

'Everything is understood viscerally: by sight, touch, smell
and [Isabel's] intuition. In attempting to express this, Mason
sets himself a tough challenge. He pulls it off impressively,
narrating the story within the limitations of Isabel's own
terms while at the same time managing to produce extremely
vivid and evocative prose. The main concern of this novel,
with its uncluttered plot and gratifying ending, is not to
highlight the brutalities of the developing world; at first,
Isabel doesn't even realise she is living in poverty. Instead,
Mason explores the ways in which modernity can complicate
traditional rural lives and create isolation'   *— Observer*

'Full of colour, immediacy and powerful imagery, this is
remarkable, beautifully crafted story by the author of the
hugely successful *The Piano Tuner*' — Book of the Month, *Choice*

A FAR COUNTRY

Daniel Mason

PICADOR

First published 2007 by Alfred A. Knopf, a division of Random House, Inc., New York,
and in Canada by Random House of Canada Limited, Toronto

First published in Great Britain 2007 by Picador

First published in paperback 2007 by Picador

This edition first published 2008 by Picador
an imprint of Pan Macmillan Ltd
Pan Macmillan, 20 New Wharf Road, London N1 9RR
Basingstoke and Oxford
Associated companies throughout the world
www.panmacmillan.com

ISBN 978-0-330-49270-6

This is a work of fiction. Names, characters, places and incidents either are the product of
the author's imagination or are used fictitiously. Any resemblance to actual persons,
living or dead, events or locales is entirely coincidental.

Some quotations in this book come from the following sources:
Osman Lins, *Retable of Saint Joana Carolina*; João Cabral de Melo Neto, *Morte e Vida Severina*;
Plutarch, *Life of Caius Marcius Coriolanus*.

The author wishes to express his gratitude to the Santa Maddalena Foundation and the
Townsend Center for the Humanities at UC Berkeley for their support during the writing of this book.

1 3 5 7 9 8 6 4 2

A CIP catalogue record for this book is available from
the British Library.

Printed and bound in Great Briatin by
Mackays of Chatham plc, Chatham, Kent

Visit www.picador.com to read more about all our books
and to buy them. You will also find features, author interviews and
news of any author events, and you can sign up for e-newsletters
so that you're always first to hear about our new releases.

For my parents

Even so, there were times I felt uneasy when I looked at her. A serenity came from within her, like the one we see in the images of saints, the coarsest ones.

Osman Lins
Retable of Saint Joana Carolina

In the valley of the village they would one day name Saint Michael in the Cane, the men and women waited, turning the November soil and watching the sky.

Clouds came, following the empty riverbeds on long solitary treks from the coast.

Sometimes it rained. Little green leaves unfurled from the dry branches, and a soft grass bloomed on the floor of the thorn scrub they called the white forest because it was too poor for color. The men and women watched the sky distrustfully then. Sometimes the rain fell so close they could smell it, but if it didn't fall again in that corner of earth, the leaves turned brown and rattled in the wind. That could kill a field, they said: a single rain and then empty skies. It raised your hopes, the land's hopes. They called it green drought and swore at it under their breath. Rain is like a man, said the women, It flatters you with sweet gifts, but it is worse than nothing if it doesn't stay.

When the rains didn't come again, the first plants to die were the grasses. Then the thorn brittled and the cactus grayed. In December, on the eve of Saint Lucy's Day, they set out six fragments of salt to divine for drought, and in the morning they counted how many had melted away and how many remained.

Finally, when the earth grew so hot that any rain would only steam back into the sky, they began to get ready. They called it the retreat, as if to settle the backlands was a foolish and unnatural thing in the first place. Most had seen drought before and knew too well the rituals of flight and uncertain return. In the dry fields, they clanged spades against the stone and combed the earth for fragments of manioc. They made calculations, checking their stores of salted meat and the levels of their wells.

As the days passed, they watched the sky, pinning their hopes on distant clouds that vanished suddenly as if bewitched. They broke fragments of dirt from the ground, caressed and crumbled them between their fingers, rolled the warm silt along the dry calluses of their thumbs, tasted it, talked to it. Coaxed, apologized, pleaded. Once a newspaperman from the coast came and wrote: *The sharecroppers know the texture of the land better than they know their own faces.* When the story was read aloud in the drought camps, an old man laughed, Of course! I was born there, I'm too poor for a looking glass, and when was there ever enough water for a still pool?

At dusk, they sat outside their homes and listened to the dry creaking of the thorn. They counted the days since they had last seen the orange armadillos, the hawk that nested in the tall drinking-tree, the night mice that made skittering pilgrimages across the bare yard. They drew thick mud from the wells, pressed and twisted it in handkerchiefs, sucked it or threw it to the goats. The goats ate the greenest plants first: the jujubes, then the delicate pinnae of the mimosas, then the palm cactus, crushing the spines with their leathery tongues. When they had stripped the lowest branches clear, the animals stood on their hind legs and walked about like they were men. Flocks of birds blackened the sky, fleeing for the coast.

In town, they met at night and talked about when they would leave. The first to go were usually those who had seen drought before, who knew the horror of retreating at the last hour, with the last-goats and the last-flour and the last-hardtack burning in their mouths. Others wanted to go but waited, remembering the long march, the hunger, the drought camps and the cholera, the barren trails where they buried children with their eyes open so they wouldn't get lost on the way to heaven.

Others held out angrily, said, *This is mine,* and stamped their feet on the packed earth. They were the last to leave and the first to return. They were also the most likely to survive, as if they had the gift of estivation: drying up, slowing, sleeping for days, rising only to take little sips of what they could steal from the wells. Like the resurrection plants, with stems like rope and black-burnt leaves, blooming again at the first sign of rain.

They watched the sky and pinned their hopes on wisps of clouds stretching languidly across the blue. They shuttered windows and covered the wells. They watched neighbors leave and listened to rumors of where the government had set up way stations, and where there was disease. They killed the bone-thin zebu cows and then the goats, the animals arching weakly away from the dull blades of the knives. The meat of these last-goats was stringy and dry; in silty water, the women made stews from the guts and broth from the hoofs and tendons. They left the healthiest ones for the long march. In the hills, they searched for the last drinking-trees, held their bird-pecked fruit, ate their withered leaves and chewed their tubers until the sweet alkaline juice numbed their mouths. Slowly, the great trees began to die, their roots torn up, their leaves scratching at the dust as the wind swirled them away.

They watched the sky and pinned their hopes on the empty blue of it. Hadn't they heard stories of rain falling from cloudless skies, last-minute interventions by Saint Joseph or Saint Barbara? What of thorn ghosts who could stream tassels of water from the bean trees or open fountains from the cracks in the empty riverbeds? They began to leave candles at the crossroads and sprinkle cane wine on the lips of their patron saints. They worshipped in tiny chapels filled with carved wooden feet and heads left long ago to pay for wishes granted. While they waited for answers, they rolled their earthen bowls into blankets and tied them with twine. They piled these along with their children onto carts and backs of donkeys with weak knees and dry mouths. The poorer ones carried their blankets on their backs and their children in their arms. Half-empty gourds of water sloshed about their necks.

They watched the sky and finally cursed it, cursed the clouds and the absence of the clouds, the laziness of the clouds, the immoderation of the clouds that refused to leave the coast with its plump women and rich black soil. They rolled their icons of Saint Joseph into the blankets alongside the bowls. They recited invocations and slipped the scripts into twig-thin scapulars around their necks. They chewed their last meals slowly, waiting for each dry lump of manioc to dissolve as if it were the viaticum.

They spent their final nights at home. These were restless nights, and every one of them dreamed of the dust storms. This, they said, meant it was time to go, when the dreams turned dry and the clouds stayed away even in the night. They woke the children before dawn and set out while it was still cool. They calculated how far it was to the coast and how much water remained.

When they spoke of those hours, they said, *We passed hunger.* As if it were a place, an outpost on a lonely road. Other times, they said, *Hunger passed through here.* As if something alive, a pale hoofed creature, who tore through on bristling haunches or ambled out of the white forest with a worn suit and a broken face, a monster or a devil.

Isabel was three when she left and four when she came home, and so her memory was only a child's memory, made of smells and light and the uneven surface of the road. What she remembered was this: the hot taste of the charqui her aunt pushed into her cheek with a dirty thumb when she cried; the difference in the warmth of her mother's body and the radiating heat of the ground; her father's hands, pink-burned and black with the grease of the engine.

She remembered the sky, too, and how she hated it with a child's hate. Her father's hands were pink-burned because the engine seized constantly and the men were too anxious to let the radiator cool. They had been lucky to find a ride on a flatbed and wouldn't be as lucky on the journey home.

What she remembered of the drought camps was: the dark shade of a government tent, the chlorinated smell of the water, novenas of soft sad songs, the sting of vaccination needles, a yellow dog that came and nosed her hammock until someone kicked it away.

She couldn't recall the trip home and wondered if it was because she was sick or too tired. They had purchased a spavined horse and a dray from a family that decided to stay on the coast. They rode until a wheel split east of Blackwater. Since there were no nails, they unlatched the horse and loaded it with their bags. The path was filled with families returning to the backlands. Later, she would imagine the camps strung out on the long roads like seeds on a rosary, but she didn't know if this memory was her own or from someone who held her.

For the next three years in Saint Michael, the rains came, the white forest blossomed in patches of olive green and light maroon. Isabel grew up playing with her brother Isaias and with her cousins. When she was older, it was easy to remember herself as one of the tiny girls with thin legs and swollen bellies. Her aunt once teased, *Like little wild animals.* She had no birth certificate, and no vaccination card despite the needles she endured in the camps. She was five when she first stood before a mirror, advancing suspiciously toward the new child with dirt-bannered cheeks and translucent lashes. Until she was baptized by a traveling priest, there was no document to say she was alive. On that day, she fought the soft hand that tried to steady her and brushed tears and well water from her eyes with the heel of her palm. The cursive loops of her name were inscribed in the same church ledger that cradled the name of her mother.

Growing up, she played all day in the dusty plaza before the whitewashed houses and the church. There was an empty fountain built during optimistic times, and a statue that had long lost all its features to the wind and dust storms. There was no running water in Saint Michael. Some said the statue was the governor, and others said it was a great bandit. The old men said that it had been salvaged from the road to the coast. At Carnival, it wore a hat.

When she was old enough, she attended a one-room schoolhouse at the edge of town. There were twenty or forty children, depending on the season. In the evenings, she walked home alone, or her brother went to fetch her.

They lived in a small house on the plaza. Four hammocks hung in one of the rooms. In the second was a worn sofa, where a visitor slept if there wasn't space to string another hammock. The walls stopped short of the underbelly of the roof. Flower-print sheets hung in the doorways. Spots of light twinkled in the chinks between the roof tiles and speckled her arms. There was a little wooden table with an altar for the Virgin and a half-dozen photos perched at uneven intervals on the walls. Above the couch someone had written, in charcoal, ROBERT S. + MARIA. It was surrounded by a heart, and had been there for as long as she could remember. She didn't know who they were. Outside, the door was chalk-marked "7" by a census taker. Then the "7" had been crossed out and rewritten "4."

On the other side of the sofa was a kitchen. There was a small raised hearth with an iron trivet and an earthen jar for water. They kept the provisions in a wooden cabinet to hide them from the flies. The table was surrounded by four stools, which her father had carpentered himself. If visitors came and there weren't enough plates, the children waited and watched until the meal was finished before taking their places at the table.

The back door opened into the thorn scrub, where a path zigzagged through the brush and didn't stop until the mountains. Drying clothes flapped on the branches. Goatskin chaps with hair on the outside hung on the wall, but they were brittle and hadn't been worn since a murrain killed most of the cattle. Outside in the center of the main square was a single telephone, installed by the family of the state phone company when one of its sons was running for governor. The token collector never came, so someone pried open the collection box. From then on, calls were free: the line engaged, the coin dropped out into the caller's hand. A single token sat atop the phone.

In the four hammocks slept Isabel, her brother, her mother and her father, in that order toward the door. They slept so close that they bumped one another when they moved.

Her mother tended the house and a small garden of manioc. A spring ran near Saint Michael, and when the earth wasn't so dry that it took all the water before it reached the surface, she tended a mango tree and a copse of banana trees as well. She had studied at a Marist school on the road to the coast and could read, but Isabel's father didn't know the letters. During the season, he cut sugarcane in the fields that grew along the distant stretches of the spring. Isabel would remember him from this time as a quiet unshaven man who rose long before dawn to eat cornmeal and leftover scraps of salted beef, refried until the strands of gristle curled up like pieces of thread.

Watching him, she learned that the natural state of a person is silence, that speaking only stirs up problems where there weren't problems before.

Her father had sunburned skin and pale green eyes. Her mother's skin was dark, and when she wore her oldest skirts, Isabel could lose her on the road at night.

When it wasn't cane season, her father found work with the construction companies, grading roads or laying pipe, at times going as far as the coast for projects in the state capital. In the cluster of houses about the square also lived her mother's mother and father, her mother's sister, the children of her mother's sister, her grandmother's sister and her children and grandchildren, and dozens of other cousins by blood and by marriage.

On the thresholds of the houses they tossed clay marbles and played jacks with goat knuckles, serrying them in little legions. When they grew tired of the knuckles, they played with the shadows of the knuckles, crouching creatures that unfurled themselves as the sun went down. At dusk, they abandoned them and swarmed the square like a wasps' nest disturbed.

Once, she had three brothers and a sister. The oldest was a young man by the time she was born, with a good job on a bus line. Her sister married a man she met in the drought camps at age fifteen, and returned with him to his home. Since then, she had come to Saint Michael once, with a baby.

They had lost the youngest brother to cholera in the camps. Isabel remembered him only from a photograph taken by an aid worker: a small boy who stood apart from the family, as if he were already getting ready to leave. She thought of this when she heard an old woman say that children who die young know it before anyone else; they behave differently, as if they have already been back and forth to the place they are going. But she always had known what would happen to him, long before she heard the old woman speak.

People said that she and her middle brother Isaias were

close because they had grown up alone together, but she knew that it began even earlier, before that first retreat. There were very few photos of her family from that time. No one in Saint Michael had a camera. The photos were taken either by a cousin who lived in the state capital or by itinerant photographers, who appeared, like the color green, in the years of rain. They lined up families against the white wall of the church and returned with the prints months later, led house to house by a crowd of children.

In the photos, Isaias and Isabel were always together: a smiling child proudly carrying a baby; a boy dangling a beribboned child upside down during the winter festivals; a young man squashing his nose against a little girl's cheek as she stood on a chair in a borrowed flower girl's dress; the pair of them at night, at the edge of the cobbled square, Isaias with a smile and Isabel wide-eyed, her lips half parted in surprise, her hand raised slightly in the air, as if blindly reaching for him the moment the flash went off. Even in a formal family photograph taken before the first drought, while everyone was solemn, staring at the camera, she was looking at Isaias, a gaze that she recognized in the old women before the statues of the saints. And Isaias, age nine then, looking back.

Once, after a summer carrying crates at the market in Prince Leopold, he treated her to a photograph at a traveling fair. They stood on stools and stuck their heads through holes in a wooden board. There was a painted dress with leg-of-mutton sleeves, a suit, a steamship and the words GONE TO 'FRISCO. It was the first time she'd heard of the sea. In the photograph, her yellow-tinged curls poked out of the hole and fell alongside the black mane of the painted woman. Isaias looked earnest, his jaw set and his lips pinched defiantly. They looked eerily similar, with the same skin, the same color hair, the same light blue eyes that ran through her family like a jagged vein through a stone. Behind the set, he held his back straight and his hands on his hips.

They said that he took after his grandfather Boniface, a thin man who wore a watch on each wrist, donned a stained white suit despite the heat, and spent the market days pining for the return of the New State with two other eccentrics and a set of dominos. Boniface played fiddle, and in his youth he had made a name for himself. At a time when schooling was a whim of the large plantation owners who hired them for seasonal labor, he taught himself to read and knew which plants to take for problems of the liver and which to take for problems of the nerves. He knew how to remove a rotten tooth with the tip of a knife and what to give for a snakebite. He was also very handsome, and the town whispered that he was grandfather to many more of the dusty children than was publicly acknowledged. He wore three wedding bands, one for each wife he had survived. From him Isaias learned to play fiddle, and to smile in a way that made girls cover their teeth and trace their bare toes through the sand.

Isaias was born in the public hospital in the nearest city of Prince Leopold. Isabel was born in Saint Michael itself, twenty minutes after her mother's water broke as she crossed the cane fields. It should have been the other way, her mother said, the pensive child born in the yellowed hospital walls, the impetuous little boy clawing his way out into the cane. But they showed their true selves within hours, the boy protesting wildly against the prodding hands of the hospital nurses, the girl uttering a single, startled cry before settling quietly into the arms of her mother, who rose and continued the walk home.

Her mother would often say: Even then, anyone could see

the difference. At that time when babies won't stop watching your face, that boy stared straight past. Not Isabel—she looked you in the eye and knew what you were thinking, but the boy's eyes were moving the moment he could keep them open.

From an early age, Isaias went alone to walk in the hills. When Isabel was old enough to keep up, he took her with him, on excursions in the high heat or at dawn, dragging her grumbling from the house to see the birds before they hid from the sun. He found her wild cactus fruit and polished the dust from it with his shirt. He made her practice the names of plants. He thrust his hands into the thorns to grab beetles, into the hot mud to scoop up toads, into the cacti to pull out vivid pink flowers that he held for her, as she squinted with one eye and then the other through a scratched watch-repairman's lens he bought at the weekly fair in Prince Leopold. He found fossil fish for her in the eroded sandstone and showed her rock etchings of men and animals. He broke off long leathery pods from the mimosas and rattled them as they walked.

He brought his fiddle. In the shade of a buckthorn, she sat on a bumpy stone and listened to him play. The fiddle had a threnodial cry, as if one could play the sound of creaking floorboards or an animal's wail. On the way back, he told her how he would become famous. It was one of the few times he laughed, and his laughter spread until it shook his whole body. Isabel lived for these moments. She lost herself to imagining his successes and boasted of them to everyone.

When he was older, he borrowed books from a traveling notary. He read to her. Her favorite story was of the Princess of China, whose hair was described as long black sails.

Once, as she ran dusty and barefoot through the house in a pair of underpants, her grandfather Boniface grabbed her arm.

'Where's your conspirator?' he asked. She was four and the word was big and unfamiliar. He brushed dust from her cheek. 'What is it, little mouse? They don't teach you anything in school?'

'Conspirator in what?' asked her mother, cutting a sliver off a rope of tobacco. 'I don't think I understand, either.'

'What's not to understand? The boy makes crazy plans and she believes them. He thinks he is a king, and she thinks this is the center of the world.' He waved a hand. 'Yes?'

Isabel sneezed and didn't have an answer. She already knew there were certain questions adults asked children only for the sake of other adults. 'Wipe your nose,' said her mother, laughing, 'and if you see your conspirator, tell him the goats chewed down the clothesline.' Boniface loosed her arm and she sprang off running into the brush.

At Saint John's festival, her mother freckled her face with dabs of dark mud. At Carnival she was an angel, then an Indian, then an angel again. Most boys borrowed lipstick and put on their sisters' dresses. Each year Isaias wore the same oversize coat of ribbons and colored buttons. He brought his fiddle to play along at the edge of the band, where he flirted with the girls who came down from the villages. Isabel trimmed her hair with tinsel, shouted, 'It's Carnival!' and whirled, glinting, as he played.

When Isaias was thirteen and she was six, her father said it was time for him to leave school and join the men in the sugarcane fields.

He went on longer walks, alone. At night, she heard him arguing. 'Let me go to the coast,' he said. 'And what are you going to do there?' her father asked. 'Play fiddle.' 'And be a beggar your entire life?' 'Not a beggar. In the cities you can make a living in music.' 'That's a lie.' 'It isn't a lie, I promise. I can play in the markets, or in a band. There are many ways.'

In the morning, she awoke to Isaias climbing out of his hammock. She rose quietly and stood behind the sheet that hung in the doorway. She watched his hunched back as he ate in silence.

He worked for the next three years cutting cane with the older men. He walked the half hour to the fields in the darkness and returned to sleep in the early evening. To protect against the sharp leaves, he wore patched leather shoes and three shirts, ash-stained, stiff with dried sweat, buttoned to his neck to keep out the spiders. He wrapped his ankles and torn elbows with rags. Fragments of cane fiber specked his clothes and hair. In the cane fields the men were joined by others brought in by flatbeds. At lunch they sat in the clearings and ate from dented tins.

Once he cut his hand. The foreman made the driver wait until the end of the day to take him to a clinic. Isabel came along. There they learned the nurse had gone home, and so they slept on a wooden bench until she came back in the morning. The nurse poked at the wound worriedly and stitched it with wide, looping bites. The next night Isaias began to shiver. By the morning, the wound had swollen at the stitches like an overstuffed sausage, and when he made a fist, one of the threads tore through the flesh. He spent the next week at a little hospital in Prince Leopold.

He asked for Isabel to stay with him. In the next bed was an old woman whose breath rattled like the withered pods they twisted off the trees. Cockroaches fell off the walls under their own weight. Since Isaias was so thin, there was space in the bed, and the nurses let Isabel sleep there. Outside a window, they could see a pair of thrushes dash along a stretch of hot earth. They argued about whether a bird's feathers were warm or cold. 'Warm from the sun, cold from the wind,' said Isaias, and this question occupied Isabel for a long time.

The hospital had no food; he sent her into the city to buy cornmeal, which he cooked on a stovetop shared by the patients. As he swatted at the flies that gathered on the crusted dressing on his hand, he told her he was afraid he would never play the fiddle again. When he could close his fist, he returned to work.

During this time Isabel went to school and began to help her mother, taking care of a baby left behind by a cousin who had gone to work in the city. She learned to carry the baby with its legs scissored around her waist and to recognize the meaning of its cries. She helped her aunt sell bananas at a weekly market in the mountains. She grated manioc, pulled the ticks from the ears of the yelping dogs, balanced bags of laundry on her head when she walked to the stream. Her hands became callused. She could break a heavy piece of manioc in two.

When she was seven, a new teacher came from the coast, a spirited young woman who read poetry about the struggle of farmers and poor working people. Isabel did not understand all of the poems, but the teacher came regularly. Alongside the other children, squirming on the crowded splintery benches, she learned to read.

One day when the cane was flowering, her mother sent her

to find her brother. It was afternoon and still hot. As she followed the empty road along the fields, she thought how she would ask him to cut pieces for her and how only God could have invented a plant that killed both thirst and hunger. The flatbeds had parked a long way down the road. She decided to take a shortcut through the cane. Her bare feet skidded on the gravel as she descended the sharp slope from the road.

As she threaded her way through the narrow passages, she sang. A rustle startled her. A snake, she thought: last year, a boy had died after being bitten. They found him in the cane fields two days after he had disappeared. They hadn't let any of the children see him.

The leaves stirred at her feet and then the rustling moved away. The canebrake was the same in all directions; the sun was almost directly overhead. She picked a faint path along one of the rows. When this was crowded out by the other stalks, she dropped to her knees and crawled. The cane was blue at its base. The air was sweet and, save the rustling, very quiet. It seemed that she was following a path, but when she looked back she saw only an unbroken wall of cane. Her eyes hurt from the shifting of the stalks. Once, she thought she saw a shadow of a person. She stopped and strained her eyes to see and then continued on. Many times, she wanted to shout *Isaias,* but told herself not to be scared. She entered a burn. Soon she heard someone cutting cane and singing, and walked through the black skeletal stalks and into a small clearing, where she saw her brother. He wore thick gloves and a handkerchief draped beneath his hat, gray with soot. His back was bent and his head was down. She followed the rhythmic motion as he embraced the cane with one arm and swung his knife.

That night, he said, 'Isabel, how did you do that?' 'Do what?' 'Find me like that.' 'What do you mean?' she asked. 'I mean, how did you walk straight through the fields and find me?' 'I don't know.' 'You don't know? There are acres and acres of cane.' She shrugged. He said, 'You knew where I was?' 'I think so.' 'Do you think you could do it again?' he asked.

It was quiet as they walked down the road. At the start of the cane fields, he said, 'Wait here and sing "Little Sparrow" ten times,' and he disappeared into the darkness. She stood alone on the road, whispered the words to the song and tore strips from a dry husk. She could hear the sound of his feet on the fallen stalks and see the swaying of the cane plumes. She waited until she could no longer see or hear him, and then she followed. The moon was as thin as a curl of her hair, and the faint light flashed off the long leaves. Above her, the plumes were pale and luminescent, reminding her of costume feathers. Then she thought of the two of them, moving about each other in the darkness, which despite the cane appeared in her mind like a great empty place.

So it was easier this time, and she found him standing in a dense copse.

He took her back up to the road. 'Try again,' he said, and again she found him. 'Again,' he said, and this time had her sing the song ten times, and ten times again. She walked straight through the cane and found him crouching, holding his knees. On the way back to the road he began to laugh. 'Again,' he said, and again she found him on a straight line from the road. 'You are following my tracks,' he said. 'No.' 'Then you can hear my breathing.' 'No.' 'Then how?' 'I don't know, Isaias,' she said, feeling the hair rising on her arms.

They went out the following night. He blindfolded her, and she found him, feeling her way straight through the rustling stalks, until he tickled her ankle and pulled her down, laughing. He brought a cousin, and told him to hide, but Isabel hunted in circles until the little boy began to cry.

In the winter of her eighth year, another drought came. There won't be a cane harvest, said the men, and they began to talk about where they could find work, and later, if they should leave. As summer approached, they were visited by government men who promised help if they stayed. 'The cities can't take more of you,' they said. 'There is no water and no electricity; there is only disease.' The men and women were cautious. Hadn't the government come before, to promise water and food at the time of elections? But this time they returned a week later, with rice and a water truck. They brought a plastic reservoir and posters of the governor. Isabel stood with her brother and watched the dogs gather around the truck to lap at the leaking water as it dripped from the fender.

Some families left, but most stayed. At home, the men talked incessantly of work, of jobs in far-off places where it rained.

It was not the first time they had left in search of work. Since her grandfather's time, rubber plantations had sent representatives into the interior with promises of wealth. Now, again, the rumors tumbled out of megaphones, rattled among the fairground gossips and spread like stains along the roads into the backlands. At first, the men chewed slowly on the news. They were mistrustful of such wet, lush places. In the markets, they huddled around photographs of fruit-laden trees as if they were pornographic postcards.

At night, when the families gathered, those who had already gone and returned told stories. I walked, I hitched, I took a flatbed to the coast, they began, and the children listened.

In the stories, the companies took the men to a city by the sea. There they wandered along the docks, stared at the shifting hips of the washerwomen and watched fishermen pole skiffs into the emptiness of the horizon. As they waited, listening to the rumors swell, they saw ships bound for Panama City, Valparaiso and Rio de Janeiro, and others that said Lisbon and Cape Town. On boardwalks glittering with fish scales, they shadowed the stevedores, watching in disbelief at the cargo, the crates of fruit and fish and boxes of grain. They learned the ships had names: *Jeanne d'Arc, Rubber Princess, Jungle Queen*. What a wealthy place, they thought, and recalled the dogs without names and the horses without names, and the children, left by emigrating families, whose names had been lost.

On the docks, they spent days at seaside bars, waiting for enough men to fill the company steamers. The companies were generous and advanced them money for liquor and plump, laughing girls. They signed the bottom of ledgers they couldn't read. The company men licked the nib of the pen for them and said, This just promises that you'll pay me back, It's not much, You can work it off in days if you work hard.

One morning they woke to a procession at sea, where a Christ with real hair swayed like a mast above an altar boy and a seasick priest. Then the company men came around and gathered them into ships. At sea, they watched schools of fish swim beneath the hulls. They nearly cried with awe, whispering, So many fish, and still we don't stop, Imagine what it will be like when we arrive. After many days, they felt the air change, grow wet and heavy, the seawater go sweet. The banks were so far away that they didn't believe the crew when they said that it was no longer the ocean but a river. They disembarked on the mildew-stained docks of a cobbled city with a golden cathedral and markets reeking of rotting fruit. In the evening, when the market had closed, they walked barefoot over a boardwalk thick with the slush of papaya. They fought the cats for scraps. They had been fed by the companies, but still they were hungry, as if hunger were an old habit that couldn't be broken.

Isabel and Isaias considered the stories quietly. From there we took more boats, said the men who had been and then returned. These boats were smaller, with ribbed railings that reminded some of us of skeletons and some of us of jails. We worked on the plantations, or we fled and tried to mine gold. We fell over each other in massive muddy trenches torn into the earth. We carried everything we owned. On our backs. Like the Indians, who speak strange languages, and keep a distance when they come to trade.

In the deepest reaches of the jungle, the migrants met men who had never heard of the sea. They looked at the men with incredulity and thought, I spent my life before *seeing* the sea, but there is no one who hasn't heard of it. They repeated: sea *sea* seeee SEA ocean séa sèa sêa Ocean pacific atlantic, sea sea sea and the others shook their heads. A river? they asked. No, not a river, Bigger than a river. With clear water? Clear, yes, but not sweet water, salted water. Salted? Yes. By who? The salt is there already. But who put it there in the first place? Distrustful now, stepping back. In the first place? said the migrants, You could say God, and thought, Or the Other One. The men who had never heard of the sea said, Then people there don't have to buy salt. No. You don't have to trade for it? No, there is more salt than you could ever want. That must be good. Yes, said the migrants, thinking it over, That is good. But is it water you can drink? the others asked, and the migrants answered, No, it's poisonous. The last word soaked with such hatred that it terrified them.

In the great rubber plantations they cut chevrons into tree trunks, collecting the white latex in rusted cans. They melted it in large kettles and dipped string into the boiling milk, pulling the rubber out to dry. Then they dipped it again, until they held soft swollen spheres that grew slick in the rain, reminding them in their loneliest hours of the breasts and bellies of the girls they once lay with. They stared at the walls of the company shops, decorated with torn magazine photographs of beautiful women whose hair blew behind them. They tried to recall their wives at home, but their memories had withered. In the plantation canteens, they began to pay on credit for the company of Indian girls, who held their hands and followed them through the darkness of the camps.

Then the rumors of gold came, real gold, not rubber gold, and they fled their debts and the rubber plantations, following barroom whispers up the rivers, where they found cities of rafts. They asked for directions to the mines. You're here, came the answers. They stared down at the river, with the water black and clear above the rafts and brown below.

They began to spend days in the river, mining. They became hose men. They attached pressurized tubes to their

swimming masks and, at the bottom, scraped the bank with a vacuum, sucking up the mud to a raft above. At times they went down at night, but it didn't matter: even in the day, the bottom was completely dark with the dye of rotting leaves. They emerged at dawn, the black water streaming from their bodies. Below, when they were thirsty, they removed the masks and drank from the river. All night long, animals passed, sliding over their necks or between their legs: anacondas and electric eels; giant catfish that could grip an arm with pumice-like gums and pull them under; pink river dolphins with vaginas like women's, seducers of men.

There were other times when screaming came up through the air hose and the water went red with blood. Caimans, they whispered the first time it happened, but the others shook their heads: No—needlefish, they'll strip any meat not covered by your suit or your mask. Down below, they imagined themselves surrounded by schools of the fish, felt them tickling their skin. Still, they loved the river, and broke into laughter below, imagining that they had once lived in a place with no water at all, that now it was easier to drink than it was to breathe.

In the canteens, their fingers still pruned from the water, they sang songs from home, told jokes from home and recited dry backlands stories. In their off hours, when they lay in the hammocks with the Indian girls, tickled them and smelled the oil in their hair, they tried to tell them why they had come. They told long stories about the drought. The girls nodded and said, We, too, have months here when it doesn't rain. No, said the men, Not months, *years*. And the girls, But if it doesn't rain, how can you grow anything? And the men, That's what I am telling you, we can't, That's why we are here.

They kissed the necks of the girls, who laughed and pushed them back and asked, Then what are your rivers like? There are rivers, but they don't run all year, Mostly they are dry. Then how do the boats pass? There are no boats, The rivers are small, they come and then they go away. Then how do you bathe? Sometimes there are little ponds, sometimes we don't bathe. There is no other water? No, none, you keep asking me, and I keep telling you, It's like here, the water rises when it floods, and then the water goes away. And the girls, But the river here never goes away. I know. But your river goes away? Yes. Completely? Yes. You can walk where the river once was? Yes, you can walk there. Where does it go? Away, the men said, stroking the smooth skin, tired of the questions. It goes away, it disappears. Like you, said the girls, all at once, giggling in the hammocks, on the back creeks, in the shelter of the rubber trees. Like you, an echo. Running their fingers over the narrow faces, their cheeks against the rough beards. So you came to a place where the rain never stops.

With the end of the drought, Isaias began to work again in the cane fields.

Isabel was nine. She spent the mornings watching the children. Slowly, she learned that if a child was colicky, she only had to carry him on her hip and soon he would quiet. It was normal, she thought, but the other women said she was different. Once, as she hushed a baby, she caught her mother staring. She asked, 'What's wrong?' but her mother said, 'Nothing,' and stroked her hair.

In the afternoon, she went to school. She noticed that on his rare free days her brother took longer walks in the hills, always with the fiddle. She heard it wailing from their house, from the street, from the tangle of brush that led down into the valley. If it cracked, he shimmed it with chips from dry branches. He composed his own music or played traditional backlands folk songs and songs from the coast.

On Friday evenings, he walked ten miles to Prince Leopold, where a group of old men formed the Remembering the Past Regional Band, with an accordion, tambourine, triangle and drum. Sometimes there was a man playing clarinet, with a register key fashioned from cut tin. They played long into the night. For the first few warm evenings, nearly the entire neighborhood gathered to watch them play. Over time, they went back to their radio sets and their rocking chairs, until only a few remained: Isabel and a simple man who laughed at his own secret joke; the wife of the triangle player; a pair of mangy dogs who stirred the dust and chewed at the flaking pads of their paws.

Once, toward the end of winter, Isabel saw a little boy wandering on the dusty road above town. He was covered with long glass-like hair, and he chirped when she approached him. A week later, she fell sick. She shook with a fever, calling out, dreaming of people with strange faces taking her into the ground. Her mother made a poultice of leaves to press against her chest. Isaias came home in the evenings and lay next to her in her hammock. The fever broke.

A week later, she saw the boy again. Again, she became ill, and dreamed of running on the surface of a river, leaping on rocks made of faces that bobbed and sank beneath her feet.

Her mother took her to Prince Leopold, and then on a second truck to a small town farther out in the thorn scrub. There, they waited outside the house of a man who was said to move easily between worlds. There was a long line of trembling old men and women with screaming children. At last, they walked into a dark room, and her mother unfolded a crumpled wad of bills from a knot in her skirt.

The man was heavy and unshaven. Isabel thought he would have incenses or cowrie shells to cast, but he sat alone on a chair with a missing back. On a table behind him were scattered cloves of garlic, a dead bird tied to a little wheel, brown bottles with rolled newspaper stoppers and a cut-metal pipe with punched eyes, pointed ears and thin wire arms. Bunches of herbs hung from nails hammered haphazardly about the room. A calendar read AUTOBODY PRINCE LEOPOLD. He called her 'Isabel' without asking for her name, and told her everything she had seen.

To her mother, he said, 'Her body isn't closed.' Her mother nodded. The man recited an invocation. It was a strong prayer and would protect her now. 'But you will have to watch after her,' he said, and prescribed a special prayer to Saint George.

On the trip back her mother told her how there were certain people for whom there was less of a barrier between this world and the other one. Who needed prayers to close their bodies and protect them. These people could become healers or poets or could hear the word of God. They could see and smell and feel what others couldn't. But they were vulnerable to everything: they were haunted by spirits that others couldn't see, felt others' sufferings, fell ill more easily and often. Prayers could close a body, although some people didn't wish for their body to be closed: they risked the hauntings in exchange for their awareness. If a healer closed your body, you could no longer know which plants cured and which were poison. Anyone's body could be torn open, by too much sadness or too much suffering. It was why, with the death of someone close, the world seems different, the light changes, we can see and understand what we never saw before. 'Once,' said her mother, 'when my sister died, I became sick, and saw a headless mule outside our house. In my dreams, a woman in white told me that our dogs would get distemper and the next year they did. They said I cried for two weeks, but I don't remember crying at all.'

There were those, like the healer, for whom no barriers existed, for whom there were no limits of knowledge or suffering. 'That isn't you,' said her mother. 'In you, the walls are there, they are just thinner. My grandmother was like you. Even when she stopped seeing spirits, still her body wasn't closed. She could read people. She knew cures and could calm children. Then, when the drought came, she began to see more clearly: she knew how to find water, and whether rain was coming. Some said she was lucky for it. But it wasn't easy; she felt the sadness of others, too. She was like that her entire life.'

She paused. 'Except when my grandfather was sick: then she was blind. Everyone knew he was dying, but she didn't believe it. With him, it was like her vision was blurred.'

Later, she added, as if from nowhere, 'Being blessed and lucky aren't the same.'

In Prince Leopold, they stopped at a little store that sold incense and icons. Rows of saint icons lined the shelves. Handwritten labels curled from the bottles. Isabel read them slowly. There was *Find Employment Soap, Soap Bring-Him-to-Me, Spell-Breaker Soap, I-Dominate-My-Woman Shampoo, Sham-*

poo Beauty, Shampoo Goodbye-Evil-Eye. At home her mother washed her in a bitter solution that stung her eyes. They set a laminated card of Saint George on a shelf next to a rosary and a photo of the Cathedral of Our Lady of Tears in Blackwater.

Isaias watched Isabel from a distance. 'Why are you staring?' she asked. 'I'm not.' 'You are.' 'It's like performing miracles,' he said. 'Like magic.'

'Not magic at all,' snapped her mother. 'Just seeing.'

He asked Isabel, 'Does it scare you?'

'No,' she answered, not certain if this was true. She thought, Does it scare you to see farther, to hear better? 'I'm not seeing anything that isn't already there,' she said.

Her grandfather Boniface considered the diagnosis silently. They repeated the prayer for three Fridays.

She didn't see the little boy again. At night, her dreams were quiet dreams about her family and the white forest, dry and empty recapitulations of the day. She no longer heard snakes moving close to her on the trail. In the market, it was easier to pass the beggars without feeling their sadness. She could still calm children, but it took longer now. Somehow the old drought songs weren't as lonely anymore, and she knew that if she tried, it would be harder to find Isaias in the cane.

The burning season came.

In the fields, the men set fire to the cane. The long blades flared, blue and yellow, the nestled leaves fanning like pages of a burning book until only the sweet core remained.

At night, Isabel could hear the crackling of the fires. Sometimes she went to the edge of the road and watched the men herd the flames over the hills. At sunset, the smoke turned the horizon as red as a rooster's crest. She joined the other children as they ran down the long road to the burns, where they felt their faces prickle in the heat and squinted at the silhouettes of the cutters moving gracefully against the fires.

The harvest began as soon as the long, sharp leaves crumbled to cinders. The workers came home with their nostrils black, their eyelids dark with ash like kohl. Spiderweb tattoos laced the wounds on their hands and striped the chapped crevices of their lips.

The days were long. She saw little of her brother. She waited for him to resume their walks in the final moments of light. But each day he said he was too tired, and so she stopped asking. At night, his coughing kept her awake. She found black stains in the handkerchiefs she washed in the stream. In his absence, her world narrowed and quieted.

When the season was over, the men collected their final wages from the foreman. The canteen ran a swift business. Some of her uncles visited a house in the city, and at home their wives cursed them. Once, her father went along, and in the morning, Isabel woke to her mother shouting, her voice hoarse from crying.

It was about this time that Isaias disappeared.

At first they thought that he had gone to a cousin's in Prince Leopold. Later, they found the fiddle was also missing. Her parents were furious, but Isabel imagined him playing in faraway plazas, before massive crowds. It was two weeks before the telephone in the square began to ring. She heard a girl's voice answering and then footsteps toward her door.

She cupped the receiver as if she were whispering into his ear. 'Where are you?' she asked. 'In the capital,' he answered. 'Tell everyone I'm fine, I joined a band that plays in the market.' She whispered, 'They're going to *kill* you. Father curses you and Mother cries all the time. You should've called.' 'I couldn't, I didn't have the money to call, but now I do.'

She wanted to ask, Why didn't you tell me? 'What's it like there?' she whispered.

'There aren't words for it, Isa, it's so beautiful, I will tell you everything when I come home.' 'When's that?' 'Soon, before the cane season starts, I promise. You'll be happy I went. You'll understand.'

She could see her mother lingering at the door to their house. Isabel asked, 'Do you want to talk to anyone else?' 'No,' Isaias said, and she could see him standing at a pay phone by the sea. On the shore, a white bird cocked its head inquisitively, a group of men struggled with the thin filaments of a net. The wind was wet and smelled of salt. 'Just tell them I'll be home soon. I'll explain everything then.'

On the wall of the schoolhouse were multiplication tables, an alphabet and a map of the state. The state capital was only two hand widths away from S. MICHAEL and the dashes that showed the river that sometimes ran. Both had been inked in; there was nothing else but blank space. The capital had a star and printed letters that stretched into the sea. Now Isabel daydreamed of going there, imagining a place filled with fiddlers, markets, automobiles. In the evenings, she took the goats to graze and visited the places Isaias used to take her. She made a collection of pods and oddly shaped stones.

Sometimes, when her parents were fighting, she said that the land near the house was too dry for grazing, and she walked the goats a day into the scrub.

It was easier, alone in the white forest. There was no shouting and she could imagine her brother was with her. She brought manioc flour, found cactus fruit to eat, foraged bromeliads for the water in their hearts. The nights were cold; she slept on beds of dried leaves. She could hear goatsuckers screeching and the pods of the bean trees exploding as they cooled and coiled. Twice she saw a will-o'-the-wisp catch fire near the watering holes, but she had seen them many times with Isaias and so she wasn't afraid. In abandoned plots she found dried pieces of corn and beans, which she collected to bring home to plant. She slept curled up with the animals and awoke with their dry dust on her lips and in her ears.

Once, one of the goats stirred up a fer-de-lance. She stood still and watched it hiss, and then she killed it by striking a rock against its head. The goat smelled the snake on her hands and bolted. She found him tangled in the thorn, braying, his eyes wide and ears tucked back. She unwrapped him from the thorn, and again he tried to run. This time she grabbed his ears, twisted his neck until he fell to his pasterns and wrestled him to the ground. She could feel his heart pound beneath her knee. His eyes were wide, flecked with mucus and dust, his neck lined with little bulbs of swollen ticks. She stared at him, feeling his warm breath on her face. She waited until his heart slowed and she let him stand.

Another day, she heard her name whispered. She gathered the goats and walked four hours home. When she arrived, Isaias was coming up the road from the dirt highway. It was two months since he had left. She walked the last length of the road with him, as if she had been with him all along. At their home, she entered at his side to see her mother turning, wiping her hands in her skirt, her father rising from his hammock.

Isaias leaned the fiddle case against the wall and without saying anything put a short stack of bills on the table. Her father counted them. 'This isn't much,' he said, but he put them in his pocket. 'Planting starts soon.' He turned to let Isaias pass.

That night, when Isabel asked him about the capital, Isaias said he had joined a band performing for tourists at a seaside hotel. He said a man told him he had a true talent. Isaias's eyes twinkled. *You will go far* were the words the man had used, and the next day, Isabel repeated them to the other children.

Over time, he told her about nights in plazas lit by long strings of bare bulbs, dances that went on until dawn. He described tips falling so fast that they rang in the plastic bowl like a shaking tambourine. He had a girlfriend there, a beautiful girl with long black hair, and Isabel imagined her to be like the Princess of China.

Their walks resumed.

One warm night, when the villagers dragged their chairs into the street, Isabel was with her brother by the empty fountain. Two men who worked with him in the cane fields came and sat next to them. They were drinking. 'Want some?' said one, raising a half-empty bottle. Isaias shook his head. 'Why not?' said the man. 'No reason,' said Isaias. 'Just don't feel like it tonight. I have to play at a wedding tomorrow.' The man took another swig from the bottle. '*Isabel,*' he slurred, 'why does your brother think he's better than us?'

'He has to play, in Prince Leopold,' she said.

The man snorted. 'Bullshit.'

'Don't talk to her,' said Isaias. 'There you go,' said the man, 'thinking you're too good for cane cutters.' 'I never said that,' said Isaias. He took Isabel's hand and stood to leave. 'Where you going?' said the man, lurching up, his machete clanging against the chair. Isaias tried to push past him, but the man grabbed his shoulder. Isabel could smell the liquor on his breath.

Suddenly, the man spat. 'That's what I think of you,' he said. Then Isaias hit him, falling on him as the bottle clunked in the dirt. An uncle pulled him off. 'What's going on?' 'Said the rest of us are dogs,' sputtered the man. 'Said nothing,' shouted Isaias, his face red. Isabel could see tears in the corners of his eyes. 'Easy there, music-star,' said someone, and Isaias turned and took swift strides toward the thorn.

He began to spend more time in the hills.

It was summer, and hot, and people began to whisper of another drought. When Isabel went with him, he talked about a different place, a city in the south.

She couldn't remember when she first heard of the city. In the earliest geographies of her imagination, there was Saint Michael and Prince Leopold, and beyond the mountains, the state capital by the sea. The city in the south had a name, but when they spoke of it, they called it simply *the city*, as if it were the only city in the world. She had learned of it in school: a place of kings and fleets of caravels, sea monsters, corsairs and cold southern squalls, a single cross erected on cliffs above the coast. On the school map, it sat on the underbelly of the country, and she imagined it at the end of a long descent down a great plain: when people left to work there, it was said they had 'gone down to the city.' A shuddering descent, like falling from the sky.

As she got older, she imagined a vast, shifting place, a light, a rush of noise. The old men who had been there spoke of mansions built on great avenues, elegant ladies who carried parasols with their long white gloves and wrapped themselves in mantillas against the fog. Their sons told of automobile factories and rising skyscrapers. Their grandchildren spoke of a different place, an endless cinder-block city with gangs of angry young men. On the single marketplace television in Prince Leopold, mantis-thin women sipped glasses of bubbles before a shimmering skyline. Until she was five, Isabel thought that in the city the sky and land were somehow reversed, until her brother explained how the lights could stretch forever beneath a blanket of clouds.

Each year, the men debated whether to take the ship for the jungles or the flatbed to the city. They drew up the merits, dangers and possibilities of each: rubber plantations versus auto plants, gold strikes versus the mansions, malaria versus city thieves. As they sewed bags with sisal and shaped roof tiles over their thighs, they spoke of impossible factories. They said, In the city in the south you don't go hungry. In the city the clinics have doctors, the schools have paper, the stores have food. In the city, families put their maid's children through school, babies are bigger. In the city, the poor are rich, minimum-wagers are kings. The men don't cheat on you in the city, they aren't powerless, they don't drown themselves in drink, they don't hit. The women don't get old before their time. In the city, if you are thirsty there are fountains, I've seen them myself, big fountains, with water spraying from horses' mouths. In the city, they have markets every day, they have rain.

At first the men went, and then some of the women, including their cousin Manuela. When Isabel was eight, an entire family bundled their belongings in a knotted sheet and climbed onto one of the flatbeds they called parrot perches for the metal bars that the passengers clung to on the long trip.

The following year, another family left. They were one of the poorest in Saint Michael, and abandoned a wattle house out in the thorn forest, latching the door with a string and a little stick. On their walks, Isaias took Isabel there, where the wind whistled through the cracks in the walls. Inside, he ran his fingers over the grooves worn into the beams by swaying hammocks. Sometimes they waited out the heat of the day together in the shade of the rooms.

As he spent more and more time in the hills, Isabel often found him in the empty house. Someone took its door away, and the chinks in the wattle widened. Once they surprised a pair of rhea. The birds screeched and hurled themselves about the room in panicked, scratching loops until they leaped through an empty window. For days Isaias imitated them, shoving his fists into his armpits and spinning around the room as Isabel chased behind.

Usually, it was empty. A pair of anthills appeared in the floor, and the carapaces of insects swung in the dusty strands of abandoned spiderwebs. Thin centipedes formed question marks as they dried and curled.

Once she found him there with the fiddle. 'Maybe I should also go,' he said, and he played for a long time.

When she was twelve, Isabel began to travel with her aunt and uncle to an uneven hillside overlooking the valley, where they kept a pair of thin zebu cows, grew some manioc, collected wood for charcoal and led the goats to graze. The soil was thick with stones and barren except for thorn scrub and the occasional cereus cactus with sticky white fruit It was a long afternoon's walk from town. They spent days there, sleeping in hammocks strung from the low trees. They returned with plastic buckets of milk, kept warm by the heat of the day, sloshing beneath a scrim of yellow fat.

In the evenings, they watched a plume of dust winding its way into the distance until it disappeared.

One day they returned to town to find a white pickup parked in the square. In their home, three men sat with her father. There were two pistols on the table. Her uncle approached warily as a man rose to shake his hand. He wore a bolo tie, its clasp fashioned from the rowel of a spur.

'This man's from the city,' said her father. 'Says the land out by the zebus is his.'

Her uncle slowly made his way to her father's side. 'We've

had that land for as far back as my great-grandparents,' he said. 'And probably before.' 'You mean you've worked the land,' said the man. 'No,' said her uncle, 'I mean the land's ours.' 'Then you've got papers, of course,' said the man, smiling. 'Not now.' '*Not now.* What's that mean, citizen?' 'Means just that. Means once we did, but not now, with all the going and the coming because of the droughts.' 'That's the problem,' said the man. 'Because I've got papers.' He pushed a stained sheet forward. Her uncle picked it up. He massaged a long keloid that ran from his eye to his ear, a scar from a bottle slash, twice infected, poorly repaired. 'Says right there that the land's mine,' said the man. 'Right there at the bottom is the date my family bought it.' Isabel took a step closer. The paper looked old and brittle. Her uncle threw it back onto the table. 'You're cricketing,' he said, angry now. He clenched his jaw. 'It isn't yours.'

The man rose. 'I came here to tell you, not to ask, citizen. You can leave on foot, or your people can carry your body out in a hammock.' He turned angrily, and the other men put the guns into their belts and followed him out.

The man came back, three times, and each time he spoke to a different family. Each time he brought his henchmen. They didn't clap their hands outside the houses, as was the custom, but banged on the doors with the butts of their pistols. He carried the same faded papers, and he said things like 'I will let you work it if you give me half, You should thank me, Most landowners are not so generous.' Word came that he worked for even a bigger man, a general of the Federal Army, who lived in the capital and controlled great swaths of the state.

In town, the men searched old chests and the backs of

closets. They shouted at their wives to find the records, although everyone knew there were no records to be found. 'The man's papers are fake,' her uncle told them. 'Fake's only fake if people think they're fake,' said others. 'They look real.' 'That's a lie,' said her uncle. 'Fake's fake, I know their tricks, I'm not believing some piece of paper just because he left it in a box with a pair of crickets to piss and shit on it and make it look old.'

On their walks, Isaias was silent. Once Isabel asked, 'What's going to happen?' He answered quickly, 'We're still here, aren't we? Do you think this is the first time this has happened? Do you think it's the first time someone has tried to scare us away?' The words sounded rehearsed, as if he was repeating something someone else had said.

A week later, two dogs were found at the edge of the town, their heads shattered, sticky and covered with flies. At night, the men ate silently, and the women uneasily eyed the sacks of beans. In the weekend markets, they heard similar stories from other towns. They began to see the three men everywhere, driving into towns with pistols in their belts to pay visits to families who refused to sign the old sheets they couldn't read. She watched the old people circle them cautiously, an arm's reach away.

Later that month, on a small farm on the outskirts of Prince Leopold, someone strung up more dogs in the thorn and cut off the udders of a milk cow. They gouged out the eyes of a herd of goats and left them to tangle themselves in the scrub, hissing at the birds that made swooping dives at sockets clotted with blood. The goatherd was tied to a post and left in the sun, muttering through blistered lips. On the old road to the coast, a man who stayed on his land was found outside his little house with a stick stuck in his throat and the crotch of his pants brittle with blood.

In some towns, they heard, there were those who resisted, gathering at the entrances of their lands with sharpened hoes before squadrons of the Military Police. Late at night, in Saint Michael, Isabel's uncles and father sat around the table alone. From behind the sheet in the doorway, she heard the clicking of guns as they were cleaned and loaded. The sound brought a soft cry from her mother. She has seen this before, Isabel thought. When she couldn't sleep, she looked over to her brother and watched him staring up at the specks of sky.

At the crossroads, offerings appeared, scattered corn and half-empty bottles of cane wine.

They waited for the priest. When he didn't come, they opened the church. In the gray shadows, Isabel stood by her mother in a row of women with bowed, kerchiefed heads. An old aunt put a worn prayer card of Saint Michael to her eyes and began to wail. The others fell to their knees, pressed callused hands together, whispered, *Protect us, Saint Michael Archangel, warrior who thrust the devil into hell, Defend us in our battle against our enemies, Crush Satan beneath your feet so that he may no longer hold us captive, Spare us, Saint Michael, Have mercy on us in the hour of our trial, Assist us in the dangerous struggle we are about to endure.* Out of the corner of her eye Isabel watched their lips moving. She felt herself part of a long line of daughters. She knew her mother had once kneeled where she was kneeling and her grandmother where her mother was kneeling, shifting through the pews as each daughter came in and took her mother's place.

'You aren't praying,' said her mother, and Isabel pressed the base of her thumbs to the top of her head. She imagined Saint

Michael smelling of dust and feathers, diving toward the earth with his wings tucked behind him. She saw him perched on the church tower, preening his feathers and waiting. She imagined him with talons, scratching on the roof tiles above her, red dust filtering down; she heard the crackling uncrinkling of his feathers as he folded and unfolded them; she saw him pacing the plaza and letting the children stroke his wings, sharpening his spear on the stones and tucking his head into his down at night. She watched him waiting for the cars, and when the cars came, unfurling into a great bird and, with a single clap of his wings, tearing up plumes of gravel, overturning the pickups, unpeeling the roads and hurtling the henchmen into the white forest, their pistols fluttering harmlessly down.

They locked up the church again when they left. They waited through the long days and watched the shadow of the statue sweep the square and stretch up the walls like the silhouette of a stranger.

Isabel's uncle continued to go out to the land, although her aunt stayed home. At night Isabel could hear them shouting at each other in their house across the square. He became silent and sullen, and at the weekly fair, he bought a scapular and an invocation against bullets. He sat in the square and with his thumb broke the spines from a spray of thorn. Her father told him, 'Be careful, or we'll find you with a mouth full of ants.'

Then, in a bar in Prince Leopold, a drunk whispered that he was already marked. The men in the family began to escort him everywhere. When it was Isaias's turn, he brought a sharpened cane scythe, choked up on the handle and let it sway cautiously as they walked off down the road. Her mother waited nervously by the door, but to Isabel, it was inconceivable that Isaias might be hurt. 'He knows strong prayers,' she said, to comfort her mother.

A week later, her uncle didn't come home. His wife wailed and rolled on the ground, tearing at her hair until the women came and sat on her and rubbed her chest with herbs and holy water. When they found his body out on the road, his mouth was open and his tongue was stuffed into the pocket of his shirt. The men went and carried him back in a hammock. As the women fell over him, Isabel turned away, frantic, to look for Isaias. He wasn't home or at the fountain. The schoolhouse, where sometimes he went to read the few books, was empty. At last she found him, alone on a trail above town. His eyes were red and his lips trembled when he tried to speak. Finally, he said, 'Don't cry. There is enough crying already.'

She went back down the hill to her house and curled into the cool cup of her hammock. Twice she heard her uncle speak to her, and she whispered him away. She squeezed her fists, pinched her eyes tight and felt the fabric beneath her face grow wet and warm.

They completed a novena of mourning.

When the nine days were over, she began to hear different words in Saint Michael. They no longer spoke of the droughts, but of false papers and boxes of crickets. I will be run off my land by cricket piss, they said, and no one laughed. Their conversations dried, as tinder dries and becomes ready to burn.

She was awakened by her parents' arguing. 'What do you want me to do?' her father said again and again. 'I have no choice—they have taken away my choices.' At the weekly market in Prince Leopold, she joined the crowd around the canteen television. Images played of massive settlements made of black plastic tents, clashes between landless men and the police. One day, a young mother stared from the screen with such defiance that Isabel turned to look behind her in the square.

The days passed, but the henchmen didn't return. Slowly the men put their guns away. Someone said there were bigger fights over better land elsewhere. 'I never thought I would thank God for worthless land,' said her father, smiling for the first time in months. That summer the men still found work in the cane fields. When the foreman offered them the same pay as the year before, one of her cousins shouted, 'But prices have doubled!' 'I think there are many men who would be happy for your job if you don't want to work,' said the foreman.

In November, a family who lived near the highway locked the door to their house and boarded a parrot perch to the south, and two weeks later another followed. The older people cursed them as cowards. They asked, 'Who will do the work if all the children have gone away?'

In December, on Saint Lucy's Day, they set out six chips of salt at night. In the morning, four had dissolved: it would rain by February.

Now when her family gathered, they spoke only of the city in the south, as if the calm had cut a path for the rumors to pour in. Everyone had a story. In Isabel's mind it ceased to be a place; it was the static in the background of the radio programs, the flickering on the television screen, a press of crowds, a screech of tires, a chorus of hawkers' shouts. On the news, a reporter stood before a bus station, where families dragged bags over concrete floors. He spoke of numbers, first tens and then hundreds of thousands, numbers she didn't understand. In her imagination, the television's forest of great glittering towers shattered and fell about the city. In their shadow grew a tangle of planked slums and brick escarpments, a city of cement and broken cement. It was a heaven and a terrible place, an emptiness, a tomb, a place to beg alms, a whorehouse, a street child's playground, a floodland, a stink. Shimmering at the end of the great descent of her imagination.

One night Isaias shook her awake. 'Come,' he whispered, and she swiveled her legs from the hammock and followed him.

Outside, the square was empty and blue. He said, 'Isa, I'm going. There's a perch leaving for the city early tomorrow from Prince Leopold. If I leave now I can catch it.'

Sleep still clung to her. She stared at him mutely. 'I am going to go mad here, Isa. I am going to die if I stay.'

She was quiet. He said, 'Isa, you understand. I can't take it.'

'Those men aren't coming back. Things will be better—' she said, but he shook his head. 'That's not it. If I thought they were coming back I'd stay. But I'll spend my life here. I'll die in the cane if I don't leave. At least I'll have a chance.' 'At what?' 'You know: a *chance*. I'll play music, I'll perform, I'll get a good job, I'll send money. You don't know the stories I've heard. I'm going to send you letters, and color photographs. I'll make wishes for you at the cathedral.

'Isa . . .' He paused. 'Are you all right?'

She nodded slowly and looked into the square. She wished something would happen: that a dog would pass by or someone would start yelling somewhere, or the sun would come up and break the moment into day. She felt her lips tighten. She looked down at her feet.

'Isa, I'm not abandoning you.'

'I didn't say you were.'

'But it's what you're thinking. If you're thinking something, you should say it.' He watched her face for her reaction. 'When you're older, you'll get it. You'll see. You'll understand that a person can't just wait and let things happen to him.'

She traced a flagstone with her heel.

'Isa—listen. What do you want? A brother who's just a cane cutter? Another broken-back?'

She saw then that he had shaved, and his hair was combed. He wore his best shirt. The fiddle rested against the wall.

'Where are you going to stay?' she asked.

'With Manuela. She has a new man, you know, but he works at sea. There'll be room for me.' 'When are you coming back?' 'Soon.' 'What's soon?' 'Months, just months.' 'Yes?' 'Yes.' 'Why didn't you tell Mother, then?' 'Because she won't let me, Father won't let me. They think a person can cut cane forever. I'll tell them when I get there. When I have my first job and they can't say no.' He laughed. She said, 'But you promise you're coming back?' 'Yes.' 'Say you promise, Isaias.' 'You'll be okay here,' he said. 'I'll write letters to you. It will be like you're there with me.' 'Say you promise, Isaias. Say: "I promise, Isabel."' 'I already said I did. Now you are acting like a child.'

She looked away and bit her nails. Her hand was trembling, and she put it down. 'I promise,' he said. He kissed both her cheeks, her forehead. 'Tell everyone not to be mad.' He laughed and poked her. 'Come on, look up . . . Imagine your brother, like on the radio: *Isaias, the King.*' Her cheeks were hot; she wouldn't smile.

Two weeks later, the phone rang again in the empty plaza. This time her father retrieved it. He white-knuckled the receiver. 'Where did you get the money to pay for the trip?' he shouted. 'How long is it going to take you to make that much? Doing what? I don't care what a man once told you, those kinds of things are not for people like you.'

When Isabel took the receiver from him, Isaias said, 'You wouldn't believe it, there are buildings as far as you can see.' He spoke breathlessly about the city and its crowds. At last he stopped. 'I have to go, my token's going to run out.' 'I'll call you back,' she said. 'It's free.' He paused. 'I'll write to you,' he said. She could hear the echo of his voice, like a ghost in the line.

'Are you okay?' he asked finally. Then: 'Isa, you there? You all right? Is everything there all right?' 'Yes,' she managed, but her voice began to break. 'You sure?' he said, quieter now. 'I'm sure,' she said, turning to watch a cousin leap from the doorstep of a house, run across the square and disappear laughing into the brush.

Saint Lucy's salt was off by one month that year: it rained in January, in the mountains. So the spring ran and the cane fields bloomed.

Isaias wrote after a month, a long letter in a bounding hand, his words clipping the lines. He described the buildings, the maze of highways, how he took buses without stopping just to watch the city from the window. *I began to perform in the city park,* he wrote. *There are other performers too, street magicians and rhyme singers, and they are all from the north, although from other villages far away. It's like everyone is fleeing the drought and bringing home here. A city built of drought,* he wrote. He said he was staying with their cousin Manuela. *Most of the time, she lives at her employer's and comes home only on the weekend. She is well, she works very hard.* He said little else about her. Isabel imagined her as one of the soap opera maids on the market television, in a mansion like a marble palace, with a pressed apron and her hair in beautiful curls. She carried the letter with her and read it over until the words came easily.

Since her uncle was killed, they hadn't seen the cricket men. They returned to the hillside, to graze the goats and zebu cows. But they no longer stayed overnight, and as they walked, they squinted constantly into the horizon to look for new trucks.

Despite the rain, Isabel felt a new, vise-like fear grip the village. In the market in Prince Leopold, they saw the cost of goods rise each week. Her relatives who crushed their own cane found fewer buyers for their sugar because the merchants argued that the new roads made it cheaper to buy from the coast. The money her father earned from the harvest disappeared. Someone stole one of their chickens. They wrote relatives in the state capital and asked for help, 'to tide things over.'

As the bean and manioc stores dwindled, they began to hunt, to lay traps for turtles and armadillos. They loaded shotguns with gravel and rose at dawn to kill the antwrens that came to pry insects from the tree bark. In the market, they haggled fiercely. Hunger's returning, they said. Isabel listened suspiciously. Hadn't the government promised that this wouldn't happen? Hadn't it rained? Hunger was a beast from years ago, when the houses were built of wattle and thatch, not now, not with brick houses and cobbled streets, a telephone in the square.

They began to cut down the forest, burning the white wood to make charcoal to sell in the market. On the hillside above the village, the land became bare, quiet, sick. The zebu walked over the empty fields, loosening clods. Dust curled off like smoke from something burning slowly.

In the day, Isabel led the goats to graze. The slope was hot, the air stale; she often needed to stop to rest. Each week, she had to walk farther. The animals grew so skinny that she could see the arteries pulsating in their necks. When the rain did come, coffee rivulets wound down the hill and fouled the stream.

Once, one of the charcoal burnings flamed out of control. The fire crackled in long waves over the hillside. They beat at it with spades and doused it in sand. It licked up the hill until it was contained by a high rock seam that ran through the white forest like a wall of defense. Angry accusations broke out. They blamed an uncle named Ulises, and he blamed it on his three-year-old son. Under her breath, Isabel cursed him as a coward.

Her mother cooked a little less with each passing night. A week went by with no meat, and her parents debated in low voices about whether to kill a goat. There were four of them, and then one became sick. It was small and ringstraked and once her best climber, but now it walked in circles and fell on its left side, kicking its legs and lurching its neck as it tried to rise. They killed it and flayed the dark red carcass of its skin. The lidless eyes bulged from their sockets and watched her wherever she walked. They ate the meat, boiled the hoof for broth and chopped up the innards. When the second goat fell sick, her father killed it, and then killed the two that remained. He salted the meat to dry in the sun, where Isabel whisked a rag at the bottle flies. They found their guts full of sand, scraped them clean and dried them on the thorn.

They finished the goat meat. The zebus' humps thinned and hung limp. They began to flavor the rice and cornmeal with stringy meat from birds and armadillos. Isabel was ashamed when she saw how little meat came from a hummingbird, but for the first time she could remember, she was hungry all the time. With her front teeth, she scraped the meat from the gleaming breastbones and crushed the wings with her molars. They caught lizards and bull toads fleeing the dry creek beds in search of water.

Two months after he left, Isaias sent money through a family member in Prince Leopold. It was enough to last them several weeks. In his letter, he said it came from performing at restaurants. They bought beans that very day because the prices were rising. Her father got drunk and said, 'To my son the musician!' Isabel told everyone of his success. They waited for him to send more.

Later her father went to Prince Leopold to look for work, but the flatbeds that passed were already full.

They began to search for tubers and cactus fruit in the hills. They sharpened their knives on stones, held one end of the cactus with their teeth and the other with their fingers. They slit them open as though they were animals' bellies and ate the white meat inside. She helped pull spines from the palm cactus flesh, swiftly plucking them until her thumbnail splintered and she had to use the knife. They ate the leaves of the hogplums. They followed woodcreepers to leaf-cutter-ant columns, the ant columns to the colonies, broke open the colonies and collected the swollen abdomens of the queens.

The smell of the roasted ants was sweet and made them hungrier. When there was enough to drink, they oversalted the food so they would fill their bellies with water. They got drunk, dizzy on the water. She tried to think of her brother in the city, but hunger dominated her, followed her everywhere like a thin dog. Alone in the thorn, she fantasized that she could smell meat cooking. The world separated into categories of things that could and could not be eaten.

She began to have a recurring dream of eating a sweet melon. She could taste the melon and feel the juice run over her cheeks as she laughed. In her dream, she was ravenous, not even scraping the peel but biting the honey centers from an endless supply of identical melons. She awoke crying. She began to kneel by her hammock before sleeping, to pray that the dream wouldn't come, *It is making me sick, I don't want it anymore, just let me go hungry but don't drive me crazy like this.* One night she awoke in the kitchen, coughing on uncooked beans. She wondered if she should wake her mother. She wanted a prayer or a candle to stop the dream, but she was ashamed to ask. Who ever heard of that? she thought, A prayer against dreams of eating a melon?

She awoke with headaches that wouldn't go away. One of her infant cousins became sick from eating a dead carrion bird he found in the scrub. Her grandfather began to complain of night blindness and grew too weak to leave his hammock. She had to help him turn, and wiped his legs of sparse, pungent urine. On his back they found an ulcer like the yolk of an egg. Her first impression was not disgust or sadness, but disbelief that there was enough meat for the disease to take hold.

Even the youngest children grew quiet and listless, and their skin grew soft lanugo hair. A baby developed pale marks like lichen on the skin of his groin. When Isabel held him, his swollen legs pitted in the shape of a hand. Plump, translucent lids covered his eyes. When the families pooled together to feed him, he didn't grow fat, but withered until his face was the face of a little old man.

Her mother began to cry, without warning or provocation. They waited for Isaias to send more money. When none came, they began to mix earth into the beans. It was the first time she came to see earth as food, and her mother had to teach her how to recognize the right kind. She found it satisfied an unfamiliar hunger, and soon she was craving it. On one of her walks, she fell asleep in the sun and woke up lost and disoriented, her skin burned and peeling. She had never fallen asleep in the noon sun before. In the market, they bought scraps of skin and zebu nose, haggled harder. She cut herself trying to dig up a bromeliad, and the wound wouldn't heal.

Once, she came across a hogplum with low-hanging leaves. She ate one, and then another, and then she began to stuff her mouth with them, faster than she could swallow, the sweet taste making her salivate and quenching her thirst. Her mouth filled with leaves but still she stuffed herself. She ate until she vomited a heavy mass of fiber, and then heaved again and again until her stomach was empty. She understood that it was punishment for her greed.

Now each week there was news of someone else leaving. The teacher stopped coming. There were rumors that she had fallen sick and stayed in the city. Others said the landowners were angry that she was teaching poems about the retreat and backlands prophets. Others said she had just grown tired of the place.

Two months after the end of the harvest, someone heard there were foreigners distributing free rice in Prince Leopold.

Isabel rushed home when she heard the news. As she told her father, she began to laugh uncontrollably. Her father listened quietly and said, 'I'm not taking anyone's charity, especially foreigner charity,' but three days later he led them along the long road to the city. There, where the streets ended, they found a crowd from the villages. They looked for the food, but a man told them the foreigners had come to first build a church, and there would be a dinner when they were finished. He said, 'If we feed you now, you'll go away.'

While her father worked, Isabel stayed with the other children. She watched a tall pink teenager with a crew cut hand out toys from a cardboard box. He had a mechanical toy car with a long wire and a lever that made it move. He stood in the center of a crowd of children with swollen bellies and chased them with the car. A woman handed out shirts with many colors. Isabel chose a green one with a picture of an orange-haired man in a fighting stance and words she didn't understand. It had beautiful green letters, and she wore it over her dress.

There was a toy truck with a ladder on its flatbed and a doll whose eyes opened as they lifted her. Another doll could be filled with water, and when the boy squeezed its belly, a stream of urine arced out. The children watched first in amusement, and then in nervousness and silence as the water made a muddy puddle on the ground.

It took three days to build the church, and they spent the nights with a cousin. She slept with two other children on a stretch of leather hammered onto a frame with old black nails. It was age-burnished and tan in the stretches around the nails. During the night, the children slid toward one another in the center and awoke in a tangle.

On the second day, her mother asked a man in a tie, 'Where

is the rice?' 'Soon,' he said. When the church was finished they stood and listened to a sermon on living water and the Samaritan woman at Jacob's Well, and then a truck came and gave out bags of rice and sugar, which they carried home as night was falling.

After a month, her father found a job building a police station north of Prince Leopold. She was still always hungry, but they were able to afford beans. With money from an aunt, they bought a pair of goats. Now when Isabel grazed them in the hills, she was usually alone. She no longer passed other goatherds, or old men leading mules laden with handwoven baskets, or the children who used to run alongside her. The houses where she used to stop for a glass of water were empty.

Once, as she balanced her way along a rock outcropping, she came across a pair of black high-heeled shoes. Around her, the gray expanse of the forest spread up the hillslope, unbroken but for the cacti and the rare umbrella of a drinking-tree. She had just turned fourteen. She thought how she had never worn shoes with high heels. They lay wedged in a crack; she had to lie on her belly to reach them. The rock was sharp and dug into her breasts. When she couldn't reach them, she broke a branch from a buckthorn. Then she hesitated. There were forest spirits who dressed as women when they came down into the villages. She withdrew her hand and whispered an invocation against ghosts, along with three Hail Marys and an Our Father. She could hear the tlingaling of goat bells somewhere in the brush.

She ran off as the day was ending. Her legs were warm with the radiating heat of the ground, but her shoulders were cold. She found the goats and ran them home.

Another day, she passed a small cross. They were common in the backlands; she didn't know why she had stopped. The cross had been painted, but the paint had worn away. Before it, someone had placed a pair of heat-wilted candles and the bottom half of a green plastic bottle, shredded along its length, with the end of each strip painted with a dash of nail polish, like a little bouquet of flowers. On the cross was carved a single word, IZABEL, with no dates. Perhaps it was a baby, she thought, or an old woman whose last name was forgotten. The thought of the marker bothered her for a long time, as if below was not one Isabel but many, perhaps every Isabel in the world one day found her way to this spot. Later, she avoided the cross and the path that led there.

Isaias wrote again. The city was hot and crowded, he said. He sometimes found work playing alongside an accordion and a drummer at an open-air restaurant. He couldn't send money this time. It was more difficult to find jobs, he was earning only enough to get by, but that would change. He used city expressions, such as 'things are on the up-and-up.' He promised to send money soon. When his letters came, she first scanned them slowly for some mention of when he would come home, and then returned to 'Dear Isabel,' and read them word by word.

In his third letter, he wrote of seeing a beautiful girl. He was playing in the Cathedral Square, and she stopped and listened to him play. He didn't know her name. He filled both sides of the page, and in a thin blank space at the bottom he drew little buildings like the skyline of a city.

Isabel read the letter twice, folded it and took it with her on her walks. She broke the rattling pods angrily and kicked at the loose stones. It was a week before Carnival. When the festivals began, her family walked to Prince Leopold to watch the processions. She said she was sick. She stayed home and pushed herself back and forth in her hammock with her foot.

Her family came home late at night, their hair crisp with starch that children tossed at passersby in tiny wax balls. They laughed and recalled the processions, the girl who was the princess, the costumes of glitter and ribbon. The high point, they said, was a fight that broke out between the Procession of the Three Kings from Prince Leopold and the Great Lion of God, a marching orchestra that had come all the way from the coast. An angel punched the king, a drunk in a priest's cassock smashed a bottle over a Fierce Indian, a man on a cardboard horse purloined a kiss from the princess.

The story cheered her. She went with them the next day. Her cousin wore wings made of real feathers. The street flashed with sequins. She marveled at the wondrous costumes, but it was different from the years before: quieter, emptier, and the drunks were angry. Because so many men had left for the south, the girls danced mostly with one another. I live in a world of women, she thought. She whirled, her hands in her mother's.

Only once, a man in a woman's stockings came close to her. His chest was bare and he wore lipstick and tinted glasses. He spun around her, his hips moving faster and faster, until they were a blur. She turned and he was gone.

In late March, not long after Carnival, they spotted a file of dust plumes on the horizon. Word came that they were building a highway from the coast. A representative of the governor

came and erected a sign that said PROGRESS INTO THE BACK-
LANDS IS PROGRESS FORWARD.

Over the following weeks, the highway came closer. When
the wind shifted, they could hear the roar of the machines.
Clouds of dust swept through town, coating the windows and
the uncovered food, tinting the white walls a light orange that
the children blew away with puffed cheeks. It formed soft
slopes in the corners of doorways and settled in films in the
water jars.

In the afternoons, Isabel went with the other girls to a hillside overlooking the highway. They watched huge vehicles
drive through the white forest with a scouring chain slung
between them, tearing through the trees as if they were nothing but dry twigs. In places, the crew followed the old road
that wove its way around the thickest copses; in others, they
pushed straight over them, the bulldozers crushing the brush,
the backhoes clanging against the stones.

Isabel could see men below, tiny against the machines.
They shoved sticks of dynamite beneath the largest rocks and
exploded them, or drilled them, screeching, until they shattered apart. The children stared with amazement and chased
one another, repeating the noises. There were soldiers, too,
with helmets and rifles, pacing the road and watching the
hills. At night in town, her family talked about the soldiers,
and why the government thought the roads needed to be pro-
tected, and from whom.

At first, the children watched warily from the bluff, but
each day they made their way closer. The construction men
were friendly. They showed them the machines and let them
play on them during their noon breaks. The children asked
where the asphalt was, and the men said that it was coming

later, that they were just clearing a path, 'We go first, It's a harder job with the stones and thorn.' Isabel stood uneasily at the edge of it all, watching a little cousin as he clambered over the seats and slid down the dusty concavity of the bulldozer's scoop, whistling with surprise at the heat of the metal in the sun. She noticed that some of the girls began to wear lipstick and their best clothes, and hold their shoes in their hands as they made their way barefoot down the hillside. They sat in the shade with the men, laughed with them and took short drinks from label-less bottles.

There was one man who smiled at Isabel when she sat alone, watching from beneath a buckthorn not far from camp. Once, when he approached, she stood quickly, brushed off her skirt and took the hand of her cousin. She retreated up the hillside and watched the man shrug and move back to the camp. Another time, when her cousin disappeared to play in the cab of the bulldozer, the man came and stood at the edge of the tree's shade. He offered her a bottle of soda. 'It's cold,' he said. There was only one icebox in Saint Michael, in the canteen, but it was unplugged and usually empty. She let him sit with her. The rock was wide, but his leg pressed against hers. 'From the town?' he asked. She nodded. 'Not much here,' he said, 'It must get lonely.' 'It's all right.' She didn't know what else to say. He continued, 'Where I'm from, we've got a lot more green than this, although not much more money.' He laughed. 'If we did, I suppose I wouldn't be out here. What's your name?' he asked.

When she finished the soda, she held the bottle against her arm until it wasn't cold anymore and then handed it back to him. His leg was still against hers, and he put the bottle down at his feet. She realized they were alone. She could hear only scraps of the children's distant voices, and she couldn't see the other girls. 'Why are you so frightened?' said the man. 'I'm not frightened.' 'You aren't? You remind me of the little birds that flit about the edge of camp.' She laughed a little. He smiled. 'You have orange soda on your mouth,' he said, and placed his thumb on her lip. She felt her heart race, but she didn't move. His hands were dry and heavy and reminded her of the machines. He ran his thumb along her lip, slowly lowering it to where it was wet with her saliva. She could taste the soda on his finger. Suddenly, she pinched her mouth closed. 'Hey,' he said. 'What's wrong?' She started away, but he grabbed her wrist. 'Sweetheart, take it easy! Have some fun.' She twisted her wrist from his hand. His grip was tight, her skin burned. He pulled her toward him, but she broke his grip and ran, pulled her cousin from the hot hollow of the bulldozer plow and fled up the hill. She noticed then that she was crying. Farther up the hillside, the tears became hacking coughs. She stopped, and spit and spit and wiped her mouth with the edge of her shirt. Her cousin stood a few feet away. When she stopped crying and wiped her eyes, she said angrily to him, 'This is your fault. You will never go back.'

At home, she looked at herself in a small hand mirror her mother had been given by the foreigners. She tried to see what the man saw. Her eyes were red and swollen. She felt strangely distant from the girl in the mirror, as if she were staring from far away, as if, by blinking, the girl would vanish. There was still a smudge of the orange soda on her chin. She spit on her fingers and rubbed it away.

After two days, her mother said, 'Something happened. You're acting strange.' She shook her head. She thought: It was my fault, I went down there and let him give me the soda to drink, I should have accepted no charity, I should have stayed away. A bruise bloomed around her wrist. She wore her single long-sleeved shirt despite the heat.

In town, they whispered about the girls who began to visit the camp and dance with the men. When the wind was right, they could hear the radio music coming up from the valley. A girl came to Isabel and said, 'Why don't you come anymore? You are a prude. Your friend asks about you every day.' Another girl said, 'She already has a boyfriend. It's her brother.' Isabel wanted to strike her. Later, she imagined the moment over and over. You can't just be quiet all the time, she told herself. She wished for her brother's facility with words. She wished she had said, It is not that, it isn't anything that you can understand. If he was here he would explain.

In the evenings, when she came home with the goats, she looked for a letter from Isaias and asked her mother for any news. But the mail came rarely; the postman waited for letters to collect for many days before he made rounds to the remoter settlements. There were weeks in Saint Michael without mail.

She tried writing to him. She took paper from the schoolhouse and wrote slowly, making her capital letters big so they filled the lines. She spelled out the words on her lips. She wrote, *Isaias you should come home It is much better here than the city You make Money yes but Here is better Many people left There are places to farm I can help I know how to take care of everything now.* She crumpled it. She wrote, *Isaias I am very lonely Why If you were here I wouldn't be so lonely.* She crumpled it. She wrote, *Isaias Mother and Father say you should come back Why did you go away You can't* She didn't know how to spell *abandon,* and she stopped.

Again she crumpled it. They were a little girl's words; she felt stupid. She had used up the paper, so she returned to the schoolhouse. As she walked, she asked herself why it was so difficult to explain. Why can't I just say it, that without you there is nothing here, suddenly we are poor and there is nothing, suddenly it is empty but it was never empty before. She found brown wrapping paper and used it to trace a school calendar, going over and over the numbers until the graphite broke.

Like the last time he left, she began to spend more time alone. She found that the solitude of the white forest rendered her invisible, that in the empty place that remained, her imagination flourished: Isaias returned, the rain came, the white forest flowered, the gray smothering heat lifted off Saint Michael and the backlands. She had always daydreamed, but now the dreams consumed her; there were hours she walked without knowing where she was.

As soon as she awoke, she would take the goats into the hills. The rest of her days withered until all that remained were her imagined hours with her brother. She told him about the road, the forest burning, the migrations. When she told him about the construction worker, she asked him to accompany her through town and to the road crew so that everyone would see she wasn't alone. She fantasized about Isaias hitting the worker so hard that his teeth rattled like a fistful of pebbles.

He left her at the edge of the trail. She wondered, Does he know? Is he really with me on these walks, Is part of him here, somehow do my questions find their way to him, through some strange thread, some web, some hidden channel to the south? Or are they my own questions and my own answers? Is it him or is it my memory of him? She wondered, Does everyone feel this? Or is it different, is it like hunting for him in the cane, like that strange and impossible game?

In town, the other girls talked about upcoming festivals and the men they met in the marketplace. They crowded around an old beauty magazine that one of them had brought from the coast. Isabel avoided them. She worked harder, grating the manioc furiously, deliberately filling the buckets to the brim when she carried them up from the river. Once, as they washed the dishes, her mother said, 'Things will be better, Isa,' and when Isabel tried to speak she felt her throat thick and heavy. She turned her face to the gray water and hid in the arbor of her hair.

In the little hand mirror, her cheeks were gaunt. She wore through a sandal and resoled it with goatskin. The pencil tickled as her mother traced the outline of her foot. When the phone rang, she ran to it, but it was always for someone else. Once, she returned from a walk to the news that Isaias had called. She called him back, but the line rang and no one answered.

When the parrot perches passed through town, she stood in the crowd that gathered to bid goodbye. The men lingered, discussing the road and weather. The children clambered over the tires and the passengers stared out through the slatted rails. When they finally left, and the wind took away the last of the ridged tread marks, she imagined her brother waiting in an identical square at the end of the long descent.

In the valley, the road crew moved on, and the plumes of dust disappeared into the backlands. A week later, another crew came, with different machines. They laid hot black tar over the broken path. These men were different, humorless. They drank heavily at night and shot at the thrushes and snakes. They drove into Saint Michael and sat in the canteen until they were very drunk, and then veered away into the night.

With the new roads came more trucks, dragging huge containers toward the big cities of the interior. The children went down to the verge. They kicked the flattened carcasses of the bull toads across the asphalt or played soccer with a sack stuffed with rags. They lay in the road to listen for the vibration of the trucks, and then lined up like a little gallery of race spectators to watch them pass. They set out cacti and cheered as the tires pulped them. They gonged stones off the container siding.

Once, a little boy arced a stone into the air before a hurtling truck. It seemed to hang momentarily in space before the windshield disintegrated into a rain of glass. Ahead, the truck stopped, the children scattered into the thicket. A door creaked open and the driver walked back down the road. He stared into the scrub. A wind picked up, stirring the shards of glass. Suddenly he seemed afraid. He drove away. The children rushed the road, laughing, hurling stones.

Two weeks later a roadblock appeared. A pair of troops from the Military Police paced in the heat, stopped cars and banged their rifle butts against the sun-hot trunks. The children joked that they were hunting the little boy, but their parents were somber. The children were prohibited from leaving town. An officer came to ask questions. He sweated heavily and wiped his brow with his forearm. They were looking for highwaymen: someone, he said, was rolling boulders into the road and pistol-whipping drivers out of their cars. He watched everyone carefully as he spoke.

A week later he returned with reinforcements. They arrested two men. When they released them a month later, one had a clouded, useless eye and the other woke at night screaming. Then one day the men disappeared into the thorn. Later, on a back road outside town, Isabel came across an empty red car. There were no license plates. The window was smashed, and a thrush ate spilled bits of manioc flour from the floor mats. A snake stirred in the shade of the fender. She told her father.

'Don't tell anyone you saw that,' he said. 'And if the police come again and ask, keep your mouth shut about what you saw.'

Down in the valley, the cane began to grow again, but word came that they would be hiring fewer men this year because of a new reaper that could drive straight over the piles and scoop the stalks into its belly.

At home, her father paced the house and drank. One night, as Isabel tried to sleep, she heard him whisper to her mother in the other room, 'Send Isa.'

'And be alone?' her mother answered.

'We are going to be alone if she stays here. Look how thin she is. There's not much of her left.'

'Don't say things like that.'

'There is barely enough food for you and me. She could work in the city.'

'She's fourteen. Think before you say those kind of things. She knows nothing about the city. She knows nothing about the world. You worked in the capital. The city is even bigger. Can you imagine her there, the way she is, quiet and watching all the time?'

Her father interrupted, his voice angry: 'Then what do you want? For her to stay here and keep disappearing into the thorn? Fourteen's old. Girls are married when they're fourteen. Maybe she'll meet a man in the city. She's pretty when she's not so thin. But now she's just getting strange. Since—'

'Since Isaias left,' said her mother. 'I know. Don't think I don't see it.'

'But you think things are going to be better.'

'That's not what I am saying.'

'It's what I'm hearing.' Her father's voice broke. 'You think it's going to get better. If not, you better think about what you're saying, because it's what I'm hearing.'

There was a long silence, then her mother's voice began again, trembling. 'I can't. I can't do this. Who's going to take care of us later? I had four children, and now there is just her.'

'Just her? They're not dead. Isaias isn't dead. You are talking about him as if he's dead.'

'No, I'm not. You know I'm not. But he's not here, either. You think children come home from the city? How many children have you seen come home from the city? What if the perch turns over? What happens then? What happens if she gets sick?'

'Her body's closed. She knows which prayers to say. She's never said anything since that day she saw the spirit out in the forest. It isn't the same in the cities.'

'I'm not worried about a spirit, I'm worried about real people.'

'She isn't weak. She knows the backlands as well as I do. She's smart.'

'She's smart like an animal's smart. Like an animal knows what's near and senses things before they come. I don't know what good that does in the city. She can barely write—you've seen her try.'

'I—' began her father, and then he cursed. Her mother muttered something else, and then her father said, 'Of course I don't want that. What father wants that?' and then they both were silent for a long time. Isabel strained to listen. She thought she heard her mother crying. Then pacing, then the clatter of bottles.

'Put that away,' said her mother.

Without warning, she heard a pot slam against the wall. 'You think I want this?' he shouted. 'You think I asked for this?' 'Shh, don't scream, I didn't say—' The pot clattered across the room. 'Don't you understand? They've got my face against the ground.'

'Who's they?' Her mother sounded as though she were speaking to a child.

'*They*. The people against us. The situation.' He said the word slowly. 'The whole situation that's against us.'

Again there was silence.

'And if she doesn't want to go?' asked her mother, at last.

'She'll go. She's wanted to go since her brother left.'

They moved outside and Isabel caught only phrases. She welcomed the sudden calm.

More days passed. Her father's drinking bled into the day-time. Twice, he shattered stools in anger. He paced the house and collapsed into tears. Her mother hid the plates, cups and saints so he wouldn't break them.

One night in late May, he came home with his face swollen and bruised. 'Who did this to you?' said her mother. When she brought him water, he hit it away. Isabel undressed him. His clothes smelled of cane liquor. She rocked him and wiped grease and little specks of food from the ruddy stubble of his beard. When he fell asleep in his hammock, her mother took her outside.

For a long time they were quiet together. 'We can't do this much longer,' said her mother.

She looked old and very tired. 'I spoke to Manuela,' she said. 'She has her own house. She says it would be hard for you to get work in a factory, but she has a baby. She has been paying a woman to watch it during the week. You could take care of it until you found some kind of work. There's a perch next week.'

'And Isaias is there.'

'Yes, Isabel,' said her mother. 'Yes, he is there. But he's working, too, remember. Don't expect so much from him. It's hard if someone expects too much of you.'

Isabel telephoned the city. A man answered. She could hear loud music playing in the background. 'This is Isabel, Manuela's cousin. I want to speak to my brother.'

'I'll get him,' said the man.

She hung up the receiver and looked out at the empty square. Many of the houses were shuttered. A pair of children played, but the plaza was otherwise empty. She called again. 'Hello?' Music blasting, a loud bass sound. 'It's Isabel.' 'Couldn't find your brother, love. Haven't seen him for a couple of days, actually.'

'He must be working on the coast,' she said.

At meals they said little. In a canvas bag, among her clothes, she packed her long knife, its blade narrowed from sharpening. Her mother said that in the city there was nothing to cut. 'Not cactus?' asked Isabel. Her mother shook her head. Isabel left the knife.

Later, she walked to the edge of the thorn, broke off a smooth gray piece and placed it carefully into her bag.

As the days passed and her departure grew closer, she began to suffer attacks of vertigo. She wished her mother would change her mind. Then, later, when rumors came that the price of the trip had risen, she worried she wouldn't go at all. The rumor was false. Again, vertigo seized her. She began to worry that someone would ask, *But do you want to go?* and she wouldn't have an answer.

Finally, she kissed her aunts and uncles and cousins and, last, her father. 'Be good,' he said only, but looked away when she tried to meet his eyes. She walked with her mother to Prince Leopold, to the bus station where the flatbeds passed. She had walked the road many times, but it was different now, as if the light were somehow clearer. The thorn forest turned to fields, to dusty roads, to tin shacks, to chipped whitewash and pantiled rooftops, to walls painted with advertisements and names of political candidates. The day was very hot.

At last they reached the station. The ground was a hard burnt soil, and the station was ringed with pensions for those who missed their buses. At the snack bar, a pair of flies flitted over a sagging cake.

They sat on a concrete bench near the ticket offices and watched idling buses discharge passengers in the spray of diesel. The bus lines were called *Progress,* the *Princess of the Farmlands* and *Good Hope,* but Isabel knew they were all too expensive. Her mother stared at the station clock. The air was heavy with the heat and exhaust. A boy climbed out of a concrete trench, where he had been toiling at the undercarriage of a car.

It grew hotter. A group of old men set out chairs and lifted their shirts above their bellies. A middle-aged woman fanned a child and slumped forward, her face damp and drawn. A filthy cat wandered along the edge of the station where the sun met the shade, changed its mind and settled in a patch of weeds.

A cashew vendor passed. Usually, Isabel would beg her mother for cashews, but now she was too afraid to be hungry.

She began to feel ill with the heat and waiting. She wanted to open the top buttons on her dress, but she felt the half-lidded eyes of the men as they sat back in their chairs with their chests and bellies open to the air. A trickle of mechanics slunk between the shops that surrounded the station. She went and looked in the concession stand. It sold good luck charms, Saint Christopher invocation cards, wooden fists and rosary beads. A small black-and-white TV played a channel where a preacher inveighed against beliefs in backlands spirits.

Night came. The men went home. The station was empty except for the two of them and an old woman. Isabel took out Isaias's letters and arranged them in a row on the bench. 'Put those away, or you'll lose them,' said her mother.

'I'll bring him home,' said Isabel.

'Sleep,' said her mother.

Isabel slept with her head on her mother's lap. She awoke strangely happy.

It was very quiet, and in the distance was the stain of sunrise. The flatbed idled in the square. It was crowded with bodies and blankets. The huddled figures moved silently aside to give her space.

It took the flatbed a half hour to reach the outskirts of Prince Leopold, winding through unpaved streets of cinder-block houses. The driver hung out the window, his low song *tothesouthtothesouthtothesouth* coaxing dawn-shadowed figures from doorways and street corners. The new passengers swung bags onto the dirty planks and settled among the others.

At the edge of the city, the truck accelerated. Fresh air rushed over the back. Outside, the scrub ran to the base of the mountains, where a thin trail threaded to a summit chapel. The road was potholed and the driver never stopped swerving.

There were no benches. The passengers slumped against the slatted railing or curled up in the center. Their faces were burnt and lined with a gray dust that covered everything. The truck had come from farther north, Isabel knew. She wondered how many days the others had been riding. She found a gray wool blanket that didn't seem to have an owner. She checked it for spots of blood and bedbugs; it seemed clean, so she wrapped it over her shoulders. She flexed her toes uncomfortably. Her shoes were a size too small, but they were her best pair, black store-bought loafers with the words *Daisy Girl* printed on the insoles. She had promised her mother she wouldn't lose them, and she kept them on.

They passed through a little town. A crowd of schoolchildren swirled around boys riding bicycles with wooden blocks bolted to the pedals. On the outskirts, a billboard showed a smiling couple at the edge of an emerald swimming pool. Where the poster was torn, she could see scraps of other posters: a leg, a little owl, a woman's painted mouth, the word VICTOR. Insouciant dogs trotted through the cacti and yapped at the truck. At times, she could hear music coming from the cab.

In the afternoon, a pair of men at the railing began to point. 'A pilgrim,' someone whispered. She saw a lone figure dragging a cross, its base worn smooth by the road. The truck slowed but the man didn't look up. Some of the passengers crossed themselves. The scrubland stretched to the horizon, white like a dusting of ash.

Down the road, a man in a red velvet shirt and a straw hat flagged the truck, climbed onto the flatbed and threw himself down beside her. He began to talk the moment he sat, introducing himself with an endless name she forgot before he finished. He called her *my angel* and said, 'You look like you just came fluttering down from the sky.' He didn't ask her name. He was a rhabdomancer, 'at least a hundred and twenty-seven years old,' and he added, 'Rhabdo-rod, mancy-divination. I find water in the subsoil.' He had, he told her, an explanation for the droughts.

He said the modern age was 'all Carnival and no Lent.' For many miles, he uttered proclamations about the end of the world, when a boy-king and his soldiers would return to take revenge on all sinners, a group that included thieves and girls with shirts that showed their bellies. Behind him, one of the standing boys made loops around his ear with his finger, and Isabel tried to suppress a smile.

The rhabdomancer touched her arm. 'Did you see that man up the road? I walked for two days with that citizen and his cross. Do you know why he is paying a promise? He went to work in the salt plants, where they all go blind from seeing too much white, and before he left he said he would pay a promise to Saint Lucy if he could return to see his beloved backlands one last time. I think he is blind, his eyes are clouded like muddy water, but he says he can see the road, or the end of the road. This place used to be filled with men like that. There is no faith anymore. That's why this is happening. If there was faith, we would stay where God planted us in the first place.'

He settled back against the side of the flatbed. Isabel watched him curiously. She wanted him to say more, but she knew not to bother older people with too many questions. He must know about the city, she told herself, He could tell me how it will be. She could not find the words to ask.

In the evening, a girl in a tight orange polyester top sat next to her. 'Where are you from?' asked the girl, twirling her finger in a thin chain necklace. 'Saint Michael. It's just a village, near Prince Leopold.' 'You going all the way?' Isabel nodded. 'You know where you are going to work?' Isabel shook her head. 'I'm not going to work. I'm going just for a short time, to watch a baby.' 'Everyone's going to work,' said the girl. 'My aunt found me a job as a waitress: prime job, tips and everything. I get to buy a dress, lipstick, probably get my hair done.' She paused. 'Got a boyfriend?' she asked. Isabel shook her head again. 'Me neither,' said the girl. 'Want one?' Isabel shrugged. The girl tossed her hair. 'I'm going to get one in the city. The men in the city have real style. I've seen pictures of big white houses with pillars outside. And pools. Look,' she said, and pulled out a folded photo of a cream-yellow house with high walls, a fountain and an aristocratic dog. 'This is just a magazine photo. It only looks so real because I pasted it to paper. But it's the kind I want. A girl from my village lives in a house like that now. She was a maid and the family's son fell in love with her. His parents didn't like it at first, but when they saw that it was such pure love, they got them their own house. I want a pure love like that.' The girl scooted over to the railing and looked out. After a long time, she asked, 'You scared?' 'A little,' said Isabel. 'You don't talk much,' said the girl.

The girl brought out a tin of cornmeal. 'You should eat,' she said. Isabel shook her head. She had ground manioc in her bag, but she wasn't hungry. 'At least something,' said the girl, 'or you will be sick.'

On the edge of the highway, a woman in a pink dress walked with her shoes in her hand. She waved them to a stop and climbed onto the flatbed. Her face was painted and her body filled her dress. She smelled sweetly of lavender water. All the passengers stared until she got off at a little town with a plaster statue of a horseman whose horse had crumbled away to a metal frame.

The sun set.

The girl lifted her blanket and took Isabel inside. Isabel pretended that she was sleeping and rested her head on the girl's shoulder. She liked the feeling of the girl next to her. Through the slivers of her half-closed eyes, she stared out. The mountains were blue; the night enormous. Forgetting that she didn't know the girl, she held her hand, and soon she slept.

She had left home only once before, to celebrate the New Year with an aunt on the coast. It had been a different time, of rain and good jobs for her father.

She was six. For months before, she assailed her mother with questions about the sea. She made Isaias read to her from the school's *Young Man's Encyclopedia,* its pages rank with mold and dust. In the section for Ocean were photos of eels and sea turtles and a smiling man with a crab, his white shirt faded to an empty space against a monotone of blue.

They slept at their aunt's home on a hillside invaded by shanties. At Christmas, they went to mass and then to the beach. It was also her mother's first time to the sea, and she retreated as the waves approached. Isabel stood her ground. Tentatively she dipped her palm and sipped. It was salty but not disagreeable; she drank until her throat was sore. She peered into the horizon, trying to see where it ended. Isaias told her he could see the great city New York. 'If you can't see it, you must be blind,' he said. 'I see it,' she shot back. Then she tumbled in the sand. Isaias put pieces of foam in her hair. They raced the waves and squinted at the silhouettes of children somersaulting off the pier.

That afternoon, in the fetid aisles of the municipal market, she saw her first fish, staring from a silvery pile with a clouded, deflated eye. She put her thumb in its mouth and felt the tiny teeth. Its lips reminded her of a baby's gums. Curious, she wormed her forearm into the pile and wriggled it until her mother slapped it away. There was a broad white fish that Isaias called a ray. It had a whip-like tail and a smiling mouth. She smiled back.

On New Year's Eve, her parents took them to an old lighthouse. There were more people than she had ever seen. Squawking vendors with trays of sea-damp cigarettes shouldered through the crowds. Everyone was dressed in white, and on the shore they looked like a giant flock of gulls. They crowded the beach and tossed flowers into the sea. In the pools left by retreating tides, they floated in the blooms of white skirts. Tables slouched crookedly in the sand, their white tablecloths fluttering beneath picnic baskets and bottles of cheap champagne. The algae was luminescent in the lights of the promenade.

Isabel watched the surf flap against a feathered line of broken roses. Her mother bought a rose and told her to wish for years of rain. 'How many years am I allowed to wish for?' she asked. 'As many as you like,' said her mother with a laugh. She wished for seven.

At midnight, the crowd pushed up against the shore to watch fireworks flowering from a platform in the sea. Suddenly, a rocket streaked toward land and buried itself in the crowd. There were shrieks, the crowd surged. The fireworks platform has fallen! someone shouted, It's pointing toward us! Turn it off! said someone else, laughing, but the rockets kept coming. It's an automated show, shouted another, I read about it, The newest technology! On the rocks, a small boy wore his shirt tied around his neck like a cape. He raised his arms as the tracers of colored smoke streaked past. Laughing, Isaias pointed. Don't you dare! said their mother, holding him tightly. Hurray for the New Year! shouted the children. Hurray!

Then it was over. Down on the beach, the wind was strong. The tide had risen, snuffing the cooking fires and candles.

There was more pushing, and Isabel's hand slipped from her mother's. When she turned, her family was gone. She called for them, but her voice was lost in the music and the crash of waves. The few stairways down to the beach were packed to a standstill. She ran along the shore. Around her, drunks were sleeping in the sand, couples necked at the water's edge, children danced crazily in the waves. A girl flailed in the shallows until she was dragged onto the shore by her friends. Champagne bottles littered the beach like sandy fish.

Panicked, Isabel squeezed through the crowds and climbed the embankment. She hoisted herself onto a lamppost. The beach and streets were all bodies, she couldn't see anyone from her family.

It was Isaias who found her. He wiped the tears from her cheeks. She clung to his hand with both of hers. 'Stop being scared,' he said. 'I'm not scared,' she protested. 'Then stop squeezing my hand so hard. The thornmen will get you. They eat children who are scared.' 'Thornmen don't live in the city, Isaias.' He shrugged. 'You'll see.'

They retreated through the alleyways, past discarded decorations and figures sleeping on doorsteps, the noise and light of the festival fading. A pair of dogs followed them home. At night, when she refused to go to bed, he whispered a rhyme:

> *Close your eyes, Isa*
> *Or the thornmen will get you.*
> *They're killing the women*
> *and the children, too.*

She sniffled until she fell asleep.

Back in Saint Michael, her aunts asked about the sea. Her mother showed them postcards of the churches. She kept them neatly in an envelope and insisted they hold them by the edges.

Isabel listened. She mostly remembered the darkness, the shouting, the fear of being alone in a big and crowded place. Isaias bragged that he had been on the rocks, chasing the streaking lights. She forgave him for the thornmen song and let him lie.

Later in the night, she awoke to loud voices.

They were on an empty stretch of highway. The air smelled moist, richer, but the land was still barren. Cacti lined the road. She watched them flare in the rear lights of the car and then fade into darkness. The moon was gone.

The rhabdomancer was arguing with a woman.

'Listen,' he said, 'you can believe me or not believe me. But I know water. I've been able to see it my entire life.'

'*See it,*' said the woman. 'You mean you guess where it is.'

'No,' said the man, 'I'm telling you, I see it—like I see you in front of me. Like I see my hand.'

Isabel sat up. The passing country was black. She saw only the distant light of a house.

'I don't believe you,' said the woman. 'I don't believe in this magic.'

The man ignored her. 'There's a seam running beneath us. Like a ribbon, twisting on itself. It widens there by the cattle fence. It divides out by the pasture and branches like vessels of blood. Like roots. Like I could thrust my hand into the ground and tear out a great mass of shining roots.' He paused. 'There is an underground lake at the base of those hills. Shaped like a dog, a blue sleeping dog.'

The woman interrupted. 'On my farm we paid for one of your type, and he did nothing but lie. Not one of his wells gave water.'

The man shrugged.

'What good does it do you now?' the woman asked, and then grew silent.

Later, as the flatbed rode through a long and empty stretch, Isabel opened her eyes to find the man awake. Sand dunes crept onto the roads, and the wet air smelled of her single memory of the sea. The woman was sleeping.

'You can see it, too,' he said to Isabel, when he saw her watching him. She didn't answer. He repeated, 'You see it. You see it, don't you?'

Isabel shook her head.

'I thought . . . ,' he said, and stopped. Isabel wanted to tell him about Isaias in the cane fields, but he began again. 'In the jungle, when we mined the rivers, I could find each trench in the underwater banks, even in the darkness. In the quarries, they sent me in with the drills to keep them from hitting a water seam and flooding the tunnels. In the navy, too, I dove, to search out leaks in the hulls of the ships when others couldn't find them. I can see in the city: the pipes, water mains, sewers. I can see the rivers that run below the ground. I dove there, too. In the tunnels of the waterworks, like we used to mine.'

She waited for the rest of his story, but he had stopped. She wondered what it was like to live under the water. Somehow, she imagined it like the truck's coursing, a terrifying fall through darkness, the cold currents streaming past.

In the morning, she awoke to a gentle shaking. It was the girl. 'Look,' she said.

The flatbed had slowed; the side of the road was crammed with zebu cattle. The dark fields shifted like a mirage. Isabel wondered if there had been a fire. Then she saw it wasn't a burn, but cows as far as the horizon—it was all cows, the dark brown bodies crowding the fields, turning up clods of broken soil, in such numbers that they reminded her of blowflies that covered the meat at home. She was jolted by a wave of nausea. She heard a lowing that she first took to be the engine of the truck. An animal was pushed up against the slats, its face inches away, smeared with green manure. It flapped its tail with nonchalance. There are too many of them, she thought with sudden anger, There is not enough space.

They left the cows. She saw how the land had changed. The earth was wet. They passed cane fields, the stalks higher than those at home. A group of laborers filed along a narrow red path. She remembered stories about this place: it was sugar country, tobacco country, once slave country; the earth was so fertile, they said, you could spit and it would grow a man. They passed a cane-processing plant and the site of an abandoned fairground. Swallows arced and chased each other over the fields.

The girl offered her food again, but she was nauseated with the memory of the zebu. How many days had it been since she last ate? she wondered. She was already confused about how long they had been traveling.

In the afternoon, they stopped at a hot, barren intersection, and a group of people came running from a concrete pavilion.

They piled bags into the back and climbed on. It was very crowded now, and there was scarcely any room to sit. Isabel gave her space to an old woman with a sun-worn face and a rosary made of black and red seeds.

Isabel stood and clung to the metal bar. The air was stagnant and smelled thickly of people. She felt dizzy and looked for someplace to rest her gaze, but everything was swaying. The sun was very hot on the top of her head. She thought: I should have eaten. What if I have to ride like this, standing, all the way? She saw how the wind whipped the hair of the people at the rail, and wanted to be there. She wondered if later they would rotate, how they would sleep. She was thirsty, but she was afraid that if she drank she would have to pee. She had two cane liquor bottles' worth of water, but they were in her bag, beneath the other bags. She hadn't touched them.

Farther along the road, a young man fainted, crumpling onto a pile of bags. Then an older man fell. When they stopped next, the driver argued with the passengers. 'I can't go carrying sick people,' he said. 'It's not that I am a bad person, but if one of you dies, they'll take away the truck. I have a family.' They gave the young man water and he was able to stand. The old man got off with his son at a roadside canteen.

They slowed again, for a family that waited at the side of the road. 'South! To the south!' shouted the driver, and the family crowded in. Their children were so small that they seemed to take up no space at all. They stopped again, for a lone couple. She heard grumbling. 'Hey, driver,' said a man beside her, 'what do you think this is? Are we goats?' The new passengers looked miserable. 'The last perch was even more crowded,' said the woman.

They were climbing a low hill, and at each turn the flatbed

swayed. They held tightly to the bars. Isabel felt strangely cold. She wondered if Isaias had been sick, too. She leaned briefly on a woman beside her until the woman shifted away. Her stomach tightened and a bitter taste filled her mouth. It's good I didn't eat, she thought. 'You okay?' asked a man beside her. 'Yes,' she said. 'It's only my stomach. It will go away.' She pressed her forehead to the back of her hand. Her head was spinning now, and the voices on the truck seemed distant. She took short, quick breaths, but there wasn't any air. The truck moved slowly up the hill and she could smell the exhaust. She swayed, and caught herself on the woman's arm. 'This girl's not doing well,' said a man. 'I'm all right, I—' said Isabel, and couldn't finish the sentence. Somehow she was on her knees, surrounded by legs, and then she felt her face on a shoe that pulled away. The smell was stronger. She heard murmurs and felt hands pulling on her. This girl's sick, said a voice, and another, See I told you, Someone stop the truck, Move, Give her space, You move, There's no space, Tell the driver, Stop the truck I said. There was a banging on metal and the truck slowed. 'I'm fine,' she said to no one. She heard the creak of the grate and the thudding of feet on the ground outside. A breeze, and a voice. 'You all right?' 'No she's not, she's sick. She's going to make the rest of us sick. This flatbed's too crowded.' 'Bring her up front,' said the driver. They helped her stand but she stumbled again and they had to lower her from the truck, where she took a step, and fell. 'You better take her to the next hospital,' said someone. 'I don't need a hospital,' mumbled Isabel. 'Just water.' They brought her a bottle. She drank from it and vomited.

They carried her to the cab. The seats were hot and smelled of oil. She steadied her hand on the door as the driver put the truck in gear. 'You don't need to stop,' she said. 'I'll be fine.' 'Still got another day and a half to go,' said the driver. 'As much as they talk about the backlander being a strong breed, many people die from the heat. I've seen it myself.' Isabel said, 'I didn't eat anything. I didn't drink anything.' The road was barren. 'I don't want to be left here,' she protested. She thought of her brother waiting.

Half an hour later they pulled into a small gas station. There was a single pump and a low-lying restaurant. It looked closed, except for a sign on the front door that read WELCOM. A dog sniffed its way through the lot. It stopped, snapped at a mange-black leg and then growled at them as if they were to blame for the mange. The driver led her to the door. It was locked. He rang a bell, but no one came. He told her to wait and went around the side of the building.

At the edge of the lot, a pair of carrion birds landed heavily on the ground, their nails scratching at the pavement as they walked. The dog whimpered and ran away, its tail between its legs. The carrion birds approached her, cocking their heads. She hissed at them. She reached down, picked up a broken shard of cement and hurled it. The birds hopped to the side and watched her inquisitively. Wind blew sand off the dunes and onto the lot. She saw the other passengers watching.

The man returned. 'No one in the restaurant,' he said. A whirlwind rattled an open shutter. Against the curb, dried leaves gathered alongside the torn cover of a motorcycle magazine and a broken Styrofoam cup.

He led her around to the other side, where a small door said OFFICE. 'Hello?' he shouted and opened the door. There was a cash register and an empty glass cooler. There was faint music in the background. On the wall was a six-year-old calendar with a naked girl bent over the back of a red truck. Someone had colored in her teeth; her mouth was gaping and obscene. Again the driver shouted, 'Hello?' The music stopped.

In a little room through the back door, they found a young woman alone at a desk, one hand on a radio dial. The shades were pulled, the other door shut. She held a black ink marker in her hand. She had stacks of paper around her, warped with circles of ink. She looked at them slowly. 'My lord. You're getting high,' said the driver. Dizzy from the fumes, Isabel sat on the floor.

'Do you have a phone?' asked the driver.

The woman stared at them blankly.

'This girl is sick,' he said. 'Is there a clinic?'

The woman stared.

'*Child,*' said the man, 'where's the phone?'

The woman closed her eyes and opened them. She sniffed twice and blinked again, nodding toward a phone behind the desk. Isabel could hear the other end of the line ringing and ringing. She hoped no one would answer. She wanted to keep going. She wanted to climb onto the flatbed and sleep.

The driver hung up angrily.

'It's just down the road,' said the woman slowly.

He helped Isabel back into the cab. Down a narrow side road, at the edge of a town, they found the clinic, a low building set at the back of a dusty yard. The truck parked in a driveway with loose flagstones. He helped her to the entrance, where a guard indicated where to wait. Isabel had to lie on a bench.

Finally a nurse came. She had a bored, impatient manner. 'What's wrong with this one?' she asked. The driver stood and held his hat politely in his hands. 'She was on my truck. Now she is sick.' The nurse pinched her skin. 'She's dehydrated, of course,' she said, and added, 'I'm not surprised.' The wood of the bench felt cool on Isabel's head. 'Come,' said the nurse. Isabel struggled up. 'I'm not sick, my brother is waiting in the city, I don't want to stay here.' 'You'll be okay,' said the driver. 'Let them take care of you, you can catch another flatbed.' 'I can't.' She paused. 'I can't pay for another flatbed.' The driver waited, and then said, 'Here,' and counted out a small stack of bills for her. 'It's your fare, and there is a little extra if you need it. I have to go, or else everyone will start complaining.' Isabel wanted to protest, but she only closed her eyes. He left and returned with her bag. 'You're very nice,' she said. He started to walk away, but then he turned. 'It's not too often that I get to do something good for someone else,' he said.

The nurse led her into a larger room. There were five wooden beds in a row. The floor was concrete, the walls made of unevenly laid white tile. In the corner was a metal examining table, piled with boxes. On the farthest bed, a thin shape curled up under a red blanket and convulsed with coughing.

'Lie there,' said the nurse, pointing to another bed. Isabel lay down without removing her shoes. The nurse uncoiled an intravenous line, slid the needle into Isabel's hand and brought her a glass of sugary water. Cold rose up her arm. She drank and thought she would throw up again, but she slept.

When she awoke, it was dark. The needle was gone. The nurse sat at an empty desk and stared at the door. Across the room, the figure was coughing. He was thin, with hollow eyes. A mask had slipped sideways to cover his cheek. He sat up and tried to spit into a small cup, but his cough was dry. He lay back down and covered himself with the sheets. He watched Isabel. He was beautiful in a way, she thought, with his delicate cheekbones and sunken eyes. Above his bed was a prayer card for Saint Jude. He began to cough again.

'I think that man needs help,' Isabel said to the nurse. 'He won't stop coughing.'

'You think I can't hear that?' said the nurse. 'Also, it's not a he, it's a she. She cut her hair off—I don't know why. She's always making trouble.'

'What's wrong with her?' asked Isabel.

'No responsibility.'

'I mean, what's she sick with?'

'What do you think? Like the rest who go to the city and think they can slut around. Now her family won't take care of her, so I have to.'

Isabel didn't understand. 'I think she's trying to say something,' she said.

'She's always trying to say something. She's trying to torment me. She thinks she has the right to make my life hell.' Isabel stared at the nurse, incredulous. 'Do you need anything else?' asked the nurse.

'No,' said Isabel awkwardly. 'I'm better . . . I have to go.'

'Go ahead,' said the nurse. 'You're not sick, anyway.'

She rose and lifted her bag as the nurse watched. 'Can you show me where the bus station is?'

'I can't leave. Ask one of the people waiting. They'll point you on the way. It's a small town. It's not dangerous.'

Isabel was dizzy, but she could walk. The clinic was empty. A hallway led into a courtyard. There were no lights, and she almost tripped over a chair. Outside, a guard sat and talked with a woman and a little girl. They wore matching dresses, cotton printed with red trucks. Isabel thought, Like my mother, who cut everyone's clothes from the same roll of duck. The memory of her mother almost made her cry. I can't tell her I was sick, she thought. She asked for the bus, and they pointed to the fluorescent lights of a filling station. The street was dark except for a small light at the entrance to a private hospital, a white windowless building with the name of a brigadier general.

She walked across the road and pulled herself over the divide. A truck sped past, scattering pebbles. Headlights bore down on her, but she couldn't tell how far away they were. At last she threw her bag over her shoulder and ran across the road.

It was a small station, with a high roof, three pumps and a single light. The station attendant, a thin boy with oily hair and a yellow uniform, pointed her to the bus stop, 'through the trucks, 'round the corner.' He stepped toward her and she stepped back. She saw darkness only, the shadows of the wheels and the flatbeds with heavy chains and swirls of decoration. 'Do you want me to show you?' he asked, and she shook her head.

As she left the cone of light, a large rig pulled off the highway, thundering over the gravel to a stop. Its window reflected the light of the station, the night, the boy in the yellow suit. It looked as if there was no one inside. The door didn't open.

She was in darkness now. She couldn't see anything that looked like a bus stop. She slipped between the lines of trucks, their wheels as high as her chest, teeth of tread like clenched fists. Her bag bumped against the side of the trucks as she walked, and she turned sideways to fit through. She wanted to say an invocation, but the invocations she knew were against snakes and sickness and thorn ghosts. She heard a girl's laugh and saw a figure in a colored skirt drop from one of the trucks and scurry away.

Through a break in a wall, she came upon the bus stop.

There was a single empty car, with a hand-painted sign in the window that read TAXI BLESSED MARIA DE JESUS. Across the street, she saw a half-lit placard advertising a dorm room, but the windows were dark and the shops that lined the pavilion were shuttered. In a tiny traveler's chapel, she found a strange painted statue of Mary with closed, sleeping eyes. It felt safer in the shelter of the sanctuary, but she was afraid she would miss the flatbed when it came. She found a bench outside and laid her head on her bag. The night was warm, she thought, and somehow she slept.

In the morning, another flatbed stopped on its way south. At first Isabel thought it was the truck she had come down on, with the same rusted undercarriage and the same coarse, hooded faces. The driver was a heavy man with an unbuttoned shirt and a combed mustache. 'I'm going south, to the city,' she shouted over the idling engine. 'No kidding,' said the driver. 'I wouldn't have guessed.' He laughed.

'Are you going there?' shouted Isabel, feeling sick again.

'Am I going there? No, I'm going to Shanghai.' Isabel fidgeted uncomfortably with her bag. A man in the passenger seat punched the driver playfully. The driver paused. 'You've never heard of Shanghai, have you?' The other man hit him again, laughing.

Isabel made her way to the back. It wasn't crowded, and she found space to sit. As they rode, she listened to a conversation about a factory for light fixtures, and a second about a war in a place whose name she didn't know.

In the afternoon, a woman touched her arm. 'Did someone hit you?' 'No,' said Isabel, surprised. 'I saw your cheek,' said the woman, 'And I thought—' Isabel raised her fingers to her face. Her cheekbone was tender, soft like the skin of a ripe fruit. 'I fell,' she told the woman. 'No one did anything bad to me. I didn't know I was hurt.'

The woman was sitting next to a small girl with long black hair. The girl watched them talking. There was something different about the girl, Isabel thought: she stared as if everything were new to her. After a long time she asked the girl, 'Are you going to the city, too?' The girl looked away. Isabel asked again, 'Are you going to the city?' The woman touched Isabel's arm. 'She doesn't understand you, she doesn't speak our language. Her brother told me when he left her with the flatbed. I've been traveling with her for days.'

'Which language does she speak?'

The woman shrugged. 'Who knows? Her own language. Her brother said that very few people speak their language. Very few people are left.'

Isabel watched the girl curiously. She had never heard another language. She couldn't conceive that the girl didn't understand. She wanted to laugh, but the more she watched the girl, the more frightening the thought became.

Farther along the road, a good-looking young man vaulted on. He smiled at Isabel. Blushing, she looked away.

They were passing orchards, but she didn't recognize the trees. She wondered how far they had gone. She tried to imagine the map, but she couldn't. She sang softly to herself:

> *So the boy became a fish*
> *And he swam against the rivers*
> *From the sea until the creek*
> *That would take him to his home.*

She looked at the boy who had smiled at her, but he was talking to an older girl. Once or twice he glanced at Isabel, but his smile was now the smile an older person gives a child, and she felt a mixture of disappointment and relief.

She lay on her back on the flatbed. Beneath her, she could hear the creaking of the shocks and felt grains of sand rub against her scalp. She watched the people standing above her, tall shapes silhouetted against the light. She watched the sky, how it filled and emptied with clouds, how the colors swept past, how there were stains that fled the sun and those that pursued it. She wondered what Isaias was doing, suddenly giddy to think that she soon would see him. A shorebird flew with them for a long time. Later, vultures circled in the distant corner of her eye. Tree branches flickered past, sunlight glinting through the leaves. She let her mind clear. The wind whipped up strands of her hair. When she closed her eyes, the insides of her eyelids were warm and red, and her lips tingled.

She thought of new songs to sing to herself, but all of them made her miss home, and she didn't want to cry in front of the other people. So she thought of her brother. She remembered one of his funniest stories, about a mouse that ran up the leg of a bride. Thinking of the mouse led to thinking of thicket mice, which led to thinking of hunger, so she went back and thought about the bride instead. Then the thought of the bride led to church and praying in church, which led to the landowners and to hunger. So she went back and thought about the bride again, and this time the thought led to a dress she had seen at a store in Prince Leopold, where she and Isaias used to go to clown before a full-length mirror. Sometimes, between games, she would catch him staring at himself the way a person stares at someone coming down the road from far

away. Once he said, 'Is this what I look like?' At first she had
thought he was joking, but he insisted, 'I'm not playing, Isa.
Is this what you see when you see me?' Not understanding,
she turned to him. 'No,' he said, 'not *me,* me in the mirror.'
She stared for a long time. Then she saw a thin boy with a
man's face, a worn shirt and sandals, a stranger. She didn't
answer. A customer came and the owner shooed them out. As
they walked home, she looked at him again, and the other boy
was gone.

Night came. 'Are you sleeping?' asked the woman beside
her. Isabel shook her head. The woman sat up on an elbow. 'I
know you weren't, I saw you watching the sky. I can't sleep,
either. I'm scared there'll be a storm, or the flatbed will flip, or
we'll be robbed. Once that happened to me. First time I came.
I thought, Only an idiot robs a truck of poor people, and then
I thought how I was carrying more money than I had carried
in my life, because I needed it for the city. Then, because I
thought it couldn't happen, it happened. That night, they
blocked the road with their car and lined all of us along the
highway. That's why I can't sleep.'

Isabel thought the woman would ask, *Why are you awake?*
and wondered what the answer was. Instead, the woman asked,
'Do you have family in the city?' 'My cousin and my brother.'
'What's their work?' 'Manuela is a maid. My brother's a musician. He's called Isaias.' 'A musician? He makes money from
that?' Isabel nodded. 'And you know that?' said the woman.
'Or did he just tell you?' 'He sent us money,' said Isabel. 'He
was a performer on the coast. Many people say he'll be
famous.' The woman eyed her suspiciously. 'I'd like to see this
famous brother,' she said. 'Is he going to pick you up?' Isabel
hesitated. 'I don't know.' 'So your cousin's meeting you?' 'No.

She lives at her employer's house during the week. She told my mother there's a bus.' The woman whistled. 'Your parents just sent you here, and no one's picking you up!' Isabel protested, 'I know where she lives. I have the name written on a piece of paper. My mother told me where to go. I've taken buses before.' She felt as if she were arguing with herself.

She remembered the name of the district. 'It's called New Eden.' 'Where's that?' asked the woman. 'In the city?' Isabel nodded. 'I think so.' 'You can't just think so,' said the woman. 'Is it the city or the New Settlements?' Isabel remembered: 'The second one. The New Settlements.' 'That's what I thought,' said the woman. 'You aren't going to the city at all, then. The Settlements aren't the city. The Settlements are where all the migrants go. They all have names like that: New Eden, New Jerusalem, New Grace, they're all the same.' I'm not a migrant, thought Isabel, I'm not coming to stay.

The truck slowed and drew up next to a pair of boys. They dragged a barrow with a broken wheel that scoured the road. As they walked, they talked to the driver. Then they shook their heads. The truck roared off.

'They're going, too, if that's what you're wondering,' said the woman, pushing aside her wind-knotted hair. 'But they have to walk.' The words were accusatory, as if from another conversation that Isabel wasn't hearing.

In the morning, they stopped at a rest station. The driver unlatched the bed and the passengers pattered out. A pair of men stood by the open door of a long truck. 'Look, another shipment's in,' said one, loudly. Isabel kept her eyes down as she passed them. The hills were green, with taller trees than she had ever seen. She slipped off her shoes. It was the first time she had taken them off since home, and her feet were cold and pink where the strap pinched. She took long strides back and forth along a sandy patch lined with morning glories. When she got back to the flatbed, she remembered her cheek. In the side-view mirror, she ran her finger along the raised welt; it looked eerily blue beneath the light blue of her eye. Her forehead was lined with creases of dust. She spit on her fingers and tried to wipe it clean. She boarded the truck and it left.

An hour later, it began to rain. At first there was laughter and raised hands, and two boys did a little dance. Then it grew cold. There was a canvas tarp rolled up by the cab, but it flapped wildly in the wind when they tried to cover themselves. Isabel huddled with the others in the center. She licked the raindrops that ran down her cheeks. Water streamed back on the floor and fanned up from the wheels. A thick smell blossomed, like a wet animal. Then the rain stopped and she watched the clouds scurry off toward a low range of mountains.

Someone said, 'It's coming soon.' The highway grew wider. Isabel went to the edge of the flatbed and stared at the road, waiting for the city to appear. She glanced behind her, ready to laugh, wanting to talk to someone, but there was only an old man, and he was quiet. She stood on her toes, as if it would help her see.

They passed more towns, the green spaces giving way to lots and dirt roads, fuel stations, hills of brick houses. The traffic thickened. Now and again, buildings in half-completion stood among the rest, concrete clinging to metal skeletons.

The highway joined a wide river with heaped banks and half-buried construction pylons. The water was brown, flecked by bits of floating foam. There was no green now, and the shanties seemed to cover the hills as far as she could see. At a wide sweep of the river, she saw lines of cars stretch unending into the far distance, where towers hovered in the haze.

After a while, they passed a dump across the river. She had never seen anything like it: a mountain, its base billowing against a long broken fence. Forms moved through openings in the chain links. A web of trails ran over the dun-colored swell, and the sky above was scribbled with the silhouettes of carrion birds. Its slopes seemed torn and tattered, littered with pale confetti. In places, larger scraps—a rusted car chassis, plywood, a door—hung like lone scales. Dogs trotted over the ground. Strange that they would put a dump in the center of the city, she thought, until a second thought came: Or the city has grown around it. She felt a chill and thought she might be sick again. The smell overwhelmed her, but no one else seemed to notice. On top of the massive rise she saw a row of lean-tos and two tiny figures running.

The traffic slowed without warning. The flatbed swerved off the highway. They passed a massive building covered with cracks, as if it had been dropped from a height. She thought of home and the houses crumbling out in the forest. You could take all of Saint Michael, she thought, and grind it up and pour it into this building and there would be space for many other Saint Michaels to fit inside.

Farther along, they turned onto a wide road that paralleled the arches of an overpass. On its flanks, storefronts crowded up against paint-stripped apartments with walls streaked the color of coal. Graffiti tattooed the narrow lintels, angry, spindled letters with swollen elbows. There were abandoned lots, backed by walls of advertisements and symbols of political parties, their cracked asphalt empty but for piles of concrete blocks and tangles of telephone wire. Alleyways gave onto cement towers and whorls of steel barbs. Antennae sprouted like an old man's whiskers. There was no center and no order.

The flatbed stopped at a light beneath an overpass, the crowd broke around them, she heard shouting and the roar of motors. A group of boys around a motorbike caught her staring. One made a kissing motion, punched another. 'I love you!' he shouted, touching his heart. 'Marry me!' The others joined in, elbowing each other. 'Not him! He doesn't know how to treat a country girl! He's a baby! Marry me! My love's killing me!' She began to smile, but as the cars moved on, the words turned to obscenities and they desisted only when the flatbed was far away. The girls she saw wore tight shirts and jeans, and she recognized none of the slow, familiar saunter of the women at home. They walked fast, pulling children so that they almost lifted them off the ground. The air stank of engine oil and exhaust.

The flatbed stopped, the crowd broke around them, she heard shouting and the roar of motors, the gunshot backfire of motorcycles, the rattling of the overpass. When the light turned again, they passed a giant intersection, four lanes across in each direction, the flatbed vibrating as it picked up speed. Shops lined the road. There were signs for cheap clothing, cheap burials, cheap legal work, mourning clothes on credit. There were butcher shops, barber shops, shoe shops, shops with big plush toys, bars, dark buildings with names hidden in the shadows.

As they slowed, they came up alongside a bus. Entranced,

she watched her reflection float over the glass, until suddenly they passed an open window, where a pale girl with wide black eyes stared back.

The flatbed crawled forward and left the girl behind. When they stopped, Isabel could see the reflection of the crowded flatbed, but when she sought her face she couldn't find it.

They drove and then they stopped again, the crowd broke, she heard shouting, hawkers' cries and the roar of motors. It's like I am going around and around, she thought, and she whispered to the woman beside her, 'Is this it?' 'The beginning of it,' the woman said.

They drove for another hour. Then the truck swung into an empty lot and skidded to a stop. 'This is not the bus station,' said someone. 'The flatbeds no longer go to the station,' said someone else and gave no explanation.

The passengers began to gather their bags. They filed away quickly and silently, turning into the street at the end of the lot. Isabel waited as the flatbed emptied. She went to the driver. 'This isn't the station?' He shook his head. 'The police started fining us. They say too many perches turn over.' He paused. 'You meeting someone at the station?' She shook her head slowly. Somehow she had imagined Isaias there. The thought seemed ridiculous now; she hadn't even spoken to him. 'You know where you are going?' he asked.

'They said there's a bus.'

He rolled his eyes. 'Of course there's a bus. There are hundreds of buses. Do know which one?'

Her hand trembled as she pulled out a scrap of paper where her mother had written JUNIOR / 24TH OF AUGUST STREET / NEW EDEN / NEW SETTLEMENTS. She handed it to him. 'New

Eden!' he said. He seemed to think it was very funny. 'They should hang the guy who names these.' But he shook his head. 'I don't know. Ask a taxi.' 'Ask what?' she blurted, exhausted. 'Which name is where I am going?' 'Which name? All of them. New Eden is what a priest with a cruel sense of humor called it. New Settlements is what it is.' 'It's not the city.' 'It's beyond the city. It's what's happened to the city.'

She walked slowly to the street, where a bus rattled past. She felt her face beginning to get warm. She could see a line of white taxis at the corner. A white car without markings pulled up next to her. Its driver put his head out. 'Where are you going?' She brushed back her hair. 'New Eden. Do you know it?' 'Of course. New Eden. I'll take you.' She protested, 'I just wanted the number of the bus.' He shook his head. 'Nonsense, you remind me of my cousin. You think I would let my cousin try to find her way on the bus? I'll give you a special price.' The car looked like the taxis at the corner. She considered. She still had the change the flatbed driver had given her. 'How much?' 'Don't worry,' he said. 'We can figure out the price when we get there.'

She let him put her bag on the backseat, and he opened the door for her. The car was old, the floor was covered with muddy newspapers. 'Close the door,' he said. She looked at him. 'Let's go,' he said. 'I haven't got all night. I'm not allowed to park here.'

He reached over to pull the door shut, and his arm brushed against her stomach. 'Sorry,' he said politely, but suddenly she was afraid. She waited for him to ask for the street, but he was looking intently into the rearview mirror. He put the key in the ignition. It heaved but didn't start.

He cursed, tried again. 'Wait a moment.' He opened the door and walked quickly to the hood. On the floor beneath her, she saw a crumpled blouse. Her heart pounded. She told herself, It's just a shirt, but then she grabbed her bag, pushed the door open and ran. She didn't stop until she found herself in a crowd.

She walked for many blocks without knowing where she was going. Movement calmed her. She felt that if she just kept walking she would know the way, but soon she found herself at the edge of a dark street of warehouses. She turned back.

Her shoulder began to hurt from her bag. She wanted to carry it on her head, like she did with laundry at home, but she was afraid of people knowing she was from the backlands, and worried someone would snatch it. So she switched the bag back and forth between her hands, and wiggled her fingers to keep them from cramping. She felt very small. She had never been in such a crowd, except the New Year's at the beach, long ago. She wanted to ask for help, but now she feared someone would take advantage of her. The shoes hurt her feet. The people walked swiftly and bumped her if she stopped.

Finally, she paused by a woman outside a butcher shop. The woman wiped her hands on an apron, peered at the little paper and shook her head.

A young couple at a bus stop also shook their heads. 'You're not from here, are you?' said the girl, her eyes darting from Isabel's bag to her face. Another man joked that he knew 'New Hell' but not 'New Eden,' and another laughed, 'If you find it, let me know!' They spoke with a different accent, without the lilt she was used to. She thought, What if Manuela was wrong? She thought of calling, but she would have to buy a token somewhere, which meant putting the bag down. She was now certain someone would steal it.

It was night. She stopped at a vendor selling corn, a boy her age. He stood in the street, his shirt whipping in the wake of the speeding cars. She stared hungrily at the boiled cobs. 'You're lost,' he said. She showed him the address, and he whistled. 'New Eden, huh? That's *the real thing*. I hope you know someone there.' 'What do you mean?' 'I mean not everyone there deserves to be in Paradise.' He pointed across the street. 'Bus passes there. Just look for the word *Settlements* in the window. You can spell, can't you?' 'Of course I can,' she snapped. He held up his hand. 'Of course you can, no offense. Many people can't. Even good proud people.' She paused. 'I thought maybe I'd have to spend the night here.'

'On the street!' he said. 'You?'

At the bus stop, she stood next to a pair of older boys arguing loudly in a slang she hardly understood. 'You looking at something?' asked one of the boys, glancing over his shoulder at her. She moved to stand by a black woman with a faded dress and straightened hair. Again, Isabel caught herself staring. She felt as if she was registering everything from this moment: the stench of exhaust, the pounding echo of the overpass, the boys' thin shoulders, the splitting calluses on the woman's feet.

The bus came. They passed through a grated turnstile and paid their fares. It left the wide avenue and entered a maze of empty streets with names of dead ministers and doctors and generals she had never heard of. It seemed to be a residential neighborhood, with apartments guarded by steel grates and metal shutters and shattered bottles set teeth-up in cement, but it was empty. They pitched through at strange angles, there were no straight lines.

They climbed a massive span, over a road glittering with

car lights and a distant view of a floating city. It seemed as if they were driving away again.

She lugged her bag back up the aisle to ask. The fare collector laughed. '*Easy.* I'll tell you.'

They dove back into the dark streets. She pressed her face to the glass. Now the city seemed to have been replaced by vast fields of shanties. In some places, ranks of identical row houses made patterns in the dark; in others, the shacks swarmed over one another without reason.

The bus was nearly empty when it pulled up at the base of a hill. She descended behind a pair of middle-aged women. There was a single road; the pavement ended after several steps, the rest was a paisley of cobbles, broken asphalt and gravel. A stream ran by the road, littered with trash. She ran until she caught up with the women. 'I am Isabel,' she blurted. One of them looked at the other. 'Yes? Is that supposed to mean something? Am I supposed to know you?' 'I'm going here.' Isabel pointed at the piece of paper.

They shook their heads with the name of the street. '*Love,* the City gave the streets those names. No one uses them here.' Isabel looked back at the note. 'It's across from Mr. Junior's store.' 'That's up the road. *Whose* house are you looking for?' 'My cousin—her name's Manuela.' 'Of course. *Good Manuela.* We know Manuela.' The women looked at each other. 'She's not home, though. She works all week.'

Isabel thought she heard envy in their voices. 'She told me she would give a key to Junior at the store,' she said.

She marched behind them up the hill. The street wound through houses of concrete, brick, clapboard, widening in places and then narrowing again. She stayed close to the women, afraid she would lose them. She wanted them to ask her about the journey, but they spoke to each other in low voices and she couldn't hear. On poorly lit corners, people were gathering. She could smell food, something burning. The road passed through long stretches of darkness, broken by the red stutter of street lamps.

A pair of girls walked past in bright skintight shirts covering only one shoulder. They looked Isabel over before stopping by men drinking and dancing around a radio. From an alley, a woman ran out, cackling, holding a baby above her head, away from a girl who reached for him.

The women stopped before a pair of metal tables outside a shack. A television flickered above a billiard table with torn baize, where a fat man was eating a plate of sun-dried beef. He was unshaven, and his breasts sagged in a ribbed undershirt. 'Junior,' said the woman. He looked up. 'What is it, love?' It was the voice that answered the telephone. Isabel felt she could cry with relief.

'He's a charmer,' whispered the woman to Isabel. To Junior, she said: 'This is Manuela's cousin.' She paused. 'She just arrived from the north.'

He grinned. 'My beloved backlands.' A fly crawled on his shoulder, and he shivered it off. 'I never could've guessed you just arrived.' He winked at the women. Isabel brushed her hair back with her free hand. 'I came on a perch,' she said awkwardly.

He took another bite of meat and offered her a piece, glistening on his fingers. Isabel almost took it, but she was afraid that she would eat so ravenously that she would humiliate herself. She shook her head, immediately regretting it.

Junior lumbered out of his chair and led her across the street. Several yards away, they stopped before a brick house with a concrete roof. He squinted at his key chain. 'Good Manuela. Works hard, your cousin. She's done well for herself. Good roof. Not many people have a house like this to themselves.' He patted the wall as if it were a friend.

The door was stuck against the jamb, and he had to tug up on the handle to slide it open. He handed her the key and left. *Who will be with me, on the last perch in the world?* he sang as he trudged back up the street.

Inside, Isabel set the bag down slowly. The room was small, scarcely twice the size of the single bed, a thin mattress stretched partway over its boards. A table sat against the far wall beneath a window, one of its legs propped on a stack of cardboard coasters that had been taped neatly together. On a wire shelf, a plastic clock ticked. She went to look at it. Its face showed a smiling cat, paws pointing to the numbers. There was also an illustrated Bible, a stack of old beauty magazines and news journals, artificial flowers with clear plastic drops of water on their leaves, a glossy statue of Saint Joseph with a dewlapped robe and a broken ear.

A hammock hung against the wall. Inside was an imprint of talcum powder. The baby must be with the woman who watched him while Manuela worked, she thought. Him, or her. She didn't even know the baby's name.

In a second, smaller room she found a stove, an old icebox, a washbasin and lines with stiff clothes that smelled of detergent. She was impressed: she didn't know Manuela was rich enough to afford an icebox. There was a short stack of plates with chipped rims. The glasses were from cream containers, the expiration dates still stamped on the bottoms.

On the wall was a fragment of a mirror with a single intact corner. She stood on her toes. In the sharp beak of the glass,

she could see the saint's icon behind her. The single bulb
backlit a nimbus of wild strands of hair. Her cheeks were
dusty; the bruise seemed even darker and made her irises
almost clear. She stared. What a strange sight I must be to
other people, she thought.

Suddenly, she was exhausted and very cold. She found a
sweater among a stack of clothes and went to lie on her stomach with her head on her arms. The room smelled of bleach
and rusty water. The sheets were rough with lint and printed
with ranks of identical laughing cartoon mice playing toy
drums. She stared at the mice and then pulled the neckline of
her dress up over her nose. It smelled of dust and of herself.

She slept through the night and didn't dream. When she
awoke, the room was warm and her head ached. An incision of
light rimmed the door. Runs in the curtain cast dashes of sun
across her body. Beneath the sweater, her dress was moist with
sweat.

In the washroom, she found a large plastic tub of cold water
and a floating bowl. She filled the washbasin. Her dress bil-
lowed when she plunged it in and the water grew silty with
the dust. She scrubbed until the soap made pillows of foam.
Thin trickles ran down her belly and suds settled in her hair.
The air filled with bubbles, sour on her tongue.

When she wrung out her dress, her forearms trembled. She
poured the rest of the water over herself and washed with a
cracked piece of soap.

She wrapped herself in a worn towel from the line and went
to sit on the edge of the bed. She set the soles of her feet
uneasily on the floor. In Saint Michael, everyone talked of

wanting a cement floor, but here it seemed cold and hard, not meant for walking. It disoriented her; there were no paths burnished in its surface, no bloom of dust to say how long it had been since a person came through. She thought how the floor at home thumped when she swung out of a hammock, how it breathed, how she could put her face to it and feel the cold coming off, how it stained her feet and made the room smell of earth. She wondered, Why am I thinking so much about the floor when there are important things to be done? She rolled her toes: a dead sound.

She searched her bag for clean clothes. There were two other cotton dresses, a pair of socks, some underpants, hair clips and a worn toothbrush, the laminated Saint George prayer card, the fragment of wood, a lice comb. She had folded a small rosary bracelet from her mother in a scrap of paper. Now the dust left a rubbing on the paper, like the phantom of a tiny worm.

One of the dresses was eggshell blue, with a white frill sewn onto the collar. The second was once red, now cotton-candy pink. She drank all the water from the two cane liquor bottles and ate the manioc flour. Her stomach gurgled. Immediately she was hungry again. She went to the icebox, but it was warm and empty except for a bottle of stale-smelling water. She drank it anyway.

In the bag she found a photo of her family. She sat with it on the bed. It was their most recent one, and her parents didn't know she had taken it to the south. Before their house in Saint Michael, everyone stared solemnly at the camera, except Isaias, his head turned, his eyes intent on something in the road. He wore a shirt buttoned to the top and loose slacks held by a belt. His feet were bare. Isabel was wearing the pink dress when it was still red. Her face was round; they must have made the photo before the hunger passed through. She held her brother's hand, and her mother's arm linked his elbow. Sometimes when she looked at the photo she thought he was smiling, but not now.

She imagined Isaias in the same room the day he arrived. He would have gone out and into the city—he wouldn't have stayed inside and waited like a child. Why isn't he here for me? she thought angrily. If he was working, why at least wasn't there a note, anything? The room was empty of him. He hadn't been there for a long time. Then she scolded herself: But I don't know he isn't here, I don't know the city, this isn't like home. In the north, it was easy to look for someone's presence; dust gathered quickly and smells were everywhere. She knew when a hammock had last been slept in by the stretch in the cotton, the presence of dried insects in its concavity, whether grit had settled on the hammock hook and eyehole. By the moisture in the surface of the cornmeal or the gleam on a mango pit, she knew when someone had last eaten. She could pinch the hanging clothes to see how stiff they were, look for faint changes in the color of the dirt outside to judge when someone had washed, smell the air by the latrine, look on the clothesline for dust that settled in dashes or at the trails for fresh-broken fragments of twigs. Then there was something else she didn't have words for: like ripples, or an echo, or a shadow that remains, like the lingering presence of someone who has already left, the thin line of smoke rising from a candle that's just been blown out.

She had none of this now. The position of the chairs was unfamiliar, the scent of bleach too strong. She found long hairs on the pillow, but the sheets smelled only of soap when she pressed her nose into them.

She could see passing shadows in the rim of light around

the door. She wanted to go outside, but she was afraid. She didn't understand the words the boy had used, *the real thing.* She had never seen anyone as fat as Junior. At home, fat men were landowners or lenders and to be avoided. There is no fat man who didn't make another man thin, her uncle used to say.

From the window, she could see a group of men drinking outside Junior's store. She thought of her father, and wondered how her mother would care for him alone. She dragged one of the chairs against the door.

She curled up on the bed. She heard a car roar up the hill, then music. It was unfamiliar, loud and fast. From the house next door, she could hear an argument. 'You will be the end of me,' a woman shouted. 'I work like an animal and you do this to me.' She heard a door slam.

Later, she could smell cooking. It was so rich that her mouth watered and she felt her stomach contract. She didn't get up. It was tongue hunger, not body hunger, and she knew she could wait. She stayed curled up and watched the small plastic clock. She found its rhythm comforting, and placed it near her ear. She imagined it counting down until someone came. Later, she rose and searched again for signs of Isaias but found only one of his shirts and a pair of pants folded on the wire shelf. There was no dust to say how long ago they had been left there. In one of the pockets was a scrap of paper that read PATRICIA M / APT 22 / VILA CAPRI TOWER / PRESIDENT KENNEDY. She had never heard the woman's name before. She folded the piece of paper and put it back in his pants. She watched the door and waited.

Slowly the room went dark. Isabel must have slept, because she opened her eyes to find her cousin sitting next to her in a nightgown, running the back of her finger over the welt on

Isabel's cheek. 'How did this happen?' she asked, and Isabel struggled to sit up. Half asleep, she wrapped her arms around Manuela's waist.

Her cousin stroked her hair and gently laid her back down. 'Sleep,' she said, leaning over to kiss her cheek, and Isabel curled toward her and slept again.

It was nearly midday when Isabel awoke with the sense that she was falling. She didn't remember her dream, only the feeling of being back on the flatbed. Her fists were clenched, her eyes pinched tight, her heart pounding. She had thrown off her sheets. She lay still, breathing deeply until she calmed.

In the distance, she could hear a jingling like bells on a passing cart, barking, shouts. The air was thick with the smell of warm cornmeal.

A fly tickled her arm.

She squinted into the room. She could see her open bag on the floor, an unfamiliar pair of loafers set neatly by the door, the saint icons dust-gilded in the slanting light. Although she had been in the city for more than the full cycle of a day, she felt as if she were waking for the first time.

A few paces away, Manuela was sitting at the table, rocking a small hammock strung between the bed and the wall. She sat with her back to Isabel, her shoulders slouched, her legs set sturdily apart. Isabel wanted to jump up and embrace her.

But against the light, her arms seemed heavy, her waist thick, her posture that of someone much older than the young woman Isabel remembered. She was seized with the fear that somewhere an error had been made: it was the wrong neighborhood, the wrong Junior, the wrong Manuela, waiting for another Isabel. She shut her eyes again and the fear passed.

At last, she pushed herself up and scooted uncertainly to the edge of the bed. Hearing her stirring, Manuela came to sit with her. 'How long has it been?' Manuela asked, touching Isabel's face. 'How many years? How many? You were little then.' Isabel blinked as if to answer. She stared. Her cousin looked the same, she thought, relieved: her worried eyes set deep and close together, the color of a leaf beginning to brown. Her hair, kerchiefed, seemed to have darkened, her skin to have paled. Gone separate ways, Isabel thought.

Manuela stroked her hair. 'When was the last time we were together?'

'I was ten. Now I'm fourteen.'

'I remember,' said her cousin. 'Your face was round. A little cherub's face.' She brushed Isabel's hair over her ears, studying her. 'Isabel,' she said suddenly, 'is everyone thin like you? Are my sisters thin like you? You aren't sick, are you? You didn't get sick on the way down?'

Isabel looked away. 'I'm not sick.'

Manuela pressed on. 'You know I couldn't meet you, I can't leave work during the week. But it wasn't hard to find the bus from the station, right?'

The flatbed didn't go to the station! Isabel wanted to say. But she shook her head. 'It was easy.'

Manuela stood and brought the baby from the hammock. He was soft and pale, with a serious old man's face like the

Jesus babies in the religious icons. For the first time in days, Isabel smiled without trying. 'He's beautiful!' she said. 'Strong,' said Manuela. 'Maybe he isn't as big as some of the others, but he has such a strong grip. Look!' Isabel laughed. She brushed at his hair with her fingers. Manuela passed him to her and she rocked him and nuzzled her nose into the softness of his neck. The weight comforted her. She kissed his arms and smelled his hair. 'His name is Hugo,' said Manuela. 'His father, Leo, chose it. He's six months old. Feel his grip! Can you believe it? You should tell everyone at home, because they think I am lying. They've never seen such a strong baby.' When he grasped at Isabel's mouth, she bit his hand lightly. She put her lips to his belly and hummed.

At last, he began to cry. Manuela took him to the table, where he drank greedily from his bottle.

Isabel watched her. She remembered her cousin as a quiet, serious young woman who joined the men in the cane fields. From a distance, wrapped in thick clothes, she looked like one of them, but she took her lunches in the fields alone. She was never one of the women who the younger girls aspired to be. At the festivals, she preferred long skirts even as the coastal fashions began to make their way into the interior. Only sometimes at the dances did Isabel see her sway, slightly, before catching herself and looking about with an embarrassed smile. She wasn't beautiful. Cane takes everything delicate out of you, they used to say. They said her ears had been pierced when she was a child, but she never wore jewelry. She had been married once, to a mechanic from Prince Leopold, who had left her.

Sometimes during the harvest she worked in one of the smaller mills, turning the warm cane as it boiled down. In

Isabel's earliest memories, she smelled sweetly of the paste. It got in her hair and dried to brown crisps, which she sucked on instead of washing out. It seemed, then, to Isabel, her cousin's only acquiescence to pleasure.

'So,' said Manuela suddenly, but for a long time it was all she said. When she began again, her voice had hardened. 'Isa, what's it like?'

'What's what like?'

'The drought. I don't know what to believe over the phone. But I've heard stories and I've seen the papers. Is it as bad as they say?'

As bad as they say? Isabel paused, confused by the question. She looked away. *How long has it been since you went hungry?*

'Isabel?'

What can I answer? she thought. That someone in our own village stole our chicken? That we mixed earth into the beans? That I had dreams of eating melon?

'They are digging up the trees,' she said at last.

Then, strangely, she laughed a little.

The creases in Manuela's forehead deepened. 'I've been sending money,' she said. 'Every time I know of someone going back I send a package. You get them, right? People think it's easy here, but it isn't.' She stopped. 'I've been sending what I can.'

They both grew quiet. The sound of the baby drinking seemed very loud. Where is Isaias? Isabel wanted to ask, but her cousin stood and placed Hugo in the hammock. 'You must be hungry,' she said. She left the table and returned with a warm pot of cornmeal. 'Usually I have better food, a stew, even meat,' she said. 'But not now. Not for a little while, anyway.'

Hunching over her bowl, Isabel ate quickly and silently. She took heaping spoonfuls. Grains of meal flecked her lips, and she didn't bother to wipe them until the bowl was empty. Her cousin served her again, the spoon clanging as it scraped the inside of the pot.

'Look at you. When did you last have a real meal?'

'On the flatbed,' Isabel lied. They both were quiet. Isabel ate a third bowl. When she finished, she asked, 'Where is Isaias?'

Manuela shrugged. 'Off playing somewhere. He'll be here soon. He's always away.'

In the afternoon, she took Isabel outside. They climbed the road past Junior's store. 'Here's my girl,' he said. Manuela smiled but didn't stop. The road rose sharply. It was rutted and narrow, and smaller streets dove off between brick walls. A little boy bounded past, dragging a kite of a torn plastic bag on a cross of sticks. Isabel felt a prickle of memory. She had been in these streets before, in the same heavy light, in the smell of people and crowding. I am like a baby again, back in the camps, she thought, but the memory was uncertain.

At her side, Manuela said, 'There is no reason for you to go into any of these alleys. The phone is outside Junior's store. Some things you can buy from Junior, and there's a market down the road.' A pair of men stopped talking and watched her pass. 'Don't stare,' said Manuela, pulling her on. 'I'm not staring,' Isabel protested, but Manuela didn't release her arm. 'Why would you lie when I can see you? You're not a little kid in the square anymore. It means something different, here.'

Sloping steps were cut into the road, and on the steeper climbs, clapboard houses clung to cupped hollows in the mountain. A jacaranda tilted incongruously at the edge of the shanties. The sky was crossed with laundry strings, and above the doorways birds cried from little wooden cages. At the edge of the road, flies gathered around something gray, twisted, bristled. Isabel couldn't recognize what it was. Around her, she smelled the sweetness of rotting earth and other people.

As they walked, Manuela began again: 'This is how it will be. On Monday, I get up at four, so I get the bus at five. It takes two and a half hours for me to get to my boss's house. I come home on Friday, usually around midnight. If they have a dinner party Friday, I come home on Saturday morning. On Saturday, I spend the day with the baby, unless they have a dinner party Saturday. On Sunday we go to church. I go to Our Lady of the Rosary in the Center. You will come. At least for now, before I find you a job for the weekends.'

At the top, Isabel watched the shanties continue over the hills to the edge of a green forest. A group of boys chased a deflated ball over a clearing. Manuela said, 'This used to be woods. When I arrived, none of this was here.' She took Isabel's arm and turned her. Isabel could see Junior's store, the distant road she had arrived on, a passing bus. Beyond the road, houses rose up another slope like haphazardly stacked boxes. Beyond them, a crest of towers shimmered in the far distance. 'It keeps going,' said her cousin. 'On the other side of those towers, too. I work on the other side of those towers. Even then it doesn't stop.'

They walked down to the main road. Manuela showed her a river, a water pump, the power lines where the settlement pulled its electricity. The river came from the mountains, she said, 'So it's clean. Not to drink—don't even think of drinking—but you can use it for washing clothes.' At the well, water spurted from the faucet in uncertain hiccups, but it was clear. The power lines were a tangle of wires. On some nights, she said, the power companies came and cut them down.

At an empty lot filled with garbage, she said, 'Look at this filth. Some people want to be poor forever. Go to the rich neighborhoods and you won't see them throw their garbage where they live.'

'Yes,' said Isabel, her eyes drifting along the scattered mounds of trash, no longer listening.

'Of course, *yes*,' said Manuela. 'Except your brother—who thinks he's smart—said, "No, the rich only throw their garbage where we live." That kind of thinking isn't smart at all. That kind of thinking will get you nowhere.'

'Yes,' said Isabel again, now overwhelmed by the abundance of the place, by the fragments of colored glass, the sprigs of mint growing up between the weeds, the tires, the discarded metal. There was a car door, stripped of most of its paint but otherwise untouched. Her thoughts crystallized around the door. At home, she thought, they would have fashioned it into knives and toys, nails, grave markers, oil lamps, wind chimes, costumes, saints.

At her foot glittered a doll's wand. She bent to take it, but Manuela grabbed her shoulder. 'That's filth. You are not a scavenger.'

She waved to an old woman dressed in mourning. 'God bless you, Luisa,' she said, and the old woman nodded. She had a morning glory in her hair and stopped every few feet to catch her breath.

Later, they called Saint Michael from the phone outside Junior's store. It took four tries for the line to connect. Manuela spoke until they needed a second token. She asked

Isabel's mother to call back. Isabel answered. Loud music was playing on the hill, and she pressed her palm to her ear. 'It's me, it's Isabel!' 'What is it like?' asked her mother. 'Manuela has a house. The baby is beautiful. His eyes are so bright, his hair is soft. He eats all the time. He has such a strong cry. He is so strong.'

There was a break in the music. She thought she could hear wind whistling over the receiver in Saint Michael. Isabel wanted to say *Isaias isn't here yet,* but she knew that her mother understood this already in her silence. She imagined her standing in the square in her dark dress, holding the phone with both of her hands. She turned away from Manuela. 'How long will I stay here?' she whispered.

'Is something wrong?'

Isabel pinched her lips and shook her head. 'Isabel?' asked her mother, and Isabel could hear her trying to steady her voice. I should tell her not to worry, she thought. She wanted to say: There is no space, there are crowds everywhere, it is filled with people, a different kind of people, who use words that I can't understand.

'Isabel?' Her mother's voice caught on her name.

Manuela was watching her. She tucked a blanket around the baby. 'I have to go,' said Isabel. She waited to hear her mother hang up. After a long time, she said, 'Hello?'

'Hello,' said her mother.

'I have to go,' said Isabel again.

At home, they listened to the radio until it grew dark. For dinner, they boiled beans and thickened them with ground manioc. Manuela told her about her arrival: how she began as a maid in a factory, found a job with a family, advanced from assistant maid to head maid, how she built her house. She seemed happy as she spoke. 'I was the first in New Eden to have a concrete roof,' she said. 'You should tell that to people back home.' When she asked about Saint Michael, Isabel told her about the new road from the coast. She didn't mention the men, and it sounded as if the highway had unfurled alone in a path of black tar. When Manuela asked who was left, she told her, adding the names of the new babies who had survived. She lied and said they had celebrated Saint John's Day before she departed. Manuela asked the price of rice and considered the numbers carefully.

Later Isabel asked, 'And Leo?'

'He's a good man. Not handsome and trouble like the last one. We didn't marry properly, but you have to pay just to get married. You have to pay even to be buried here. He visits once a month, or whenever he can. He works on the coast, you know, on huge ships that go out to sea.'

At night, before they fell asleep, Manuela said, 'I know it looks easy, with the electricity and the shops and the wells, but in many ways it's harder than Saint Michael. At least in Saint Michael you know which way your trouble's coming from. And if something goes wrong, someone will help you out. In Saint Michael most of the killing's done by God.'

'What do you mean?'

'I mean what I mean,' said her cousin. 'Now quiet.'

In the street, loud music played into the night.

Isabel couldn't sleep. She turned quietly to watch her cousin. She is still the same person I knew in Saint Michael, she told herself again, but now she was less certain. There was something new, a vigilance, or anger, different from the quiet responsibility of the young woman she had known in the north.

She had been the flower girl at Manuela's first wedding, and she clung to the memory now. She was five. Her dress was white muslin, and her hair was laced with ribbons. It was the height of summer, and a warm wind carried the clang of goat bells into the church. Manuela wore a long gown with embroidered cloth roses; Isabel's mother's lips were painted crimson; Isaias wore a hand-sewn tie and brilliantine in his hair. Because Manuela's father had died when she was a baby, Isabel's father led her to the altar. She played nervously with her ring, stopping only to touch her hair as if strands had come loose. Then she covered her nails; they were chipped and split and had been almost impossible to paint.

Isabel borrowed shoes from a cousin of the groom. She sat in the front pew, where dragonflies droned through the scent of rose water. On the seat backs, wreaths of plastic flowers entangled her curls. Her hem was torn from catching on the thorn when they filed down a narrow trail.

From the wedding, Isabel also remembered: Manuela's trembling voice as she repeated the oath, a drunk uncle, the clean-swept square where they danced quadrilles. At the edge of the plaza, a photographer from Prince Leopold lit the air in dusty explosions. For the feast, they ate goat's rumen stuffed with lime, black pepper, tomato and chopped heart, liver and lungs. They boiled tendons and added the broth to manioc flour. In the kitchen, glistening tripe hung from the counter like an exquisite velvet curtain.

After the wedding, Manuela moved with her husband to Prince Leopold, where they built a brick house on the outskirts of the city. In the months that followed, Isabel saw little of her cousin. When a year had passed, the old women began to whisper that Manuela couldn't conceive. They made her teas and poultices; when these failed, she traveled to a distant shrine, where she joined a line of young women, lifted her skirts and lowered herself against a blessed stone.

She returned to find her home empty save the groom's mother, who sat in a single remaining chair and knitted. Her son had left for the coast, she said, with another woman. 'It's better you learned his type now,' she added, not without kindness, and gave Manuela back her trousseau.

Manuela returned to Saint Michael. She spent long days at a neighbor's sugar mill. By then, she realized she was already pregnant. She made a pilgrimage to pray for the baby's health. Isabel was there when her cousin came home, her face bruised and her arm in a sling. She set her small bag down before a gaggle of women. 'The flatbed turned over . . . ,' she began, standing in the pale light, her voice breaking. 'You lost the child,' said her mother, and Isabel told no one that she had dreamed this two nights before.

The following year she went to the city. She was the first woman to go alone. Isabel's father had always called her Simple Manuela, and when she left, he said he didn't think she could make it a week there. But by then Isabel thought of her differently, as someone who moved through life the way she turned cane paste, steady, without stopping, head down and muscles tensed.

Isabel was seven. She saw Manuela again when she was ten, still the same woman, quiet and persistent, settling easily into washing and caring for the children. She stayed for a month and then returned to the south.

On that single visit home, she told stories about the city with words that somehow reduced it to something familiar. It was *big* and life there was *hard* but *good* if you found work.

It wasn't the city of the crime programs or the television dramas about the rich, but a place of dogged calculations: salary less rent, less water, less food, less the bus, less devotion candles, less clothes, less phone calls home. A city made of numbers, and the children were disappointed. Isaias had pursued her breathlessly. What about the street gangs, the trains, the museums, the parks, the giant markets? he asked, until Manuela turned on him with sudden viciousness, Those things are not for me, Those are for other people, That is not the city I know.

Later Isabel cornered her out by the clotheslines. Yes, love? said Manuela. What about the sea and the beautiful people there? asked Isabel. Manuela paused for a moment before continuing to hang the clothes. The sea is still far away, she said, and what would I do with the sea?

In the morning, Manuela woke Isabel for church. 'It's late,' she said. 'I was afraid you'd sleep forever.' She wore a suit of brown nylon, burnished over the elbows and shoulders. Isabel put on her dress from the trip south. It was her best, yellow with patterned blue daisies the width of her finger. It was still moist around the hem and in the shadows of the clothespins, but it was the dress she wore to church at home. Manuela gave her a sweater. She brushed her hair and tied it with a ribbon. Curls sprang loose. She wet her hands and pressed them back. Her feet were raw where the shoe straps rubbed.

At the base of the hill Manuela said, 'On Sunday, there aren't many buses.' So they took off their shoes and walked. Manuela carried Hugo in a sling. It was early and the zinc roofs of the shanties glinted with dew. Finally, a bus passed.

Manuela waved and shouted. They ran after it as it slowed, the door accordioning open with a hiss.

They changed buses at a tall sculpture that looked like a bird or a giant C. The second bus took them across a river and toward a rise of towers before diving into a tunnel. This time, Isabel stood by a young girl with blond hair. The girl's hand gripped the bar below hers. It was white and smooth, with long fingers and violet traces of veins. Isabel had never seen such a delicate hand, and at a bump in the road, she let her palm scoot against the girl's thumb. Without looking, the girl slid her hand away.

From the next bus they got off before the steps of a maize-colored church with white cornices like the icing on a cake. Inside, the church stirred with women in wool sweaters and suits like her cousin's. Isabel wondered if her parents had ever seen such lush saints, in shawls of purple velvet, real tulle dresses and nacre crowns. There was a Jesus with lustrous enamel skin and a puckered wound like the scarlet mouth of a fish. A large statue of Saint Lucy carried her eyes on a platter and turned her face to the ceiling, where painted angel heads floated on peeling strips of cerulean. Isabel looked for salt at the saint's feet, but there was none. Women came and ran their fingers over the eyes as if reading braille, then touched their own lashes.

Manuela stopped beside her and whispered from an invocation card.

Mass began. A gray priest's hand trembled on the psalter, his sermon blurring with the murmur from the street. Isabel slid her shoes back and forth and wondered if anyone had noticed them. In front, an old man in worn wool trousers balanced his hat on his lap. He kept nodding to sleep and seemed ready to topple into a woman beside him. Isabel turned with a smile to tell Manuela, but her cousin's eyes were glassy and her lips moved with the words of the hymns.

The songs were of forgiveness and everlasting love. Isabel reached over and took Hugo, who slept.

After the service, Manuela led her to a crowded shopping street with a narrow sky. Isabel had never seen such stores. She handed the baby back to Manuela and watched her reflection pass over window displays of typewriters and bridal gowns, cartoon-covered notebooks and glazed carmine cookies with candy pearl collars. But her reflection intrigued her most; it was the first time she had seen her full body since the mirror with Isaias. Behind, she watched the passing crowds.

I am a small person, she thought.

Manuela pulled her away.

They stopped on a long bridge with wrought-iron rails. Manuela bought her ice cream from a passing cart, and she licked the sweet milk as it spiraled down her wrist. When she finished, she asked for another. 'No,' said her cousin. 'You will think it's normal, that in the city people eat ice cream every day.' At a produce stand, she bought her an unfamiliar fruit. 'It's an apple,' she said. 'I had never seen one, either.' Isabel held it until Manuela said, 'Have it now or you will drop it and ruin it.' She ate it in small, cautious bites.

They walked on.

From the bridge, they descended into a market. 'The knife that cuts steel!' shouted vendors. 'The famous pencil that never breaks!' 'Best tomatoes in the world!' In a far corner, a crowd had gathered around a man in a plaid suit and a feather in his hat. His face was wrinkled; when he wasn't smiling, his mouth folded upon itself like a clenched fist. His little mustache wiggled as he spoke. As if reading her thoughts, Manuela whispered, 'Just like the north. I know. They left, too. Would you stay if there was no one left to listen to you sing?'

He was talking about a boy and a snake, or a boy who turned into a snake, or a snake who ate a boy; at first, Isabel caught only words. He held a pamphlet at arm's length, waved his free hand, stomped his left foot and then his right, darted his head toward a pretty girl and went '*Hissss.*' The girl screamed. The crowd was still laughing when he said, 'And that, my friends, is the tale of the boy who became a snake.'

The crowd moved off, and Isabel went to stand near the man. She found an unexpected solace in his familiarity. Noticing her waiting, he said, 'My angel, shall you be purchasing anything today?' She shook her head, intimidated by his elegant speech. 'And what about your beautiful friend?' he asked, bowing to Manuela.

'Oh so charming,' said her cousin flatly. 'What do you have?'

He spread a fan of chapbooks in his hand. 'I have *The ABC of Dance.* Do you like music? No? How about *The Man Who Became a Ford*—it is an industrial tale.' Manuela shook her head. '*The Life of a Married Woman Is Never Secure.*' 'Too close to the truth!' '*The Man Who Married a Mule.*' 'That's disgusting. You should watch what you say; my cousin's just a girl.' 'Then *Lives of the Cinema Stars,* about the visit of the great Bogart to this city?' 'That's nonsense,' said another woman who was looking through the chapbooks. 'The great Bogart never came to the city.' 'Of course he did,' replied the poet. 'He called it *the city of lights.* With his wife, the stunning Hayworth.' 'That isn't his wife! What kind of crazy poem is that?' The woman shook her head and walked away.

The poet shrugged her off. He sold the last of the snake pamphlets and showed his empty hands to a disappointed customer. As a new crowd gathered, Isabel pushed to the front. Around her, a group of children jostled, whispering secrets into one another's ears.

The poet whistled through two fingers. 'Ladies and gentlemen! Cowboys, taxpayers, beautiful girls! Gather around! One of you must be in God's good favor today.' He waved his hand. 'Who knows the story of the Princess and the Mysterious Leopard?' When no one answered, he clutched his chest. 'No one? Oh! Your life is only hardship. No, I can't tell you this story. Like a flood on dry soil, the joy will run right off your hearts. I must choose another.' Laughter spread through the crowd. 'No!' shouted someone. 'No!' said a tall man.

'No!' blurted Isabel.

'What's that?' said the poet, turning toward her. 'You, young lady, what did you say?' 'Nothing.' 'My dearest, I didn't hear you say nothing. Come out with it: Which story do you want to hear?' She whispered it: 'The leopard story.' 'The leopard story?' 'Yes.' '"The Princess and the Leopard"?' 'Yes.' 'The tale of passion and punishment?' 'Yes, that one.' 'The greatest story of all time?'

'Tell it, man!' shouted someone. 'Tell it, tell it, tell it!' shouted a lady, clapping her hands together, and after shyly staring around her, Isabel joined in.

'*Silence!*' said the poet. 'You are good humble people. Life has been hard for you. You're far from home. I can't let you suffer more.' There were cheers. Isabel turned to catch Manuela's eye, but a body was in the way.

The poem was about a poor peasant in a small backlands town that sounded very much like Saint Michael. As the peasant traveled to an enchanted city, rhymes sprang from the words, met each other side by side, bounced and pattered along, hid and then jumped out when Isabel least expected. The poet sang, tipped his hat and shook his shoulders. He growled and pawed the ground with his foot. He tossed little kisses to the air, twisted his face, made his eyes bulge and puffed his cheeks. He swooned and passed his hand over his forehead, fluttered his fingers over his heart and sighed, 'Aaaah.' He said, 'And so the princess thought and thought and thought. She looked first at the handsome prince, and then at the poor peasant, and said, *I have decided!*'

He closed the book.

The crowd stirred. Isabel waited for him to continue. Perhaps the girl would marry the peasant who was a prince inside, or maybe the prince who was really a leopard: it wasn't clear at all. The man tipped his hat. 'Special price today!' he said. 'Know the ending for a special price.' Someone in the crowd groaned, 'Tell us!'

'Yes, tell us!' said Isabel.

'Tell you? Sister, it's all here! Buy my book and you will know.'

Eager people elbowed forward.

Isabel cursed under her breath. How dare he! She pushed her way back to Manuela. 'I have to know.'

'Just this time,' said her cousin, rummaging through her pocket.

She went back to the poet. 'The leopard story,' she said, showing him the coin.

'Ah, my saint, you're too slow. I sold them all. But if you buy another, I'll tell you the leopard's ending. How about *The Girl Who Cursed Her Mother and Was Turned into a Snake,* or *The Boy Who Thought He Could Fly?*'

She selected the second one. It had a woodcut print of a boy with wings.

He wrapped it carefully in butcher paper, running a cracked nail along the edges.

Then he whispered in her ear. Now that he stood closer, she could see his tired eyes. He smelled of mothballs and cigar smoke. She nodded knowingly when she heard the ending. 'The peasant,' she said. 'That's the one I thought.' He tipped his hat, and with a little bow he was gone.

Manuela took her to Cathedral Square. On the steps beneath a Gothic dome of marble and verdigris, Isabel read the story slowly. It told, in rhyme, of a boy from 'a land so poor it grew only gravestones.' One day there was a great wind that carried him into the sky. He stared down at his home and saw only hunger and sadness, so he flew toward the sun. Then another wind came and blew him down, crashing through the clouds and into the center of the city, where he landed in a tree. A man, seeing that he could fly, offered him a job at a palace. But the palace was a factory, and his life was full of suffering. Isabel's mood darkened. She wished she hadn't read it.

Manuela took out a small tin filled with rice. She fed Hugo and changed his diaper, setting him between her feet as they ate and watched the crowds in the square.

They walked again. This time they stayed away from the fair. Inside the marble entrance of a department store, Manuela took Isabel on an escalator. 'Step!' she whispered. 'Now!' They rode up to the mezzanine, then down, then back up again, all the way to the top. As they walked, Isabel ran her fingers along the soft clothes. Below sale banners like Carnival coats of arms, they passed aisle after aisle of toothbrushes, perfumes, soaps.

It is beautiful, she thought, but she began to feel dizzy. The perfume banks smelled of unfamiliar flowers. The soaps were wrapped and sealed and couldn't be touched. She had never seen so many toothbrushes.

They stopped before a towering wall of beauty products, photos of faces with hair done up in creams, gels, dyes, tints, oils, sprays, pastes. There was blond hair with brown ends and brown hair with blond ends, black women with straight hair and white women with curly blond hair, hair that fanned out like dry grass, that hid a face like a curtain, that tufted in a little wave, that glistened with wetness and shined like metal. When she had the money, she would choose something for her mother, she thought weakly. She wanted to sit. Manuela browsed a row of lightening agents. Suddenly, Isabel was angry. She shouldn't have taken me here, she thought. She should have warned me so I could be ready. A girl in a store uniform touched her shoulder gently. 'I can get you a basket,' said the girl, pointing to a lace shirt in her hand. Isabel didn't remember taking the lace shirt. 'She doesn't want it,' said Manuela, and handed it back.

A voice boomed. 'Not too early to start thinking of school! Come to our children's department for the latest fashions. Make your children the envy of their classmates!'

Isabel pinched her eyes tight.

'I know,' said Manuela, taking her hand. 'Come. Let's go home.'

Isabel turned to look at her.

'New Eden,' said Manuela. 'Home.'

The next morning, Manuela was gone when Isabel awoke. She left only a note that read, *See you Friday,* and a small fold of money. Isabel didn't know what to do, so she waited until

Hugo began to stir. She spent the day seated at the edge of the bed, watching him play with a battered plastic doll, feeding him with a bottle when he was hungry. Later, she cleaned the room. She ate the beans and rice her cousin had prepared. She sat at the window and listened to sounds from the street.

The following days were the same. She stayed inside, leaving only to draw water and buy food from a market down the hill. She fed Hugo, cleaned him, played with him and waited while he slept. Watching him, she found herself wondering how he could grow up inside, alone without other children or animals.

Sometimes she listened to the radio, and sometimes she looked at the only book, the illustrated Bible, where Christ preached on a desolate mountain that reminded her of the ragged hills at home. Mostly, she lay on the bed and stared at the ceiling, watching the room fill with light and later with darkness. Her eyes followed the geckos and cockroaches, and she strained her ears for distant conversations.

At times, she paced the room, needing to walk and stretch her legs, but she didn't go outside. She was terrified by Manuela's warnings, by the noise. She had the impression that each time she opened the door she was crossing into another world, without empty space. She told herself that she would venture out once she became used to so many other people, once Isaias came. She wondered if others thought it was strange for a person to come from so far away only to sit in a little room.

As the week wore on, she found herself increasingly seized by an unfamiliar compulsion to speak. So she spoke to the baby: unconnected, hesitant stories of festivals and family, names of plants, attributes of town dogs, myths, bestiaries, spirit hierarchies, dresses she had seen on television, a garden she would plant near the stream at home, tales of bandits, the Princess of China.

They were good stories, her best stories, but soon she began to wonder if words like *drought* or *cane* would mean anything to Hugo. 'Drought,' she whispered, once, staring at his face for a reaction. After a long pause, he laughed and reached for her eyes. She said it again, but the word was odd, meaningless, as if she were speaking a foreigner's tongue.

She lay on the bed and sat him on her belly. He's just a baby, she told herself, but now she was fascinated by the thought of a person who didn't know what drought was. She wondered about other words: *cane, cactus, thorn. Thorn,* she whispered. *Buckthorn, Jerusalem thorn, gray thorn, rose thorn, whistling thorn, virgin's thorn, wet thorn, blood thorn,* I know hundreds of kinds of thorn. 'In the thorn,' she began, 'on an overcast day when you can't see the sun—' Then she stopped. The words seemed impossible now.

She found a colored sock and dangled it over the baby's nose. His eyes followed. They were green, like Manuela's, but darker. They met hers and then the colored sock was forgotten. She tried to distract him, but his gaze wouldn't leave her. He wasn't easily tricked, she thought. In the north they would say he was born old, like her. Like his mother, too, but not like her brother. Her brother was born very young; to him, everything was new.

Later, Hugo played with the doll, holding it by the hand and banging it on the bed. When he finally slept, Isabel took the short pile of beauty magazines and brought them to the bed. Back home, on market day in Prince Leopold, she and Isaias used to stop at a store with a shelf of monthlies. The man in the store didn't let them touch the magazines, but he took them from their plastic covers, set them on the counter and flipped the pages when the children said, 'Turn!' Once, as a gift, he had given her a cooking magazine with photos of heart-shaped red fruit on plates of white cream.

Manuela's magazines were filled with colored photos of thin women. Isabel stopped at a page with a wrinkled dog that licked a girl's chin, and another with a baby and a smiling mother. She read slowly, *Nutribébé infant formula — Why deny your loved ones the health they deserve?* On another page, there was a photo of a girl and boy kissing. She stared at it for a long time. The girl's hand was on his shoulder, and his was on her belly. The article's title was WHAT IS LOVE? Beneath were smaller words: *You feel empty when he's gone. You want to share everything with him. Does he feel the same?* But the article was mostly about movies, kissing and holding hands, none of which seemed to answer the question it first proposed.

She looked through an old news magazine, with men in suits and soccer stars. She stopped at a photo of a black woman and a skinny baby in the desert. There were flies around its eyes, and its lips were chapped and swollen. Its ankles were thin like her fingers, and veins fretted its head. The headline read THE END OF HUNGER? She tried to read it but her hands began to shake and then she couldn't read any more. She hid the magazine beneath the others. Then she thought of her mother for a long time.

At the window, the view was of the Settlements, the corrugated patchwork of tin and cement rooftops. She heard music from one of the houses, and from the wires, the legions of broken kites fluttered like flags.

Manuela came home on the weekend. 'This isn't a prison,'

she said. 'I said be careful. I didn't say you should curl up like an animal alone in its hole, doing nothing.'

'I'm not an animal in a hole,' said Isabel. 'I'm not—' She paused. She had almost said 'lonely' instead of 'alone.' 'I'm waiting,' she said. 'Not doing nothing.' But when her cousin left again for work, she took Hugo to the top of the road, where the view opened onto the forest, and dogs trotted gracefully through the weeds. She began to return to that spot. She spent hours watching the dogs, envious of the simplicity of their lives. She told herself that it should not trouble her that she had no friends, because Isaias would come soon. She left Hugo's sling at home, and held him close against her body.

At night, she listened to the radio. Again she read the pamphlet she had bought with Manuela, secretly hoping that somehow the ending might have changed. She stayed away from the magazine and its photo of the starving woman.

Once, she ventured as far as the soccer pitch. There she watched the boys play, firing the ball off the concrete walls, dodging gracefully through bricks and tufts of grass.

From the soccer pitch, the ball bounced into her memory of evenings in Saint Michael, when the cane workers came home, soot-covered and smelling of dust, their sweat-stained hats slung low over their eyes. It was her favorite hour of the day, gilded in lengthening shadows, the wind whistling over the windows. The villagers would gather at the field, setting out chairs or squatting on the sidelines. The players wore uniforms made of shirts donated by opposing political candidates, numbers inked in bold pen on the backs. They did battle between goalposts made of a cactus and the trunk of an old jacaranda. Isaias was a midfielder, and left-footed.

In the summer, the field was littered with little violet flowers that stirred as the players ran past.

The ball skidded over the ground, through the flowers and into the field in the city, where a foot stopped it and sent it streaking past a crowd of girls. The boys played shirtless, their backs tattooed with images of guardian saints. They dribbled over the rutted dirt and shot at a goal marked by two empty bottles.

Isabel sat at a distance and moved away when the ball rolled past. Once a boy stopped before her. He wore a threadbare shirt with a foreign word she didn't understand. He tossed the ball into the air and leaped up. His foot met it at the top of his arc, rocketing it toward the game. His body windmilled, sweat spun from his hair, his feet thudded down. He landed inches away. He was small, with fuzz on his cheeks. He turned and caught a pass, and fired it back into the empty field at home.

Slowly, faces became familiar. From a bent metal chair outside his store, Junior greeted her whenever she passed. He called her *my princess* and Hugo *my king,* and slowly her suspicion softened. She began to look forward to seeing him, finding herself disappointed if he wasn't outside. She would stand near the shop until he invited her to sit. Between customers, he told her about his home in the north, *even farther away than yours.* He had a daughter there, he said, Isabel's age. He showed her a photo of a smiling girl with long black hair. 'You two would be friends,' he said. She liked dancing and her name was Angelica, which Isabel had always thought was a beautiful name, the name she would give her daughter one day. 'She goes to school,' he said, 'in the capital. She's a star at math. That's what this store is for, to pay for her school.' A woman behind him slapped his arm. 'For her school and your girlfriends!' she said, and Junior's belly shook as he laughed.

When he saw Isabel staring at the television, he said, 'You

can come and watch anytime, love—you don't have to buy anything.' On a newscast, she watched a report on the pilgrimage at the shrine of Good Jesus of the Springs. Pilgrims walked through the dirt roads in the thorn, on their knees, with stones on their heads. They showed a map of the backlands and its geography of biblical names.

For hours in the afternoon, there was a broadcast of a preacher in a light green suit, pacing the stage of a very big church. When he put his hand on people's heads, he cured them of limps and blindness. They fell on the floor and shook like fish out of water. He liked to say, 'Everyone has a purpose! You must find your purpose! Everyone has a gift! You must find your gift!'

She stopped watching the television. The sound and noise intruded on her thoughts, hurrying them or cutting off the long paths that they took when she lay alone in the room.

One day she met a group of older women coming up the hill beneath baskets of clothes, and she began to descend with them to the stream.

They all had the same thick hips, sloping shoulders and muscular forearms. They wore layered muslin skirts, faded to brown shades of once-different colors. Their hair was tied in printed fabric; when they bent their heads together, they touched like the squares of a quilt. In the water, they gossiped and teased each other as they twisted the clothing, beat it against the rocks and squeezed soapy clouds into the river. They sang songs from the north. In the little lakes cast by the folds of their skirts, the water shimmered. It smelled dirty to Isabel, but the women didn't appear to care.

In her mind she compared them to her mother, who would stay in the shallows long after the washing was done, just sitting, letting the water wick up her clothes and into the dry air. Now, when she imagined her mother joining the women in their chore, she seemed thin and very small.

The women laughed alike, and wagged their fingers every time they said *no*. They spoke without breaking the rhythm of their washing.

'Where are you from, daughter?' they asked, stirring up the water as they scrubbed the clothes. 'Saint Michael,' answered Isabel. 'Saint Michael,' they whispered to one another. 'We don't know Saint Michael, no.' 'It's in the interior, in the mountains, near Prince Leopold.' 'Lord, that's hard land. They don't make land and people hard like that, no. We're also from the north,' they said. 'We also passed hunger.

'How did you get here?' they asked, twisting the shirts into heavy corkscrews. 'A perch,' said Isabel. 'A perch,' they whispered to one another 'We came that way, too. It's been twenty years. For me, twenty-six. Me, I've lost count. You had it easy,' they said. 'We ran out of water, we ran out of fuel, we spent our nights on the side of the road.

'How long will you stay here?' they asked, squeezing out plumes of detergent. 'I don't know. I am waiting for my brother—I'll let him decide. Until it gets better in the north, I think.' 'It's never getting better in the north,' they said. 'If you think it will get better, you're wrong.' 'I've spent the last thirty years wanting to return to my village,' said one. 'I'm going to return, if only to die. I want to be buried in that warm dry dust, not this rotten soil.'

'And what work will you do here?' they asked, pounding the clothes on a wide flat stone. 'And do you have a man?' Shaking the clothes, snapping them in the air in little bursts of mist.

They brought a new batch of clothes into the river. The conversation moved on. They spoke about the price of cooking gas and news from the north. They complained about their families. 'They call every week and ask me to send money. They think that chickens fly through the air here, already plucked and roasted, and we only have to reach up and pull one down. They want to send my niece here to work, because she has troubles with men. Imagine! Sending a girl here who has troubles with men!'

Isabel sat Hugo on the bank, where he chewed on the hand of the doll. There were anthills in the slope of the riverbed, and Isabel watched the ants carrying little boulders of dirt into the holes. Their antennae beat at the ground like tiny drummers. She put sticks in their way and watched them struggle over.

The days passed, and she waited.

In the morning, sitting on the doorstep with Hugo on her lap, she watched the people descend from the Settlements and crowd the buses to the city. They were day maids and factory day-shifters and construction men. At night, others came down: the cleaners of factory plants and girls who said they were waitresses, the night-shifters and night guards.

The buses were full in the morning. There were long lines, and the fare collectors packed the aisles as tight as possible. The buses lurched through the city, rumbled forward in traffic, swung tight curves, dove into tunnels, shook until they seemed ready to fall apart. Sometimes they broke down, abandoning their fares in worried crowds that set off walking for the nearest stop.

In the industrial neighborhoods, the factory day-shifters got off first, filing into looming steel amphitheaters. They donned light blue bonnets and face masks, and took up their places on the factory lines, where they soldered in showers of sparks, turned, clamped, cut, twisted, dipped, sprayed, bolted, hammered, lathed, until the end-of-shift bell rang, stopping only for lunch on the cold aluminum tables of company cafeterias.

The construction workers got off at crowded street corners, boarding unmarked vans trawling for day labor. On the tops of skeletal towers, they touched talismans of Saint Barbara and wrapped shirts around their heads to protect themselves against the sun.

The maids rode all the way to the Center, where they changed for buses to leafy districts with electrified fences. They stood before cameras and let the guards buzz them in. The guards were their brothers or their cousins or neighbors in the city or from the towns they had fled during the droughts. They rode service elevators up terraced apartments called Villa Italia, Le Beaumont and Edificio Cézanne, and learned to shadow the movements of gilded women in dark sunglasses. They mopped the same floors they had mopped the day before, and washed lipstick from Danish crystal. At lunch, they carried silver trays and smiled politely, and listened from the kitchen door to stories of Parisian *parfumeries* and tans in Miami. When their bosses left in chauffeured cars, they went to the balcony and watched the distant airplanes, smoked and flicked the ash with secret pleasure toward the sapphire blue of the swimming pools below.

Then the maids folded their aprons and took the elevators back down. The construction men lay down their tools, and the factory workers shook out their hair from the light blue bonnets, removed their gloves and masks, and filed out of the great buildings, where they caught the buses back to the periphery, shouldering their way out through the night workers waiting to get on.

The buses went back. Now the watchmen crowded in with the cleaning women, factory night-shifters and girls who said they were waitresses. The women who were old and free from the tyranny of once being beautiful watched the girls tug on their short skirts with a mixture of sadness and anger. The night guards also watched the waitresses, inhaling their heavy perfume as the bus swayed. They also felt sadness and anger, but they felt desire, too, which made the sadness and anger stronger. The girls who were shift workers in the factories and still not freed from beauty's tyranny watched the waitresses and saw the necklaces, nail polish, pumps and the men's eyes travel to the edges of their skirts.

The girls who were shift workers in the factories remembered the first time a friend whispered, They aren't waitresses, and learned how much they made. Time and again, they considered the possibilities but said No, which they told themselves was a final No, but each night they reconsidered as they rode into the Center. They told themselves with pride, I would never do that, They make more by suffering more, and they rubbed their elbows and wrists swollen from turning and clamping and cutting and twisting, and their rashes from dipping and spraying, and they wondered if this was true. Then they told themselves, It is a different suffering, a soul suffering, and they thought of the great cold rooms and the whir of motors that made all conversation impossible, the masks that kept the dust out but also kept them from smiling to one another or mouthing words. They told themselves, But it is dangerous, and they thought of the gears and belts and flying metal shards, and friends who lost eyes and hands to mechanical things that couldn't hear them scream.

The girls in the short dresses saw the girls in their factory clothes and remembered the first time they heard of the grinding monotony of the plants. They thought, I won't do that, I won't slave for a month for what I make in a week, and they thought of their faces pushed into the rotten carpets of cheap motels and minutes that seemed like hours. They told themselves, I would die of the boredom, and thought of the same foul words from the same men, the same musty smell below the same bellies, the same haggling, the same damp beds, the same sharp edges of broken floor tiles, the same mildewed ceilings. Then they told themselves, Poverty is worse, Minimum wage is worse, and they thought of the cost of lipstick and stockings that the stupid men tore in fits of false passion, and the price of contraception and injections of penicillin. Then they thought in the end, But I am beautiful and shouldn't work in a factory, and stared at their reflections in the vibrations of the glass.

They joined buses from other corners of the periphery as they descended on the Center. Now it was the cleaners of the industrial plants who got out first, on the corners of empty blocks with graffitied walls and barbed wire. They watched for shadows as they walked to the gates, waiting as the guards fumbled with the locks. In the black and echo of empty corridors they mopped and sang childhood songs from the north, thought of home and watched the rectangles of sky for dawn to come.

Then the night-shifters got off and took up spots on the factory lines and turned and clamped and cut and twisted and dipped and sprayed until the end-of-shift bell rang, stopping only for midnight lunches on the cold aluminum tables of company cafeterias.

Next were the guards, who left meal tins in supply closets and checked the chambers of their guns. They waited in the empty lobbies of the black-marble banks and watched the entrances. They imagined figures moving through the dark. They learned that if you stare long enough, you see men where there aren't men, that in the darkness of the empty lobbies of black-marble banks, the night-men emerge from the artificial palms, the swirls in the marble, the reflections in the floor. They knew that some guards never learned to tell the difference between real men and the night-men who appeared and disappeared and would never rob anything. They laughed at stories of friends who broke the glass on alarms or fired rounds into the marble, who, trembling, tried to explain what they had seen. They said they would never do this, and fantasized at night of gallant rescues, newspaper headlines and thankful executives who emptied coffers of gratitude into their hands.

The last to get off were the girls, who walked until they were beyond the lights and then stopped, to tug their skirts above the white triangle of their underpants and pace the shadows of the overpasses, to smoke anxiously as they walked toward cars idling at the edges of the dark sidewalks, where in the morning they caught the buses once again for home.

Over the following weeks, more families arrived in New Eden, marching up the hill beneath bags and battered suitcases, settling in homes or pushing back through the Settlements to the woods. They cleared the brush and felled the cypresses and laurel. Behind the fluttering sheets that hung as window curtains, Isabel could see sleeping bodies crowding the floors.

The city was dry, the days covered in a strange, thick warmth. Without rain, the dust stayed in the air, blurring the distant towers in the haze.

At the edge of the forest, Isabel found a quiet spot in the carmine shade of a coral tree. She began to spend hours there, watching the children play, the women hanging clothes on the branches, the boys slinking into the shadows to capture songbirds. The stumps of the cut trees were moist with sap. Clapboard shanties sprang up in the sweet-smelling arbors.

Then she went down, through the streets where groups of young men sprawled before televisions flickering with images from over the hill. During the first few weekends, Manuela showed her whom she could trust and whom to avoid, whispering, 'That one, careful of that one,' until Isabel learned to recognize the restlessness and the angry stares. At Junior's store, she began to hear hushed stories about a man named Blue Rat. On a newspaper used to wrap bottles of cane liquor, she read the headline KILLING IN THE CENTER. In the photo, a crescent of children stood around a body and stared back at the camera.

At times, her sleep was punctuated by sirens. Once, on the weekend, she and Manuela woke to screaming and then a shot, and in the morning the streets were eerily empty. Strangely, it frightened her less than it did Manuela. The stories seemed somehow to come from a parallel world, whose seething trajectory could be avoided by not asking questions and staying small. This was an old skill, from Saint Michael.

She noticed early that the police never came up the hill.

One day, one of the washerwomen said that her son had come home with a white purse as a gift. 'I refused to take it,' she said, close to tears. 'I said, son, where did you get this? and he just lay on the bed and wrapped the leather strap around his hand so tightly that his fingers were pale.'

On the riverbank, a princess flower began to drop its petals. They shriveled like crepe paper and drifted to the water. At home, Isabel carefully plucked purple stamens from the clothes when they dried.

After her third week in the city, she awoke to a small procession led by an old woman in mourning. Behind her, in a shifting crowd, a man carried a box for a woman's dress. Isabel followed. Inside the box was a baby, its lips painted and a sparkling crown upon its head. Pale blush powder covered its cheeks. Its eyes were open. The box was painted with clouds and filled with strips of tinfoil fashioned into roses.

In her light blue dress, Hugo on her hip, she joined a crowd of children following an itinerant portrait seller.

He appeared one morning by the river, lugging a bag full of picture frames, walking as if he were listening to music. When the women saw him, they rose together, tendrils of soap curling from their feet. He was whistling the melody of 'White Dove.' He finished the verse before he greeted them.

He was a little younger than Isaias, with sage green eyes and long lashes like a woman's. He wore canvas tennis shoes that looked as if they had been scrubbed clean, and a mesh baseball cap with the name of a cement distributor, its clasp repaired with electrical tape. His bag was printed with PHOTO ALIN in rainbow-colored capitals. He had a slight underbite, accentuated by his smile, and uneven teeth of which he seemed unconcerned. He had, Isabel thought, a lonely air, like someone at the edges of a dance, or a child who, because of an illness, had once been kept from other children.

As the women crowded on the bank, their hems heavy with water, soapsuds fizzing on their arms, he showed them a portrait. It was the size of his chest, and Isabel recognized an old woman named Rosa who lived several houses up the hill. In the portrait, she wore a beautiful dress and a necklace of swollen pearls; her lips were scarlet, her cheeks mauve. Her hair, which Isabel remembered as streaked with gray, had turned to raven black. Behind her was a ballroom with chandeliers and tiny couples dancing.

'They are tricks,' said the washerwomen, but Isabel already knew. Before the cricket men had come, a similar portraitist would visit the market in Prince Leopold. He collected old photos, enlarging them, coloring them, pasting them on backgrounds cut from magazines. Who wants a photo of what they really look like? he would say with a laugh, decorating them with big houses, cars, teeth, the sea.

As the washerwomen purred around the photo, Isabel saw that the young man was missing two fingers on his right hand. The ends of the missing fingers were burnished with scars like pink centipedes. Cane, she thought immediately: once, he didn't move fast enough. He caught her staring and smiled. Hugo grabbed the collar of her dress. *Stop,* she whispered through her teeth, pushing back his hand. She avoided the young man's eyes.

The young man left the women and Isabel followed at a distance. Curious children gathered as he stopped by each house and clapped. In her doorway, Dona Rosa wiped her hands on a faded gingham dress. When she saw the portrait, she laughed and threw her arms over the young man, covering his face with kisses. He described the details: 'This necklace comes from Italy. I found it in a magazine for *madames*—it's called *True Romance;* the dress is from France, it's pure silk; the hairstyle is from *Beautiful Bride,* it's special for springtime and roses. *Not for everyone,* said the article, but I knew it was for you.'

'And the ballroom?'

'Vienna, in Europe—it's Carnival. I didn't believe it, either, but that's what the magazine said. The music is a waltz. Like this . . .' He danced her a few steps. Rosa cradled the frame against her breast. 'There, there,' said the young man.

He turned back at the top of the hill. The children drifted away, but Isabel continued to follow. To her surprise, he stopped at Manuela's house and called outside the door. She took a hesitant step forward. When no one answered, he shrugged and hefted his bag over his shoulder. 'Wait,' said Isabel.

'You live here?'

She nodded. He looked at a folded sheet of paper. 'There's an Isaias, right?' 'Isaias is my brother. He's gone now. Working.' She paused and shifted Hugo up on her hip. 'You have a portrait of him?' she asked. The young man nodded and pulled out a frame scarcely larger than his hand. 'I've been carrying it around for almost a month. No one's been home.'

Isabel recognized the portrait immediately from a document photograph Isaias had taken in Prince Leopold. His mouth was set and serious, his brow faintly wrinkled. Now the photo was enlarged and colored: her brother's cheeks were pink, his eyes a bruise blue. His lips were salmon, as if he were wearing lipstick. In the photo, he wore a jacket and a crimson tie, but she knew he never owned one. There was a cutout of a violin, and the background showed an orchestra: not a backlands band, but a concert hall orchestra, with musicians in black-and-white suits. She was so close that she could see that the images were pasted, but from a distance, it looked as if he were in the concert hall himself.

Her hand began to shake.

'You okay?' asked the young man. She nodded. 'Is something wrong? I didn't mean to upset you.'

She shook her head. In her arms, Hugo reached for the photo. She held it away, and pushed her hair back with her shoulder. The baby began to cry.

The young man reached out and stroked Hugo's head, 'When you're old enough, I'll make you one, too,' he said, and chuckled, alone. Hugo buried his face into Isabel's breast.

'I'm Alin.' The young man extended his hand, but Isabel's

arms were full. She nodded shyly. The sun felt very warm on her cheekbones. He let his hand drop. 'Do you have a name?'

'Yes,' she said awkwardly, and then, 'It's Isabel.' Hugo twisted again.

'Is he yours?'

'Mine?'

'The baby—is he your baby?'

'This baby? No! He's my cousin's!' Her face grew hot. 'I don't have a baby.' Her fingers fidgeted with the frame. It occurred to her that she had spoken very loudly.

Alin regarded her curiously. 'You know, you remind me of a niece I have in the north,' he said. 'You just arrived, didn't you?'

Isabel paused. 'No,' she said.

'No? You don't have to be ashamed. I'm from there, too. Not that you would know where I'm from. Just a little village with a saint's name. Hot as sun on a black cow's back.'

Isabel felt herself smile, a little. 'My village is Saint Michael in the Cane. Do you know it?'

He shook his head. 'Not that Saint Michael, but I've heard of other towns with that name. Every state must have a Saint Michael. Saint Michael of the Mountain, Saint Michael of the Riverside, now Saint Michael in the Cane. My cousin's husband is from a Saint Michael. He used to curse that name. It was bad luck, he said. If you name your village after the saint that fights the devil, then you'd better be prepared to join him. That's what he said.'

When Isabel saw that he was waiting for her to respond, she said, 'I think it's just another name. He watches over us. We aren't unlucky. There is a stream, sometimes, and sugarcane. Many places don't even have a stream.'

'Maybe,' said Alin. 'But if he really watched over you, you would be home, not here.'

Isabel didn't know how to answer. She saw the washer-women trudging up the hill under their loads, and she excused herself and went to help them carry.

For the rest of the week, she remained inside.

Now, with the portrait staring into the room, her brother's absence became acute; the hours no longer disappeared into long stretches of dreaming and waiting. She paced and wrung her hands. She told herself: Be patient! He's always been like this, walking off into the thorn, disappearing to the coast, making fantastic plans in that house with its anthills and crumbling walls. She tried to imagine him before big crowds, with his own hand and clean white boots. Maybe he went somewhere far away: the docks, the jungle, even to sea. Maybe the phones didn't work. Maybe he'd sent a letter, the envelope overstuffed with pages, lost somewhere in a dark post office.

Then, at night, she yielded to different possibilities. He had been shot or robbed, hit by a car, killed by police; he had fallen sick with a disease of the city, from poisoned water, poisoned air, from visions, spirits, nerves, nostalgia, possession. The thoughts seized her like a fever; she had to recite invocations against her imagination. As she waited for sleep, she tried to imagine him moving through the mass of buildings, the two of them circling somewhere in its great dark spaces.

In Saint Michael, when she was a child, a little boy had been found wandering the white forest north of Prince Leopold.

A family had taken him in, waiting for him to tell them the name of his village. At first they thought he was scared, but then his silence lengthened into weeks. When they asked, Where do you live? he said only, With my mother, and when they asked, Where does she live? he said, With my father. He's simple, said some. Others argued, Why does he need to know the name of his father? Why does he need to know the name of his village if he has never seen another village?

The story had terrified Isabel's mother. She made Isabel practice her family name and the name of their town. *The cane,* said Isabel, and her mother corrected her worriedly: No! Say all of it, say *Saint Michael in the Cane.* If you say you are from *the cane,* they will not understand you. A *little girl from the cane* could be any little girl, from anywhere. To be safe, her mother took a string and tied a piece of cloth to her wrist. On it was written her family name, village and then *I am Isabel.* She imagined other Isabels from other villages wandering through the white forest. She wore it until the string grew thin and snapped.

When Manuela came home at the end of the week, Isabel showed her the portrait. Manuela carried it to the light and peered at it for a long time. 'These are very expensive,' she said at last.

'It's elegant,' said Isabel.

'It's not elegant at all. Poor people paying so much to pretend they're something that they're not is pathetic, not elegant.' She handed it back.

'Manuela,' Isabel asked. 'Why isn't he here?'

'I told you,' said her cousin. 'He's working.' But later that night, she said suddenly, as if to herself, 'Leo is coming soon. Once or twice he helped Isaias find a place to stay when he was working on the coast. Maybe he'll know.'

'Every day, the women at the river talk about their sons,' said Isabel. 'One of the washerwomen said her boy hurt a woman and took her purse—'

Manuela interrupted, 'That's different. Isaias isn't stupid like those boys. Hopeful, maybe, which is the best friend of stupid, but not stupid.'

Later Manuela said, 'I worked with a girl whose brother disappeared once. He went to the city to work because he wanted to buy a record player. He thought it would take two months. It was before they had phones. It took four years, and then he came home.'

She threw herself into her chores.

Her day became the baby. She thickened formula and boiled him rice, crushed him bananas with a bent fork. She dusted him with talcum, scrubbed stains from his clothes until her fingers ached. A health poster appeared on Junior's store—RAIN COMES SOON AND DENGUE TOO—with a drawing of a giant mosquito hovering over a sleeping child. She found a discarded mosquito net and repaired the tiny holes. She combed lice from his hair with the lice comb she had brought from the north, and when they had a plague of ants, she put cotton in his ears. She played with him, lying on her stomach and biting his hands as he reached for her eyes, or pushed her nose into the softness of his belly, hummed and listened to him laugh. She wished there were two babies, a hundred babies. She would scrub and wash and hum until Isaias came home.

One evening, at dusk, she was cleaning her nails with a knife, listening to the radio, when she sensed someone pass the side of the house and stop by the door. Hugo was babbling and banging the plastic doll against the floor. She clicked off the radio. 'Shhh,' she said, and rested her hand on the baby's head. The room was silent. In the distance she could hear the faint sound of music.

She waited for knocking or a clap, but there was nothing.

She lay back down, but the feeling persisted. *Isaias?* She stared at the lock. No, she told herself, There's no one there. It's the sound of the street, it's the wind or my imagination. She pivoted her knees over the side of the bed and walked swiftly toward the door.

In the street outside, two little boys were playing. She ran to them. 'Was there someone outside my house?' she asked. The children shook their heads. 'Yes,' said one, pointing, 'That lady.' She followed his finger to the corner, where an old woman struggled up the hill. 'Just her?' 'And a man.' 'Which man? What did he look like?' The boy shrugged. Isabel begged, 'Please, you have to remember what he looked like. Did he look like me?'

'Yes.'

Then the second boy swung at the first, laughing. 'Liar!'

'Wait . . .' she began, but the boys fell over each other, wrestling. She made her way back, not letting her eyes drop from where the road banked away. A pair of older boys were walking up the road. It's nothing, she thought. Of course there was a man—I live in a city. Isaias wouldn't come and leave.

Still she sensed something, farther now. At the door of her house she stopped. You don't know, she told herself, but she could feel it moving, flashes sinking away. She peeked into the room. Hugo hadn't moved. It will only be a second, she told herself. She closed the door and turned down the street.

She walked quickly. She entered an alley that dove through a cluster of shacks and dropped along a trickling stream reeking of sewage. She passed a group of men clustered at a corner. She felt the words on her lips, *Have you seen a boy who looks like me?* But as she drew closer she saw that they were drinking. She turned down another alleyway, down worn steps cut into the hillside, slipping briefly before she plunged deeper into the maze. The alley narrowed; at times she had to turn sideways to slip through spaces between buildings. She seemed to be following a path: even when the alleys split and re-formed, there seemed to be only a single way to go. Around her, the houses were lit by dim bulbs. Light glinted through the chinks in the brick and the slivers beneath the doors. She heard fragments of words, whistling, a moan, she saw shapes shifting, smelled rot and dogs, cooking oil, plastic burning, perfume. Birds stirred in their cages. In the shadow of the doorways, silent figures rocked slowly in hammocks or came to barred windows to watch her pass.

She entered a cleared lot. There she stopped on an old broken concrete floor with a single cinder-block wall. She saw the darkness of a half-dozen paths that ran off into a mass of shanties. It's that one, she thought, staring at a narrow alley that fell off to her right, but then she paused, filled with doubt. The light was gray. There was barking. Inside the alleyway, a shadow stirred.

She stared at the alley. She could feel him, it—the light, the shape, the sound, the warmth, the warp in the street —she could feel it moving away, winding down the hill and into darkness. You will lose him, she told herself. But her feet wouldn't move. The shadows stirred again, and three young men appeared, walking quickly toward her. She turned and stared up at the looming hill, tried to remember her path through the houses and went back in.

And if it was him? she wondered later. If it wasn't just my imagination? Why wouldn't he stay? She waited for an answer, but no answer came. She told herself that next time she would be faster, she would trust her instincts, she wouldn't wait.

When Hugo cried, she went to the door, but there was never anyone there. In Saint Michael, they believed that babies could sense what most adults couldn't, that their bodies closed off slowly, the way a skull closed. She sat with her lips against his fontanel. Sense *what*? she asked herself, searching for the words. Her mother knew, her grandfather knew; she had never needed to explain. Now, alone in the little room in the city, those moments in the cane fields seemed impossibly far and strange.

I am like the girl on the flatbed, she thought, the black-haired girl who spoke a language no one knew.

She thought of the rhabdomancer. Now she wished she could ask him how he divined for water in the city, how he saw the tunnels and underground rivers. What good is anything I know? she wondered. What does it matter that I can survive nights out in the forest? Who cares about enduring hunger when there are markets to buy food? Who needs to hear snakes in the cane if there are no snakes and no cane fields?

She had the vertiginous sensation that she was back in Prince Leopold, on the days the men of her village met the foremen from the road companies, the construction firms or the big coastal plantations. *What can you do?* the foremen would ask, and the men tallied off on heavy callused fingers: I can hunt, I can track, I can walk through the night without stopping. Then the foremen shook their heads and said, *Why would I need a hunter when I have cattle plantations? What else can you do?* I can turn a grindstone in a sugar mill, I can cut, I can carry pounds of cane. *But the sugar mills are going, it's all factories now, What's worth a couple oxen and a millstone in the new age?* I always was a farmer, I can farm even the worst, I can dig and find fertile soil where others see only stone, nowhere is there land I cannot grow. *That means little on the coast where the great fields give two crops every year, We need men who know fertile land, not that worthless land of yours, Tell me, man, what else can you do?* I can gather stones, make walls, homes. *Stones?* I know which cactus to eat, and the leaves from which trees, I know how to collect ants and cook them, I know where starch roots are found. *Those are skills for scavengers.* I can grow corn, manioc, yams. *On your little farm, you mean, you can grow those on your little farm, But no one has need for little farms anymore, Tell me, man, what else can you do?*

She cooed to Hugo until he slept.

In the middle of the week, Manuela called from work. Leo was coming this weekend, she said. 'It's sooner than I thought. Clean the house. The sheets, the dishes. And take your underwear off the line. Dust the saints and the top of the shelves.'

On Saturday morning they walked up the hill to a beauty salon, with a hand-painted shingle and a lone chair. The beautician, a middle-aged woman with heavy hips and a waddling

gait, left lipstick stains on the baby's cheeks. Isabel held Hugo as her cousin had her hair straightened. The beautician talked incessantly about the soap opera at eight and her daughter who was *nothing-but-trouble*. A third woman sat on the steps with her hair in curlers and echoed with heavy, aspirated *humph*s. The walls were covered with photos of the newest styles, torn from magazines.

An old man with a bowl haircut appeared in the doorway and bowed. The women shooed him off. 'He loves you,' said the beautician, kissing Manuela, who covered her teeth as she giggled.

Isabel could smell the perfume on her cousin as they came down the hill. They bought beer from Junior's store and prepared a stew with beans and onions, tripe and slabs of fat. As it simmered, Manuela sat at the edge of the bed and thumbed absently through a magazine. She made herself up with lipstick and blush, powdered Hugo with talcum. She sat him on her lap and brushed her fingers over his forehead. 'Daddy is coming,' she whispered. She sang it softly. Isabel watched as if from a great distance. I should be happy for her, she thought, I should not feel lonely. Soon Manuela said, 'Leo's late.' She began to pace. When night fell, they heard clapping outside the door. Manuela jumped to her feet and tucked her hair behind her ears.

Leo was a small man who reminded Isabel immediately of an uncle, a serious man who worked in the fields. When Manuela embraced him, his hand rose slowly to caress her back. He said, 'They made us work this morning, otherwise I would have come sooner.' He broke into a smile when he saw the baby. He lifted him and spun him around the room. 'My prince! My cowboy!' The baby made sputtering sounds with his lips, and Manuela laughed as Isabel had never heard her laugh before.

He kissed Isabel politely. His cheeks were shaven and he smelled strongly of cologne. She could feel the ridges of his rib cage. A little comb in his shirt pocket brushed against her shoulder.

He didn't set Hugo down even as they ate. He talked about a storm. 'You can't imagine the waves,' he said. 'You feel them even after you come to land. They follow you. In bed you think you are still at sea.'

She waited for him to say something about Isaias, but he grew silent as he ate. The only sounds were chewing, the clatter of the spoons, the clink of cups against the table. The food was warm and rich. Isabel devoured it, lifting heaping spoonfuls that dripped beans, crushing the fat against the roof of her mouth, feeling it dissolve over her tongue, stopping only to lick the grease from her lips. She felt drunk, heavy. A sweetness seemed to hang from her eyelids, and she didn't know if it was from the drink or the food. I haven't eaten like this in years, she thought. For a moment, she forgot the others and chuckled, humming a Carnival tune, until Manuela said 'Isabel?' and eyed her crossly. She ate until her belly hurt, and then collapsed beside Leo and Manuela on the bed, where they huddled around the baby. She felt as if her heart was very big, and rose to finish the beer from their cups and lick the bowls. 'Do we have more?' she asked, but they were absorbed in the baby and didn't respond.

Isabel lay on her back next to them. She moved closer so her body pressed against her cousin. Manuela's hair smelled sweet with perfume. Isabel buried her face into it, but her cousin didn't seem to notice. She decided she wanted to hold the baby, but Manuela pushed her gently away. 'No. Let Leo hold him, Isabel. You are with him all the time.' Twice she tried to stand, but the walls spun.

That night, as she slept on the floor, Isabel could hear them making love in the bed above her. Manuela whispered, *Hush,* and later, Isabel heard her moan, a soft cry she didn't think could come from her cousin. She lay perfectly still, her arms pressed to her sides. She felt her face grow warm.

In the morning, she awoke with a blinding headache and almost fell asleep again on the floor of the washroom. They dressed. Manuela let her wear lipstick. In church, she tried to see if any of the men were looking at her. She slid her shoes against the floor. On the steps, she asked Leo, 'Have you seen Isaias?'

'Not for months,' he said. 'I was going to ask you.'

They spent the day together in the Center. Leo bought Isabel an ice cream, and she ate it outside the Municipal Theater, swinging her legs from a plinth beneath a tall caryatid, watching the theater crowds. Drops of cream fell on her dress, and when Manuela wasn't looking she leaned forward and licked them from the cotton.

Before he left, Leo gave Manuela a small roll of bills. 'This is it?' she asked. 'Do you know how much last night's meal cost?' He protested, 'The price of the bus ride went up.' Manuela looked away, and Isabel imagined her calculating. She tucked the money into her bra. In the evening they took him to the station where buses left for the coast. Manuela went to the ticket window and asked about the prices. 'Why don't you trust me?' asked Leo.

They waited outside the bus. Leo held the baby until the driver said, 'Get on, brother!'

As they rode back to New Eden, Manuela cried. 'He'll be back soon,' offered Isabel. 'Two months!' said Manuela. 'My baby won't see his father for two months.' For a long time, she turned from Isabel and wept softly, her head pressed against the glass. She is crying too much, thought Isabel, She should be stronger.

Outside the window, mother-of-pearl clouds haloed the hill. She held her cousin's hand until they reached home.

That night, Isabel dreamed Isaias came to see her.

He entered the room through the door and sat on the side of the bed.

He was wearing his Carnival jacket, with tinsel and colored ribbons. His hair was combed. He drummed his fingers on the side of the bed and whistled happily. Where are you? she asked. He laughed and said, It's easy, and leaned over to whisper. She awoke with the feeling of his breath on her ear.

She tried to remember what he said, chasing the dream back until her memory failed her. Still, she was comforted. She closed her eyes and thought, Does it count, to be comforted in a dream? Does he know he is talking to me? If I remembered what he said, would I follow his advice, the dream-advice of a dream-brother?

She slept again, and Isaias was there. He left sometime in the early hours of dawn.

In late July, a month after Isabel's arrival, Manuela came home with news of work. It was election season, she said. 'The job is only on the weekends, so you can still watch Hugo during the week. You'll miss church, I know, but there isn't any other way.' She gave Isabel directions to a campaign office in the Center and woke her early the next morning.

At the office, a man asked what she could do. 'Do you know typing? How is your math? Have you worked with a campaign before?' The office was crowded with boys and girls her age. 'I can read,' she said, 'and write with a pen.' She prayed he wouldn't ask her to show him. 'You'll be a flag waver,' he said.

She didn't expect to start right away, but he gave her a shirt and cap in the colors of the party. He said, 'We drive through the city all day. If we pass you and you are not waving the flag, you will be docked half your pay. You are allowed to stop waving only when the traffic is not moving. You are never allowed to set the flag on the ground, although you can rest the base of the pole if you like. You shouldn't do anything that could reflect poorly on the Candidate. You can break to eat lunch at noon, but no more than thirty minutes. If you lose the flag or it's stolen because you're careless, you'll have the value of the flag docked from your pay. The value of a flag is three days of waving.'

She filed behind the others into a van. It stopped at the busiest intersections and let them out one by one. Soon Isabel was left with the foreman and another girl. She hoped she would be next—she didn't like how he had held her arm when he helped her into the car. When they stopped, he motioned the two of them out. He gave them both flags. 'I want you both on that traffic island—you, there, and you, there. Stay in those places. Don't talk. If you talk, I'll know.'

On the corner of a wide avenue with tall buildings, they waited for the light to turn. 'Ever done this before?' asked the girl. Isabel shook her head. 'Then watch out for the mirrors— they come close—and careful with the flag. Once mine got caught on someone's grille and almost threw me into the street, *and* it broke, *and* I had to pay for it. And we can't talk—he's serious about that. He's docked my pay before. But we can talk at lunch.'

The traffic was heavy when they took their spots on the island. The flag was gold, with the Candidate's name flanked by black stars. Carefully, importantly, Isabel smoothed out the hem of her shirt and tried to stand as tall as she could. Around her, the street reverberated with the sound of honking and roaring motors.

Scarcely a half hour passed, and her arms began to tire. She looked at the other girl, who was shimmying her shoulders as if she were dancing to music. The girl signaled to rest the base of the pole on the ground as she waved. The traffic grew worse. From passing cars, she heard whistles or boos. 'Go home!' shouted one. 'How can you work for that animal?' Another shouted, 'You are a traitor to your class!' Isabel didn't understand what this meant, but, to be safe, she waved slower.

In the late morning, they were joined on the island by a pair of old men. They wore placards that read ROCKET CHICKEN and hats with chicken beaks on the rim and tails behind. They had tired, furrowed faces that reminded her of her grandfather. The placards showed a bird running with a plate of cooked chicken on its outstretched fingers. Does the chicken know what it's carrying? Isabel wondered. She tried to make herself smile, but the more she stared, the more the image disturbed her. The men shuffled uncomfortably. Someone probably told them: No resting the placards! She thought, I'm lucky I have a flag.

The sun glinted off the sloping glass walls and formed mirages in the intersections. Soon Isabel could not see the end of the avenue for all the pollution. It was hot; the air clung to her like a wet film. I know how to bear heat, she told herself. But it was different from the dry heat in the north. By late morning, her nose and eyes were burning. She was dizzy and was afraid she might fall. She sat cross-legged on the island. Did the man say anything about sitting? But the exhaust made sitting worse than being on her feet. How many days do I have to do this? she wondered. When her feet began to ache, she paced back and forth along the island. I used to walk for hours, she thought. She crouched until her legs grew numb. The other girl had tied her shirt above her belly and turned her hat brim backward on her head. When she came close, Isabel whispered, 'You can't do that.' The girl laughed. 'Of course I can; they like it better. It's the sexy style.' She let the flag sway in her hands, spun it and let it fall, only to catch it again. She dipped it into the street and whirled it away as the cars charged.

At noon, they slumped against the huge roots of a ficus that broke through the mosaic of the city sidewalk. The girl said, 'You'll be okay. I used to hate it, too, but it's better than other jobs. The secret is pretending you're a famous star and not just a flag waver. The day goes by, you'll see.'

The girl's name was Josiane. She was sixteen. She lived with her mother in New Jerusalem, in the Settlements, not far from Isabel. She had six brothers and sisters. She waved flags for two parties, she said, it didn't matter. They paid well because no one wanted charges of cheating their campaign workers. During the week, she worked in a doll factory and sold bus passes in the evening. She was born in the north but came to the city when she was seven. 'You know, *that old story,*' she said. Isabel shook her head. 'Like you, I bet,' said Josiane. 'Drought, parrot perch . . .' She laughed and waved it away with her hand.

Black hair fell down her neck in ropy braids. She had long, thin arms, and spoke with her hands. 'Street's crowded,' she said, turning her palm up and tapping her fingers together. Or: 'Watch your pockets with that one,' this time pointing her lips to a boy with a stocking cap, placing her thumb on her thigh and sweeping her painted nails past.

With a wink, she showed Isabel a book she brought to read on the bus. It was called *Traveling Fire* and was Number 27 in the Young Passion Collection. On the cover was a shirtless man caressing a girl in jeans and a bra. It was about a girl named Marina and a traveling cowboy named Thyago Firestorm. The spine was broken at chapter seven, "The Burning Desire." It was heavily annotated: someone with a pink pen had underlined 'her burning love' and 'her famished heart,' and stars flanked 'their unquenchable passion.' In the margin where the famished Marina is prohibited from seeing Thyago, a different pen had written, *Let them be!* The pages were bent and the print smudged. She had inherited it from a cousin, who had inherited it from a coworker. She would be happy, she said, to pass it along when she finished.

Isabel's eyes drifted to the word *kiss*. She read slowly, moving her lips. Marina was panting like a mare, she learned.

Josiane interrupted, 'Do you always read like that?'

'Like what?'

'With your mouth. You don't have to say the words, you know. You look like my mother when she tries to read.'

Isabel felt herself blushing. 'Sorry.'

'Sorry? Sorry for what? Just some people might think you're simple.'

She applied lipstick with the smell of watermelon, and pursed her lips.

In the afternoon, Isabel began to cough and couldn't stop. She left the island to wet the top of her shirt in a fountain by the ficus and lifted it over her mouth. Back in the street her breath was moist and cold. She hummed through the wet fabric and tried to dance like Josiane. She gave up. She forced herself not to watch the clock. Her gaze flitted moth-like over the crowds. She occupied herself by trying to imagine the city people in the north: the men in the suits trying to make their way through the thickets, the women getting their pumps stuck in heavy mud at the creek.

Late in the afternoon, she saw a young man with her brother's gait. It can't be Isaias, she scolded herself. He's not here, he's on the coast. She ran along the island until she saw his face.

She stopped waving and then let the flag hang over her so that it shaded her from the sun. She made it flap gently back and forth over her forehead.

At the end of the day, the man in the van shouted at them from across the street. They retraced the long path through the city. The seats filled with the other flag wavers, their shirts stained and crumpled.

At the office, the man made them wait outside while he spoke on the telephone. He came out only when one of the boys banged on the window. He read their names from a notebook and thumbed bills off a roll. When he read Isabel's name, he said, 'I'm docking you half.'

'Why?'

'For wearing a mask.'

She stared dumbly. Behind her, Josiane protested, 'Mask? It was her shirt. It wasn't a mask!'

'Same thing. It was a shirt serving as a mask. It's against the rules.'

Josiane shook her hands at the ceiling. 'Since when was there a rule against wearing a mask?'

'It's part of the rule about shaming the Candidate.'

'How does a mask shame the Candidate?'

'He's the incumbent—it doesn't reflect well on the cleanliness of the city.'

'Man! The *air* doesn't reflect well on the cleanliness of the city!'

'Rules are rules, don't worry, there's always tomorrow.' He turned to Isabel. 'Do you always let your friend speak for you? You shouldn't hide your pretty mouth.'

The girls took the bus to the New Settlements. On the way, Josiane cursed the foreman. Isabel bit her lip and stared around the bus with horror. 'Come on,' said Josiane. 'Get it out of your system.' Laughing, Isabel repeated the words. She cursed the Candidate, too. Josiane cursed even louder. Isabel cursed so loud that she almost shouted it. An elderly woman turned with a stare that reminded her of her mother, and she was quiet the rest of the trip home.

The next morning, she wore her good shoes and arrived early to work, hoping to meet her friend, but Josiane arrived just as they were boarding the van. This time, she held Isabel's hand. They sat at the back and again were the last to descend.

At lunch, Josiane spoke without stopping. 'You wouldn't believe it,' she said, 'but I just had a baby four months ago.' She lifted her arms. 'Not bad, huh? She's at home with my mother. I had to spend two weeks in the hospital before she was born. I should have spent more time, but the private hospitals wouldn't take me. Thank God things came out all right, because the baby pitched her tent a bit too close to the door.'

'What?'

'Well, that's my explanation. Something about the sac not setting down in the right place—you're from the country, so you probably know.' She put her hand on Isabel's knee. 'Of course, I spent a lot of time wondering: How did that happen? Then I figured it out: it's because I had sex in a hammock. Don't look so embarrassed! I know what you're thinking. You're thinking: in the north *everyone* has sex in a hammock. Of course! But *there* the body gets *used* to putting the baby in the right place, like a sailor learns to walk on a boat. But *here,* we sleep in beds, and we aren't used to it, and if you get impulsive like me and insist on doing it in a hammock'— she tapped her fingers against the ground—'if you haven't thought through the consequences like I have now, the body doesn't know where to put the baby.'

'That sounds complicated,' said Isabel.

This generated a long series of stories from the hospital, about a girl who gave birth to a clump of grapes, two babies attached at the nose, a baby with a single eye, another who entered the world with skin like a Carnival jester. She stopped talking only to catch her breath.

For lunch, Josiane mixed powdered formula with drops of water until it became a sweet paste. She gave Isabel a taste from a spoon. 'It's from an aid center for the poor,' she said. 'I told them I had twins.'

A man in a suit came and unfolded a little piece of paper by a pay phone. When Josiane began to talk again about her baby's birth, he put his hand over the mouthpiece and said, 'Hey, can you keep it down? Not everyone needs to hear your disgusting story.'

'Not everyone needs to use the phone next to me,' she snapped. Isabel flinched, but the man left.

Josiane described a fair in her neighborhood. There was a Ferris wheel and a ride called the White Tornado. 'I bet you've never seen anything like the White Tornado,' she began, and then she looked up at the clock. 'No! Just like yesterday. I talk and talk and now we're late. To be honest, I hate this. Yesterday I made it sound like I didn't mind because you looked desperate, but now that we're close friends, I'll be honest: I'm not very good at this. I'm better at impatience.'

Back on the island she twirled the flag above her head. Once again the cars swarmed. 'Hey, sweetheart! I like it just like that!' shouted a man as his car idled at the light, and Josiane stopped and, smiling, flashed him her middle finger.

At the end of the day they collected their pay. Isabel tucked it deep into her pocket, and Josiane took her arm. 'You don't have to go home yet, do you? Can you stay with me? I don't want to go home now.' She led Isabel to a plaza where a day market was being dismantled. Heavy ropes of tobacco scented the air. 'Is this what it's like?' Josiane asked. 'What?' 'The north. I was so little when I left. But everything they sell in this neighborhood is from the north. They even used to have musicians on the weekends.'

'Not anymore?'

Josiane shook her head. 'No, the police chased them away.'

'All of them?'

'All of them. Why are you so excited? It's just music. I have a radio if you want to listen sometime.'

Josiane went to flirt with a clerk in a grocery store and returned with a bag of hard candy. She gave a piece to Isabel. They sat on a bench and watched the store shutters rattle shut. Josiane broke piece after piece of candy in her teeth. She told a story about her aunt from the north, a laughing old woman with bead-wrapped wrists that clattered as she moved. She had moved to the coast, where she had grown fat. She owned a little black mutt who curled into the folds of her skirts. For two years she hadn't eaten breakfast because a doctor said she suffered from the Sugar and the Blood. She had great pillowed breasts and seemed weightless when she danced. 'They said she was my favorite aunt. That I would be like her, if I stayed.'

Josiane paused. 'It doesn't matter, though. It doesn't make me sad. One day everyone will have to come. People weren't meant to live in such a place, my uncle says. It's not natural.'

'We've always lived there,' said Isabel.

'Not always,' said her friend. 'You had to come from somewhere. Your people were from somewhere before your village. Do you think you just appeared out of nowhere, grew up out of the ground? You think you're made of dust?' 'I didn't say that.' 'Then where did you come from?' 'I told you.' Josiane shook her head. 'You're not listening. Think, where did your grandfather come from?' 'Same village as me.' 'And his father?' 'Him, too, I think.' 'And his father, what about him?' Isabel frowned. 'I don't know. I think he was born there, too.' 'You don't know anything about him?' Isabel paused. 'No. Only that he was the grandfather of my grandfather. And he must have had a grandfather, too.' Josiane waved her hands in frustration. 'But if you go back far enough, there was a place without people. That's the point. That's what I'm saying. That's why it's not natural. It's well-known.'

She grew quiet. A cat rooted in a pile of husk left by a cane-juice vendor. A paper scavenger ran past, pulling a cart stacked with cardboard. A little boy was perched on top. The man swerved through the traffic, took bounding steps and let the cart glide.

Across the street, a girl in a bright pink shirt called.

'Hey!' Josiane's smile returned. She ran and embraced her. When Isabel approached, she said, 'This is Isabel. I told you about her. My newest friend, from way back in the middle of nowhere.'

The girl's stare made Isabel feel small again. 'Hey, Miss Nowhere,' she said, and laughed.

Isabel sat next to them and listened as they talked. The girl said that she'd found a toad with its eyelids sewn shut with green silk thread. 'It's a spell to cuckold a man, of course,' said Josiane. 'My sister knows it.'

The girl nodded thoughtfully. 'Do you know spells for men?' she asked Isabel.

'Look at her,' Josiane interrupted. 'She's a kid. She just got here.'

Isabel shrugged. 'I've heard of people doing that, but they didn't in my village. We only have bull toads, and I would never touch them. Only really hungry people would touch them.' She added, 'They belong to the devil.'

'We're talking about spells for men,' said Josiane. She turned to the girl. 'She doesn't know. She's very innocent.'

'Why are you protecting her?' asked the girl. 'I knew all about men when I got here.'

They stayed with the girl until dark. Sometimes Isabel listened. Other times she watched the street, staring at the faces in the crowds that passed. After a while, the girls began to talk about the soap operas. Isabel found herself transfixed by a description of a beautiful maid called Cindy. 'She's really a maid?' she asked. 'Yes,' said the girl. 'She's from the interior like you. But she's tall, and her skin is fair. She combs her hair in the curly way. She is so lovely.' Isabel didn't know what to say. She stretched her legs so the girl could see her shoes, but the girl said nothing. The girl left.

On the bus to the Settlements, Josiane asked, 'Who do you live with?'

'My cousin,' Isabel said. Then she added, carefully, 'And my brother, but he hasn't come home.'

'Hasn't come home?' Josiane frowned. 'What's that mean, hasn't come home?'

'He was here, but when I arrived he was gone. Almost two months now.'

'Just disappeared? Have you been to the police?'

Isabel shook her head. 'We don't go to the police where I'm from.'

'Neither do we. But the police for disappeared people are a different story. Some of them, at least. I went once, so I know.

When my boyfriend, my *ex-boyfriend,* the father of my baby, didn't come around, I went to the station in the New Settlements and they told me to go to the Center, where they specialize in missing people.' She paused. 'That's where I learned that most people who disappear want to be disappeared, if you know what I'm saying. That's the worst part, almost worse than hearing something bad.'

Isabel didn't know how to answer. Suddenly, she closed her eyes and pressed her face against the cold of the handrail. 'Hey, hey, didn't mean to upset you,' said Josiane. She leaned forward and whispered, 'There's a happy ending. I revenged myself. I got his sister to dip a strip of my nightgown into his coffee. So he came back, but I didn't take him.' Isabel didn't look up. 'Hey, I'm just trying to cheer you up,' said Josiane. 'Just trying to make you laugh. You'll find him, I promise. Does he have any friends? Do you know anyone he worked for? Did he leave anything?'

Isabel wiped her eyes with her palm. 'I looked. When I came I looked in the house. Maybe not everywhere. But I didn't think he was gone.' She felt suddenly the need to tell about the flatbed ride to the south, about her first days in the room, waiting. The bus slowed. 'This is my stop,' said Josiane, and descended with a kiss on her cheek.

Later that night, Isabel remembered the little scrap of paper she had found on the first day she arrived. She was ashamed she had forgotten it until now, but at the time it had seemed unimportant. She took it from the pants. PATRICIA M / APT 22 / VILA CAPRI TOWER / PRESIDENT KENNEDY.

She showed the paper to her cousin. 'Well, well,' said her cousin.

Isabel didn't understand. 'What's wrong?'

'Nothing's wrong. But this neighborhood is . . .' She shook her head. 'Maybe he was looking for work.'

'We could go,' said Isabel. 'And ask.'

'Are you kidding? You can't just visit a person like that because you have her name on a piece of paper.'

'Maybe the lady you work for knows her.'

'My boss? Maybe my boss knows her? You think they are friends because they both have money? Do you know every poor person in the world?'

'I didn't say that—' Isabel began, and in his hammock Hugo began to cry. They both went to him, but Isabel reached him first. Her cousin watched as she rocked him. 'And what would she know?' Manuela said. 'If Isaias was working for her, he would have told us, right?'

Later, Isabel asked, 'What is she like?'

'Who?'

'Your boss. You never say what she's like. You never say what the people you work for are like.'

'You are still thinking about going.'

'No.'

'Then why are you bothering me with questions like that?'

'I just wanted to know.'

'You don't need to know. She pays me and you eat. That's enough. Why do you want to know about something that has nothing to do with you?'

The next weekend, when she returned to wave, Isabel showed the note to Josiane. Her friend whistled. 'What was he doing *there*?' It was lunchtime, and they were sitting on the sidewalk, beneath the ficus.

Isabel shrugged. 'I just found it.'

'See? I told you to look.' Josiane bit her lip and peered at the piece of paper again. 'Did you go and ask?'

Isabel turned away.

'What is it?' asked Josiane. 'I don't understand you. You won't go to the police, and now you're scared.'

'I'm not scared,' Isabel protested. 'I can't just go to someone's house because I have their name on a piece of paper.'

'No? There's a law about that?' Josiane tugged angrily at a weed that sprouted through the sidewalk. 'I know what you're thinking. You're thinking that because she lives in a neighborhood like that, she's above you. She's nothing. She's like this—' She held up her little finger. 'If it was me, I'd be shaking her gates. I'd stand outside and scream until they took me away. Your problem is that you're too meek. My relatives in the north are like you. Waiting people. You probably think the answer will come to you in a dream. You think waiting will solve everything. You think praying will solve everything. Maybe it would if you were rich. If you were rich, your brother would be in the papers. *Isabel's brother missing!* they would say. *Top news!* But you're not. You're nothing to them. You could die and they'd walk right over your body.'

Isabel dug her fingers around a pavement stone.

Josiane said, 'You don't have enough hate in you. When you hate them, you won't say such stupid things.'

'I never met anyone like that,' said Isabel, weakly. 'I wouldn't know which one to hate.'

'Not *which one.* All. They don't care. Don't you understand? You can get skinny watching others eat. You'll see. Being hungry and watching someone else eat is a lot worse than just being hungry.'

'I don't know,' said Isabel. 'I've seen people eat when I was hungry.'

'*She's nothing.*'

'I don't know,' said Isabel again, and they returned to wave.

Back in New Eden, Isabel listened to the washerwomen's gossip. She remembered that the daughter of one of the women was a maid in a wealthy district. 'What is her boss like?' she asked. 'Her boss?' the woman answered. 'She paid for my grandson to go to school. She paid our hospital bills. She buys us bus tickets when we need to go home.' She swirled a shirt through the water. 'Why do you want to know? You want to be a maid? Because you have to remember, they're not all like that. Long ago, my boss burned me because her husband liked to put his hand up my skirt. She knocked over a pot of boiling water.' She lifted her hand to show a scar. 'She said it was an accident, but I knew.'

In the quiet of her room, Isabel sat and stared at the letters of Isaias's note. The ink ran dry at the *c* of Patricia, and the *n*'s in Kennedy reminded her of distant birds. She waited for a dream to tell her what to do. She listened to the radio. They played old country songs and ran advertisements for bus tickets to the north, sold in installments. One afternoon, they played a song by a famous music star, a fiddler whose photo her brother carried in his pocket. She watched Hugo bob his head with the music.

When the song stopped, Isabel wiped tears away with the neckline of her shirt. She could hear her father scolding: *You do not come from crying people.* She took the baby outside. What is it, she asked herself, that is making me so afraid?

The next morning, she took a bus to the Center, where she changed for another. She wore her yellow dress and carried Hugo in his sling, in a clean blanket of napped, printed felt.

On the way, she turned to the window and practiced speaking. Say all the letters! she told herself. Don't call her Patricia, call her madam and don't stare. They don't understand silence, they think it's simplicity, they think the natural state of a person is to talk. It is what Isaias would have told her. Isaias . . . she felt a surge of joy pronouncing his name. I am really going to see him, she thought. Even if he isn't there, Patricia will know. She will know the next step. When she descended, she asked a taxi driver for the name of the building. He pointed to a nearby tower. 'Tall one there.' He spoke with a heavy northern accent. She paused, fighting an impulse to confide everything in him. 'Visiting someone?' he asked curiously. 'Yes,' she said, and saw the doubt on his face.

She found the building, its name in brass curlicues on a white wall. It was very tall, set back behind a fence topped with razor wire. Bougainvillea garlanded the glass eye of a security camera. She hesitated by the buzzer until the intercom crackled. 'Hello?' came a man's voice. Startled, she looked up toward the camera. 'I am here to see Mrs. Patricia, in apartment twenty-two,' she enunciated carefully. 'Are you the applicant for the maid's job?' asked the voice. She paused. She had invented a story, partially true, about her brother, the drought, a turned-over flatbed.

'Yes,' she said slowly, 'I'm the maid.'

There was a mechanical click and the door opened. She found herself in a barren walkway, before another set of doors. There was a guard-booth with blackened glass. Suddenly, she wished she hadn't lied. The door clanged shut behind her. The booth opened and a man came out, swinging a key chain. 'I need to search you,' he said. He patted her down with the back of his hand and peeked inside the sling, where Hugo was sleeping. He opened the second door for her and led her across a long driveway and into a lobby with gleaming floors and real flowers. Classical music played from a hidden speaker. A second, stocky guard motioned her into the elevator and pressed the top button. He had light blue eyes like her brother. He crossed his arms and stared at her without looking away.

The same music from the lobby played as the lift rose. It was plated with a gold-tinted mirror and the lights were low. She studied herself. Now, she was ashamed by how old her dress looked. On the hill, she had combed back her hair, but it had begun to spring from its clasp. Hugo's sling suddenly seemed dirty; she had washed it only yesterday. She realized she had no idea what she would say: the words she rehearsed on the bus seemed ridiculous, and now she'd lied. She wanted to stop the elevator but didn't know how. Her stomach was tight; she was glad she hadn't eaten.

Hugo stirred. Don't wake up, she thought. Please, be quiet. Please don't make trouble.

The door opened. There was a small vestibule with a vase of violet irises. A maid waited by a second door. She glanced at the baby in Isabel's arms and smiled politely but distantly. She reminded Isabel of the girls at home, but she wore a stiff apron and her hair was tied tightly back. She led Isabel into a room with a wooden floor, where a cream leather couch stretched before a long glass table. In a painting on the wall, a man with smooth gray hair stood by a seated woman in a strapless white dress and pearls. His hand rested on the arm of her chair. Her hand rested on his, but didn't hold it. Her thin lips were scarlet. A gray dog with the face of a rat stared contemptuously from her side. An identical woman sat at the far end of the room by a glass door that opened onto a patio. In the distance, Isabel could see the skyline of the city. The woman wore a white dress that ended at her knees. It was cut low over her breasts, which were tan and sun-mottled. On the table beside her was a plate of wet grapes.

She held an unlit cigarette and slouched. Her bare arms looked unnaturally smooth.

'Sit,' she said. 'You don't expect to bring that baby here when you start working?'

Isabel's eyes were still taking in the room: a basket of gigantic lemons, a liquor cabinet, three vases of pink, naked lilies and a brass statue of a woman. There was a television larger than any she had ever seen. A low credenza sat against the far wall, set with crystal that glinted in the incoming light.

She didn't know where to sit. To get to the couch required walking across a rug that was blindingly white. She found herself staring at the woman's arms.

'There,' said the woman, pointing with the cigarette. Isabel walked along the edge of the carpet and perched at the rim of the couch, careful to keep her back straight. She rested Hugo on her lap. The baby stirred and then settled. The woman flicked her wrist. 'Remind me: Which of my friends recommended you?'

'Recommended?' said Isabel, awkwardly. 'No one did, I . . .'

'*No one,*' said the woman, imitating her singsong. 'You haven't been here for long, have you?' She laughed. 'You have pretty eyes, you know. *Who* was it that sent you?'

'No one. I'm not here for that.' Isabel looked down. 'I'm looking for my brother,' she added, but her voice was so soft that she wondered if the woman could hear. She prepared herself to say it again.

'The guard said you want to be the new maid. So you're not here for the job?'

'No.'

'Speak up, I can't hear you. *No* you're not saying that, or *No* you're not here for the job?'

'No I'm not here for the job.'

The woman let the cigarette drift slowly down. 'Then how did you get into the building?'

'The guard let me in.'

'*The guard let me in?* What kind of game is this?' She turned to the maid. 'Get me my phone,' she said. The girl handed her a handset and backed away.

She stared at Isabel as she dialed. 'Hey, genius,' she said when the line engaged. 'What do you think this is, the municipal market? You let every girl in off the street? Yeah? Yeah, I don't care what she said. Why don't you just give the whole world the keys? You read the papers? You hear about the robbery up the road? They killed her, *slit her throat.* We are living in a war, okay? Oh, you searched her. Now, I feel real safe.'

She hung up. 'You can go.'

Isabel watched the woman return the handset to the side table. She didn't move. Her whole body seemed suddenly extremely heavy, her tongue numb. She looked past the woman to the city. The buildings stretched for as far as she could see. I can't go, she thought. She is my only link to him.

'You hear me?'

She stared as the woman leaned forward.

'Hey,' said the woman. 'You dumb?'

'I'm here for the job,' she blurted.

'I thought you *weren't* here for the job.'

'I'm here for my brother.'

'What?'

Now her words were clearer. 'I'll go. I promise. Just tell me. Did you see my brother?'

'Your brother? How would I know your brother?'

'He had a piece of paper with your name.'

'A piece of paper? That's helpful. Come on. Am I your brother's keeper?' She forced a laugh.

'He—'

The woman interrupted. 'Look, he probably applied for a job . . . Months back I had to interview some wait staff. For a week, this place was full of people like you. But he isn't here now. I hired two girls.'

'But he *was* here?'

'You think I pay attention to people I don't hire?'

'He's Isaias. He—'

'Listen, even if he was the prophet Isaias, I wouldn't remember. I had about eight guys here, and every one of them looked the same . . .' She paused, and then staring Isabel in the eyes, added, 'Short, with the same flat head and voice as you.'

Isabel's face burned. She fought to keep her words steady. 'But you must remember—'

'*You must remember. You must remember,* little girl, that you are breaking into my apartment, and if you don't get that filthy baby out of here, I'm going to call the police. I've been nice enough. This is not a place for you. What you want isn't here.'

Without setting her cigarette down, the woman reached

over to the table. Isabel thought she would call for the guard, but instead she broke a grape from the bunch and lifted it to her mouth. 'Go,' she said as she chewed.

Isabel didn't move. Something inside her seemed to have shattered. This is the anger, she thought, and now the memory that came to her was not her conversation with Josiane, but her uncle back home. Tears brimmed on her eyes. She wanted to scream. I am back with the cricket men, she thought.

'That's enough. Go. Get out.'

Isabel's heart pounded. For a moment she forgot Isaias. She felt as if someone else had possessed her. She wanted to hurt the woman. She was exhilarated by the anger, drunk and dizzy with it. She felt her legs shaking.

Now the woman grabbed the phone. 'Listen, it's bad enough you people have taken over this city. But not my apartment, understand?'

Isabel didn't hear. She sat back against the cushions and clenched her jaw. The rage was hypnotic, searing. She was aware suddenly of the strength in her hands. I'll kick her, I'll break her arm, she thought. I'll smash the phone into her face. She knew, with certainty, that hurting the woman was the solution to everything that had happened to her since she left the north. The logic was impeccable, crystal. She felt her hands clench, until Hugo began to twist.

'Hey,' said the woman, lifting the receiver. 'Go.'

In her mind, Isabel stood and shifted the baby to her hip. She spat, she overturned the table, with swift strides she crossed the room and screamed, picked up the phone and slammed it through the glass door of the patio, swept the vase off the table and swung it into the air.

She sat for a few moments longer. She imagined the vase shattering, the glass raining over the woman. Then she stared at her knees, trying to think of something to say, but the words didn't come. She stood and walked over the carpet and out of the room, as the baby began to wail.

On the way home, on a sudden steep downhill, the window open, the bus mostly empty, Isabel had a view of the city and the vivid sensation that she was falling from the sky. She put her head out and felt the cold air on her lips. Wind-tears coursed across her cheeks. At first, it seemed like she was falling over a great stone outcrop of the backlands, streaked with carpets of moss and rusty brown soil. Then she recognized it: the stiletto towers like hyphae, the canyons of the streets, the waves of brick and cement that crested over the hills for as far as she could see.

The baby curled into his sling. She lifted her arms. I'm really falling, she thought, and she somersaulted, spun once and then again, felt her hair break from its clasp. She laughed, a funny sound that seemed to bubble out and vanish somewhere in the air above. Her tears lost themselves in her hair. The wind whipped her dress against her calves and spun off from her fingertips. She wondered if they could see her from below, a tiny fluttering speck in the sky.

Again she looked out over the city. It seemed impossibly distant; she didn't expect it to be so beautiful or so still. Where was the stink, the crash of light and sound and shadow? The roaring of the cars? The rumblings of the factories and footsteps? When would she feel the warmth of it, the heat of the city rising up against the cold passages of her descent? Would it be like this all the way down? Or would it come suddenly, in a great rush of brick and noise? Where, in it all, would she land?

Finding him should be easy now, she thought, with her speed and her beautiful view. Let me fall, she thought, and the bus shuddered. Let the wind or his gravity shift me, spin me, tumble me down, into the shadowed corridors where he's waiting.

J uly passed and soon August.

On the weekends, she returned to the Center to wave flags. To fill the other days, she carried Hugo through the Settlements, wandering for hours, wondering if she should descend into the city. Once, the washerwomen asked what she was looking for, but she didn't tell them. She realized that her walks were revealing too much about herself, but she could no longer bear waiting. When she walked, she rarely stopped. The coral trees dropped all their blooms, and the arbors where she once waited had been cut away.

There was still no word from her brother.

Since her arrival, it hadn't rained. The day sky grew dark over New Eden, and, in the evenings, she could taste the bitter powder of the haze. The drought followed me here, she thought, superstitious, searching her dreams for premonitions of rain. She began to recite invocations for clouds, and invocations for the clouds to break.

A dry, barbed cough began to wake her at night, and in the early dawn, Hugo woke wheezing and wouldn't stop until she held him upright against her chest. Outside the door, gray dishwater slithered over the thin mucosa that lined the sewers.

One afternoon, she heard a commotion in the street. At Junior's store, a little boy propped his arms on his knees and thrust his chin forward. He breathed with strained gasps. A woman crouched beside him. 'Where's the ambulance?' she shouted, and a man punched frantically at the phone.

At night, Junior's TV replayed images of the city taken from a distant hill. It looked as if it were under the siege of a sandstorm. Standing in the stalls of a produce market, a reporter showed vegetables covered with soot. Not a single neighborhood of the city has been spared, he said. In a hospital on the periphery, rows of mothers held oxygen masks to wan children laboring with each breath of air. The doctor said they were overwhelmed with cases of asthma, bronchitis, pneumonia. 'We are creating a generation that can't breathe,' he said. 'And when you run out of masks?' the reporter asked, gesturing to the room. 'God save us,' said the doctor.

Dust settled on the cars and windowsills and left an oily film on the tabletops. Isabel cleaned it from Hugo's bottle, turned over the cups and draped Manuela's saints. At night, she wiped a black grime from her ears.

She stopped going outside. In the little room, she lay on the bed, spending the days remembering the rare rains that broke the backlands droughts. She would climb the hill with Isaias to watch the clouds slide over the mountains, gray-bellied, pawing the earth in streaking downpours. Down in the village, the rain turned the dust slippery and warm. It left brown stains at the base of the walls, so that the white houses looked like teeth pushed out of gums of earth. It unleashed on the banana groves, shredding the wide fronds into ribbons, tearing petals from the purple bulbs. The mango trees surged and swayed, their leaves shimmering like tossed wet hair, their heavy green fruit slingshotting off, ringing the zinc roofs, exploding the mud like shells and cracking on the cobbles in gleaming yellow scraps. Beneath the awnings, their pants cuffs growing wet and heavy, the old men watched the children streaking through the blur. The goats brayed. In the shelter of the trees, the zebu cows endured the falling fruit with snorts and whisks of their wet tails.

In the backlands, they had prayed to Saint Joseph for the rain. She moved his icon to the windowsill.

The first rains in the Settlements came after ashen clouds hung over the city for days. She was at home when she heard a rumbling she thought was a truck passing, and then one two three drops on her window, before the sky opened. The rain fell swiftly. Heavy drops shattered on the sill, drummed the zinc and rose back as steam from the hot roofs. Her window was open and fine spray floated in, carrying the ripe smell of the street.

With the first drops, she laughed convulsively, as if by reflex. She stayed at the window until she began to shiver.

Inside, she ran her hands through her hair. Her fingers caught her curls, and she pushed them back. She went to the mirror. Her face was wet and she turned from side to side, catching the glints of light on her bare neck. She forgot the rain and stared. Her cheeks had begun to fill out. *I will be fat,* she thought, incredulous. When Isaias comes he won't recognize me. Her reflection in the low light made her feel glamorous.

.   .   .

That afternoon, it rained for two hours. Outside, the rainwater ran in streaming sheets down the road. The sewers swelled with water and overflowed into pools hemmed with white cigarette butts and foam. In the street, people swept pillows of water off the thresholds of their houses. They dug narrow trenches, funneling the run-off into frothing, coffee-colored streams.

When the rain stopped, Isabel went out, barefoot. A crowd had gathered in the cool air to watch a television report. There was flooding in the Center; the flickering screen showed a bus stuck in the middle of the road and passengers worming their way out the windows. A band of boys danced on the roof, waving their soccer T-shirts like flags. There were power outages throughout the whole city. An official warned of the risk of rat sickness. The television showed men in hazard suits leading a woman with a wool cap and swollen eyes into a white van.

In the afternoon, it hailed. Thumb-size balls of ice pounded on the windows so hard, Isabel thought the glass would shatter. They drummed off the roofs, splintered on the sidewalk and rolled into the gutters, where they glistened like piles of wet marbles.

Isabel went to the door, put her hand out and withdrew it when a hailstone stung the tip of her finger. It seemed impossible, balls of ice falling in such heat. She turned her palm up to catch them and stare as they melted away. They left numb pink welts. At her feet, the baby reached for the hailstones. She scooped him up, caught more in her hand and slipped them into his mouth.

It rained again that night. The sheets were damp. She watched the rain in the distant static of a single street lamp.

The following morning, the rotted beams of a shack up the road gave way, and a sagging roof of tar shingles collapsed on a room of sixteen people. Leaving the baby with Junior's cousin, Isabel joined a crowd that helped pull out muddied sheets and ruined photographs. Families began to abandon their clapboard shacks and crouch beneath tarps. The rain dissolved a wattle hut down the road, leaving only a soaked, tangled hammock and a pan. Then more rain came, a southern squall that they could see thundering over the city before it struck, the air salty like the sea. Men rolled their trousers to their knees, women tried awkwardly to hike their skirts with fingers twisted around plastic bags full of belongings. Below, the little river swelled into the road. The air turned foul. Word came around not to use the water pump. By noon, the water in the street overflowed the narrow trenches and ran across the floors of the houses. Isabel tried to sweep it back, but it was useless. She took everything off the floor and set it on the table and bed. In the washroom, roaches swarmed from the drain, and the toilet flooded. Her clothes wouldn't dry; Hugo wailed when she wrapped him in wet diapers that she had tried to clean in the stream that ran outside the door. Later, a man parked a truck at the bottom of the hill and sold water from a plastic tank. It smelled strange to Isabel, so she didn't give it to the baby. The next day, many people were sick. The man didn't return.

Now on TV there were images of landslides, women weeping, a pale baby being pulled from the soil like a muddy tuber. Most of the footage was from the Settlements, the thin brick walls crumbling into the new rivers, the clapboard slipping apart and floating away in hesitant rafts. But some images came from rich communities on the coast, and the news played a video of a white house tearing free from its foundation and sloughing off into the sea.

Isabel stayed at Junior's store and watched the news. A famous movie star had a heart attack in the back of his car, and the closest hospital had been closed. They showed the paramedics pulling him out, his face a brilliant violet. On the highway by the river, a supermarket delivery truck overturned, and hundreds of chickens floated away into the river. The health commissioner went on TV, warning people not to eat them. The next day, the same thing happened with a truck carrying detergent, and the news showed bubbles overflowing the banks. One newspaper ran a photo with the headline NEW WAY TO CLEAN CITY.

She wished Manuela would call from her work, but the phone was dead.

That night, a gleaming car skirted the base of New Eden and tried to push its way through the flood at the bottom of the hill. It was a common sight: tryst-seekers took the road as a shortcut to motels near the highway. Isabel was at the window, unable to sleep. She saw a fan of water rise up, and then the car drift to a halt. The driver seemed to be struggling to open the door. Beside him, a bare arm began to point. Isabel was amused. The other houses gave her only a partial view of the road, so she leaned out the window to watch.

It was then that she saw the others: a pair of boys advancing toward the car, wading slowly through the inky water. In the light of a single street lamp, they seemed to float, legless. Their chests were bare; they wore their shirts wrapped around their heads. She saw a third boy move around the other side of the car, his face hidden by a woolen mask, a gun in his outstretched hand. 'My God—' Her hand went to her mouth. The boys pounded the hood, gesticulating madly. Give them the money, she thought, give them the money, just give them— But there was a shot and then another, and then the window exploded.

The black water foamed. The tallest boy tugged at the door and then plunged headfirst into the car as a horrible, inhuman screaming shot through the dark. She could see struggling— a second boy began to swing his arms as if he were striking someone inside. They took off running in long, crashing strides. Without thinking, she ran to her door and opened it. Someone shouted; she saw the boys sprinting up the hill, struggling against soaked jeans, panting, their thin arms pumping madly. One boy's shirt had come undone from his head. Briefly, his eyes met hers as he sprinted past, his face contorted. The wiry muscles on his back streamed with water, droplets flew from his arms. Ahead, a smaller boy fell, struggling at sagging wet pants that were too big for him. He tore them off, threw them onto the roof of a house and lunged up the hill.

From the doorways, cries followed the boys as they scattered into the shanties. Isabel had a sudden and cruel thought, They aren't crying for the people in the car, and she went inside and vomited into the washbasin.

For two days, the car remained in the flood. In the brown water, its windshield gleamed like the onyx eye of a caiman. When the flood rose, it shifted slightly, drifting until the water poured through the window and it settled again.

In the streets, people whispered nervously to one another. They said the driver had been dead when they reached him, and the pale woman beside him mumbled and never spoke until she was helped away. They said the boys had come from another neighborhood. They repeated this over and over again. From her window, Isabel watched the car and wished it would float away.

The rain relented. The electricity returned. The women swept the brown water out of their houses and into the street. Isabel left footprints on her floor and swept them away as they dried.

A van came in the afternoon and skirted the shanties. It had the markings of a TV station, and that night there was a report that a city councilman had been killed in the Settlements, with images of New Eden taken from far away. It took a moment for her to recognize the brick-wall labyrinth beneath the cluttered roofs. The councilman's wife, an older woman with tan, heavy arms, moved slowly through gritty footage, weeping as she was escorted from her house. On the program a pair of experts discussed the Rise of Violence. They asked, Is it human nature or is it poverty? On a call-in to the show, a woman shouted, 'They're animals! They come from the north to ruin us. They just make children and waste and destroy this city.'

In an interview, the police commissioner promised to get the killers. He said that trafficking rings were operating out of the Settlements and the woods. He used the words *wipe out* and *exterminate.*

No one came to take the car. The water rose and fell, leaving a thin berm of dirt on the windshield. Children played in the driver's seat. A man waded out and siphoned the gas tank. Then one morning the car was gone.

Manuela came home for the first time since the shooting.

'I've been watching this on TV,' she said. 'The phones have been dead, you know, and I couldn't leave. The city's angry. I think something very bad is going to happen.'

The next morning, the police raided New Eden. It was still dark when a searchlight rose up the hill, its long beam illuminating the rain. Isabel awoke to footsteps. She started toward the door, but Manuela pulled her back. 'Stay down.' Isabel crouched and peered through a run in the curtain. A phalanx of police made its way up the hill in riot gear, raindrops shattering against their helmets and shields.

They were not far from her door when the firing began. Erratic outbursts came from up the hill. The police took shelter in the doorways and behind their shields. Bullets exploded the hollow bricks of the houses and thudded into the mud, clipped the kites on the wires, smashed the birdcages, tore sharp lips into the zinc. Out of the back window she saw a figure running away on the rooftops. There was a burst of gunfire. He spun about, clasped his leg and fell awkwardly from the roof. There were more shouts and then a long volley of firing. They were right outside the door; she could hear the scraping of riot shields against the walls. The door rattled. 'Open up!' Dust sifted down from the walls. Manuela lay on the bed and curled around the baby. He shrieked and struck his fists at the air. She put her hands over his ears. 'Don't squeeze so hard,' whispered Isabel. 'Shut up and stay away from the door,' hissed Manuela. 'Let them break it down, let them take anything, just stay out of the way.' The banging stopped.

Isabel crawled to the window. She saw figures moving through the street. It was still dawn.

The police spread, clanking through the alleyways. Shots

came from the backstreets, and she thought she smelled fire. An officer came come down with two young men in handcuffs. Behind them, a woman followed, cursing and pointing at the sky. The police herded the children out of the way with their rifle butts. An hour later, they brought down more boys.

In the late morning, she saw a figure lying on the corrugated rooftop of the house next door. He looked very small and flat, as if somehow he had pressed himself into the zinc. He was naked except for a pair of rain-soaked underpants, and had a blurred tattoo of the Virgin on his back. He was only feet away from her, and when he saw her staring, he moved his lips, but she didn't understand. 'There is a boy on the roof,' she told her cousin, who didn't answer. He was still there when she returned. It rained, and she could see him shivering, his skin prickling, his knuckles white as his fingers tensed against the corrugation. She didn't know if he was trying to hold himself from slipping off, or just to stop shivering. The metal sheet rattled softly.

Later when she looked, he was gone. There was only a dry outline of his body, striped by the black lines of the corrugation and the rain.

In the road below, the police vans roared away.

That night, rumors swarmed the hill. Two boys had been killed, they said, or four. Someone said a policeman shot a boy in the head as he lifted his hands in surrender. A girl was hit by a stray bullet in one of the backstreets.

There were angry arguments outside Junior's store. 'I didn't come all the way from the north for this,' shouted a woman. 'Those boys are scum. They are making our lives hell.'

'These boys have no work and no school,' a man shouted back. 'What do you expect in this filth?'

'I had no work and no school,' spat the woman. 'And I don't shit where I eat. I don't have those dogs chasing after me with their stray bullets flying everywhere.' She saw the mother of one of the boys coming down the hill. 'You!' She lunged at her. 'If you weren't drunk all the time, this wouldn't have happened.' 'Easy,' someone said. *'Easy?'* spat the woman. 'We're turning into beasts. *Easy?* I've survived six droughts.' She raised three fingers on each hand and shook them. 'Six. You think I stole or killed? What happened to pride?' *'Pride?'* scoffed the man. 'You think I can afford pride? My kids are skinny like my finger, and some scum shows off his car in my face? I'd put a bullet in his mouth. I'd put a bullet in every one of their mouths. I'd bury every one of them.'

On TV came more images of young men in handcuffs, trying to hide their faces from the camera. Isabel recognized some of them; one was the son of the woman who washed by the river. She told Manuela. 'Good,' said her cousin coldly. 'I hope they got all of them. I hope they never come back.'

That night someone killed Junior with a shot to the neck. Isabel awoke to the sound of the gunfire and went to the door when the screaming began. In the morning, a crowd formed a cautious circle around the house. 'Informer,' someone spat. Isabel took the news numbly. From her room, she could hear Junior's cousin wailing. Then someone said she was lucky they didn't kill her, too. She stopped wailing. They burned his mattress in an empty lot.

When the weekend came, she descended slowly from the gray mist of the hill.

At the campaign office, Josiane took her by the elbow. 'I

was so worried. I saw the television. Did you see? They called it a war. *War in Eden.*'

Isabel said nothing.

'What about your brother?' she asked. Isabel pinched her lips and shook her head.

That evening when they dropped off the flags, Josiane took her to the Center and stopped outside the offices of the Civil Police. It was closed. 'Monday,' said Josiane. Isabel protested: 'I can't leave. Especially after what happened. Manuela would kill me.' 'No, she won't. She's just as worried as you are.' Isabel shook her head. 'I'm not sure she thinks about Isaias. I don't know. I think she is angry at him.' 'For what?' 'For disappearing.' 'Angry for *disappearing*? Are you angry?' 'It's not his fault,' said Isabel, quickly. Josiane pressed on, 'Are you scared of the police because of what I told you about my boyfriend?'

She relented. When Monday came, she wrapped Hugo in a blanket and descended the hill. She wandered for nearly an hour until she found the station again. Inside, a guard pointed her toward a row of elevators. She got off, alone, in an empty hallway with a wilted philodendron. A sign read DEPART-MENT OF DISAPPEARED PERSONS. She followed a corridor with high ceilings. The floor was laid with loose wooden tiles that knocked against each other as she walked.

At the end of the hallway was a bank of vinyl chairs. Two middle-aged women in pastel dresses sat together. Isabel paused. 'It's there,' said one of the women, pointing with her lips toward an open door.

Inside, a girl sat behind an empty desk. 'Yes?' she asked. 'My brother—' Isabel began. She took a deep breath and spoke as calmly as she could: 'I want to know about someone who is missing.'

'Do you have a Bulletin of Occurrence?' asked the clerk. 'They gave it to you at the precinct. Did you go to a precinct first?' Isabel shook her head. 'I didn't know.' The clerk said, 'How can you expect us to help you if you don't help us? What if the whole city came looking for someone and no one had a Bulletin of Occurrence? What would happen then?'

Isabel waited for the clerk to give her an answer to the question. She will make me go somewhere else, she thought, but the clerk pointed back to the hallway. 'Wait there,' she said.

She sat across from the women in the pastel dresses. The older one had a Bible on her lap, and every so often she lifted it to scrutinize a word. Then her hand shook and she set it down again. The other held a handkerchief. The rest of the hallway was empty. On the chairs, tongues of foam protruded through tears in the vinyl. Hugo began to writhe. Isabel set him on her knees. He reached for a strip of foam and stretched his mouth toward it. Roughly, she extracted it from his hand and tried to stuff it back into the seat. He began to cry. 'Shhhh,' she whispered, pulling him close to her.

'Boyfriend, right?' said the woman with the handkerchief. 'Can't tell you how many stories I know like yours, of girls coming to the city looking for their boyfriends. My advice is to forget it, go home, find a new man but forget him. You don't want to see where he is.' 'It is my brother,' said Isabel. 'Sure, sweetheart.' 'It is.' The woman stared at her for a while. 'A brother is something else,' she said, and the other woman looked up from the Bible and nodded.

The clerk came out of the office and called the two women inside, leaving Isabel alone. She listened to an argument in another room. 'She is going mad,' said a man. 'She can do nothing but look for Carolina. It's all she thinks about.'

A wooden cross and a poster hung on the wall. The poster

read HELP FIND US and showed a map made of little faces. Isabel looked at them until the clerk appeared and led her past a broad file cabinet to a room behind frosted glass. Everywhere smelled of dust and old paper. A man sat at a desk. He wore a shirt with a tie loosened at the collar, cuffs rolled up over heavy forearms. He lowered a pair of reading glasses as she entered. 'Yes?' 'This girl wants to file a report,' said the clerk, motioning her to sit. 'She hasn't filed a B.O. yet.' She turned to Isabel. 'This is the inspector. Don't take too much of his time.' She left.

The inspector had heavy bags under his eyes. To Isabel, he said, 'You are here to report someone who disappeared.' She nodded. 'Usually,' said the inspector, 'we advise people to wait twenty-four hours. Most missing people return home in twenty-four hours.'

'He disappeared three months ago,' said Isabel.

The inspector closed his eyes and rubbed them with his fingers. After replacing his glasses, he took a pen out of his shirt pocket and pulled a leaf of paper from a short stack. 'Your name?' She answered. 'Family name? Age, Name of the disappeared, Identification number of the disappeared?' At that moment Hugo began to babble. She shifted him to the edge of her knees to bounce him. She looked up. 'Sorry?' 'What's your brother's identification number?' the inspector repeated.

She paused. 'I don't think he has one.' 'What do you mean?' 'I mean I don't think he has one. Where I'm from, we don't have them . . . I don't have one.'

The inspector stared over his glasses before continuing. 'Very well . . . Name of parents, Age of the disappeared, Hair color, Eye color, Tattoos, Typical clothing, Height approximately, Weight approximately, Date of disappearance?' There she stopped. 'I don't know.'

'You said three months, right?' 'Maybe. He lived with my cousin. Three months was the last time she saw him. But she works. It could be less.' 'When did *you* last see him?' 'Me? Many months ago. In the north. I just arrived here.' 'Because of the droughts?' asked the inspector. 'What?' 'You came because of the droughts?' She considered the question. It had rained last year. They had gone hungry for other reasons: the landowners, the price of sugar. There is a trap, she thought, but said, 'Yes, because of the droughts.'

He turned back to the paper without acknowledging her answer. 'And when you spoke to him, did anything seem different?' 'No.' 'No mention of anything unusual.' 'No, just good things.' '*Good things.* Like what?' 'Things that were going well. With his work. He's a musician. He plays fiddle.' Then she added, 'He's one of the best in the state.' The man didn't look up when she said this. 'He played in bars,' she pursued. 'And by the sea. He even sent us money.' Now he looked at her. 'Was he in a band here?' 'He was going to be in a band.' '*Going* to be in a band?' 'Yes.' 'You mean he played alone?' 'Yes . . . I think so.'

'And that was his principal employment.'

A statement, not a question. She shifted awkwardly.

'Did he have another job? A factory job, a construction job?' 'No,' she said sharply. 'I told you. He didn't need to.' She knew immediately that this was a lie.

Hugo had stopped his babbling. Now he reached for her breast and began to cry. She struggled to find his bottle with her free hand. 'He yours?' asked the inspector. She stared at him. 'No. He's my cousin's. I watch him because it's my job. I don't have a baby.'

'Very well,' said the man, picking up his pen.

'It's true about his music,' she said.

The inspector ignored her. 'Has he disappeared before?' 'Yes.' 'But this is different, of course.'

'Yes, it's different,' she snapped.

'I understand,' he said, holding up his hand. 'I'm just asking.'

She looked away. She realized she had shouted.

'Can you tell me about the other times?'

'The other times he left? Once, back home, he went to the state capital. It was for two months, and he performed there. He came back with money he made. And then here, a couple of times, he went away to the coast, to play at bars. Good bars. My cousin's boyfriend lives there, but this time he hasn't seen my brother.' 'Do you have his phone number?' 'Who? Manuela's boyfriend? He works on a ship. He doesn't have a phone number.'

The man rubbed his eyes again. 'Okay,' he sighed. 'I can see where this is going. Just a couple more questions. Where are you living?' 'At my cousin's.' 'And the address there?' 'It's in the Settlements.' 'Do you have an address?' She shook her head; she had forgotten the street. 'No one uses addresses.' 'Any number? Number of a house, apartment?' 'I said there isn't an address. There isn't a number or an address.' 'What's the name of the neighborhood?' She paused. 'New Eden,' she said.

He looked up. 'Oh . . . that New Eden? Your brother . . . was he . . .' 'He wasn't one of those boys.' 'Easy. I didn't say he was.' 'It's good they got those boys,' she said, repeating her cousin's words.

'It is good,' he replied, without conviction. He paused. 'You don't have a photo of him, do you?' She shifted Hugo to the side and reached into her bag, where she had brought the portrait of Isaias. She handed it to the inspector. 'He doesn't look exactly like that. The artist, he touched it up a little.' An amused smile played over the inspector's lips. 'Now I see,' he said. 'Was this made in the north?' 'No, here. The portraitist came to the hill.' 'It's well done,' said the inspector. His voice softened. 'He really was going to be a musician, wasn't he?' She heard compassion in his voice, which frightened her more.

He set the photo down. When he spoke again, he weighed his words. 'Listen . . . Isabel. There are a lot of things I can tell you. The first is that we are going to file a report, and I'll take this case myself. But I have to be honest with you. There isn't much I can do.

'We have,' he said, picking up a pen and tapping it on the table, 'thousands of people reported missing every year. Granted, we handle the whole state, but most cases are from here. Thousands of people in a city with ten million or twelve or fifteen, depending on where you draw your lines. And those are just the ones we hear about. I don't want to venture how many boys in our system have your brother's name. I've seen enough Isaiases to make a whole army of Isaiases. I've worked here twenty years, and if I've learned anything, it's that there are more ways for people to disappear than you can dream of. Most of them come home, thank God. A boy runs off with a sweetheart. A girl gets in a fight with her parents, heads into the street, decides it's too cold and goes home. But others decide not to come back. Not saying that isn't a problem. But disappearing isn't a crime. Many people who disappear chose to disappear—'

'Not Isaias,' said Isabel.

He pressed on. 'Fair enough. But there are a lot of people

who come here thinking they can be someone else. Who think of their lives back in the country and want to escape.'

'He isn't like that.'

'I didn't say he was,' said the inspector. 'I'm just telling you what I tell everyone. I would—'

The door opened a crack, and the clerk put her head in. 'Inspector? Do you have a moment? Miss S, from this morning? She's back and acting crazy. Can you come outside and have a word with her?'

Without finishing what he was saying, he rose and followed her out.

Isabel waited. She watched the minute hand of a clock move slowly. Hugo had finished with the bottle, and she set it on the floor. She looked about the room, at the bare walls and the dented metal cabinets. She had to move, she thought. She had the sudden impulse to run. She could be out of the building in seconds, over the hills. She imagined herself capable of incredible speeds. She didn't know where she would go, but it didn't matter.

She stood, and began to pace. 'He is not ashamed of me,' she said aloud, to the baby, and the thought was so painful that she forced her mind away from it and back into the room. She wondered where the inspector had gone, who Miss S was and who she was missing. On the far side of the room, above a shelf, she saw a single piece of paper tacked to the wall. She went to it. Her lips moved as she read,

> *And if we are all just Severinos*
> *Who are equal all in life*
> *Then our deaths are also equal*
> *Just one more Severino death.*

It was an unfamiliar poem; she didn't know if it was by the inspector or if he had copied it down from somewhere else. Below it was a box full of photos. She looked back to the door, but there was no sign of the inspector. She hiked Hugo higher on her hip. He started chewing her hair. She touched the top photo on the stack. It showed a little boy in sailor clothes. He smiled a big toothless smile and reached for someone behind the photographer.

The next photo was a girl her age in a graduation gown, with dark black skin and long curly hair with glints of gold.

In the next photo, a greenish Polaroid, a young woman held a baby up to the camera. He wore a hat typical of country singers. On the bottom was written, in hesitant script, *Music Star.*

Isabel wanted to stop, but she couldn't. She looked at the next photo, a boy in a soccer uniform, and then the next, a boy and girl at the beach. An inked arrow pointed to the girl, who had her fist on her hip and a sassy cant to her head.

She looked up, her chest tight, and read the poem again. She returned to her chair, but her eyes kept dashing back to the box on the shelf. She forced her gaze away, and it settled on a folder. A girl's name was written in black ink. She looked over her shoulder, then swiveled the folder toward her. She opened it awkwardly, pushing Hugo's hand away as he grabbed for its corner. In the front was a photocopy of a Bulletin of Occurrence with the same questions the inspector had asked.

PERSON REPORTING: Maria O.
RELATIONSHIP TO DISAPPEARED: mother
NAME OF DISAPPEARED: Eliane O.

AGE: 17

PROFESSION: waitress, nightclub

SUMMARY: Mother called station, 22 July, last year, stating that the Disappeared, who had been in the city for a year, had ceased answering her phone.

States that her daughter called once a week, prior to 22 July. Says her daughter left home state in the north to come to work with a cousin in the city. Says daughter worked in a factory in the North Zone for four months, before finding a job as a waitress at a nightclub in the Center. Thinks the job was going well. Daughter sent money home several times. Doesn't remember the exact amount, but denies anything excessive or unusual. Very agitated by this question. Denies daughter ever reported depression, drug use. Denies daughter receiving supplementary income related to waitressing job. Nothing unusual about last conversation. Says she waited two weeks to call cousin in the city, who said that the Disappeared had moved out two months prior and was living in an apartment in the Center.

Cousin unable to offer further information. Mother calling every day.

Isabel turned the page. More testimony, phone numbers, police reports. She thumbed through the pages until a paper-clipped photo caught her eye: a smiling girl in a brightly colored swimsuit, laughing, holding her arms high.

The door opened, and Isabel slammed the file shut. A second, gray-green photo slipped out and slid across the floor. In two steps, the inspector picked it up and placed it upside down on the desk. He took the file from her. 'This isn't yours,' he said.

She blurted, 'What did that photo show?'

The inspector began to say something and stopped. '*Isabel.*' He took a deep breath, put his fists on the desk and leaned toward her. 'Why are you looking for sadness? Why do you want more sadness? Worry about your brother, but don't go looking for more, understand?' He placed his hand on the file. 'This didn't happen to your brother. It happens, yes, but not to him. There are so many people here, and most of them never see anything like this.'

He sat. 'Listen, it's late. About . . . Isaias . . . I will file the report. We'll give his name to the hospitals, the city morgue, the rest of the police department. You can get in touch with us anytime, but I advise you to be patient. If you want to look, usually we tell people to go to the big hospitals, the police precincts near your district, any place he used to go.'

'By myself?'

'Yes.'

'That's it?'

'That's it. I want to help. I'm just telling you. For the last hour I had a woman yelling at me as if I made her son disappear. No one here wants someone to be missing.'

He sat back. She thought he would send her away, but instead he closed Isaias's folder, removed his glasses and set them on the desk. He stared as if he were staring into the distance.

'You know,' he said suddenly. 'Last week, in the papers, they had an article about the migrations. They said everyone's leaving the country for the city now. They had photos of the flatbeds, people crammed together like cattle. They said whole towns have been abandoned. I knew, of course, but I hadn't thought about it like that, like it was a story worth writing about, like it was history.'

Isabel wrapped her arms around the baby. 'A lot of people left my village.'

'I'm not talking just about your village. I'm talking about the whole country.' He paused. *'The whole world.'*

She shifted nervously. Desperately, she wanted to leave.

'What do you eat on the flatbeds?' he asked.

'What?'

'What do you eat? I started thinking about that. They said the flatbeds don't stop.' 'We bring food. Or we don't eat.' 'Don't eat? Those things take four days.' 'It isn't so bad.' She clenched her teeth. 'Other people have it worse.'

'And your parents are still in the north?'

She nodded, her head hot.

'And they're making it through the drought?' 'Yes.' 'They say people are starving.' 'We're not starving.' 'They say people are eating cactus.' 'Eating cactus is not starving,' she said angrily, and he stared at her for a long time.

Then he said, 'It's late.' He looked much older. She stood and hoisted Hugo against her shoulder and let his sling hang loosely at her side. She kept her eyes away from the poem.

The inspector opened the door for her and accompanied her into the elevator. Several times she thought he would say something, but he was silent. At the bottom floor, Isabel said, 'I know the way.' But he walked with her to the exit to the street.

It was early evening. People were getting out of work, and the streets were crowded. She didn't remember how she arrived, so she just walked, looking for a familiar sign. She stopped at a concrete planter to give the bottle to Hugo and watch the buses. He drank greedily. The lines were long and the buses were full. She couldn't imagine standing for the two-hour ride home in traffic and left the stop to wander again.

She waited for thoughts about Isaias, but nothing came. She thought maybe she would cry, but she couldn't, so she just kept walking, and soon found herself in the square outside the Church of Our Lady of the Rosary. Inside, it was mostly empty. She sat and stared at the painted angels, the little heads floating on clouds and feathered wings. A nun had taken the saints down and set them in the front pews to clean them. Many of them were the size of children, and from where she sat, it looked as though they were praying, too. They had cordoned them off with a rope. A woman came and reached for Saint Roch, but he was too far away. She almost fell. The nun came and unlatched the rope for her. 'Thank you,' the woman said when she came back. 'Look.' She lifted her sleeve above her forearm. 'I can't get out of work to see a doctor, and it's already infected. I had to see him today.'

Isabel stayed until Hugo became restless. Then she went back to the lines for the buses. She was standing behind an old woman in a gray sweater when a piece of paper on the side of a pavilion caught her attention. It was a photo of a young boy. MISSING, it said, and gave his name and a telephone number with a distant city code. It was the first time she had seen a Missing poster, and thought, I must be noticing them only now. She stared at it for a long time, and then, farther along the street, a paper on a light post fluttered. She left the line for the bus and approached it, it said MISSING and showed the face of a girl, and a name and a number. As she looked at the girl, there came suddenly a sense of something tearing: a strange sense that seemed to have come to her from a far country, and she knew that this girl wouldn't be found, just like she had known what would happen to her second brother in the photo taken long ago. She left the lamp, and on a wall there was a paper, it said MISSING and showed the face of a woman, and a note, I FORGIVE, PLEASE COME HOME, and she knew this woman would be found, but not for a very long time. Then she turned, and on a newspaper booth was another, it said MISSING and showed the face of a boy, and the words WE ARE TOO POOR TO OFFER A REWARD / YOU WILL BE THANKED BY THE GRACE OF GOD AND THE BLESSINGS OF MARY, and she realized not a single poster promised a reward, and she turned, and on a telephone pole there were three stapled papers and they each said MISSING and one had a photo of a young man and said GOES BY 'LITTLE ANT' and another had a photo of a woman and said SHE NEEDS HER MEDICINES, and the bottom one said nothing else, it was a grainy snapshot of a baby that looked as if it had been in the sun for some months, and Isabel knew that the young man would be found and the woman would be found and lost again and the baby would never be found. She turned, and on the back of a bench was a photo of an old man and it said MISSING and on the side of a passing bus was a photo of a girl and it said MISSING, and she stopped, and littered on the ground were torn papers and photos and fragments of words. She ran to the steps of the church and tried to catch her breath, but from behind her she heard the drone of a Hail Mary, and looked up to see a woman with sign-boards hung over her chest and back like a chasuble and a sign in her hand. The signboards were posted with photos of a little boy, the word, repeated, MISSING. She ranted, and Isabel ran again.

She stopped before a bank of phones and hid inside their hoods. Suddenly, she took out a phone token, grabbed the receiver and dialed the number of the plaza phone in Saint Michael. Her fingers were shaking, and she kept pressing the wrong buttons, dialing again and again until finally the line engaged and she heard a static and a distant ringing.

After many rings, a woman answered. 'Hello?' 'It's Isabel, it's me, can I speak to my mother?' 'Hello?' said the woman again. It sounded like her aunt. 'It's me! It's Isabel!' she shouted. 'Hello?' 'It's Isabel. Can't you hear me? Shit phone!' She hit it against the booth. 'You shit shit phone!' She shouted into the mouthpiece, 'It's Isabel! Please hear me!' 'Hello?' said the woman, and the line went dead.

She called again. This time, a different voice, and she recognized her father. He sounded tired. At the sound of his voice, she began to cry. 'It's me!' she shouted. 'Father, it's me, Isabel.' 'Hello?' 'Yes! I'm here.' She hit the phone. 'God God God, it's me, it's Isabel.' 'Hello?' 'Please, hear me, you can hear me, you can hear me shouting.' 'Hello? Who is there?' 'It's me,' she cried. There was a long wait, and then her father said, 'Hello, Isaias? Isaias, is that you?'

Fog came.

Lolling in great white tongues, the mist crept up from the sea and slunk through the city. It wrapped the spires and carpeted the hills, deadened the rattle of the buses and muted the distant music. It streamed down the narrow backstreets and blanketed the soccer pitch. Below the jacarandas, drops stained the ground like shadows.

In Manuela's house it crept through the window and dewed the mirror. With her finger, Isabel wrote the letters of her name, ISABELISSABELSIBELBELISSA, until she reached the sharp edge. Then the mist filled the letters and the letters wept.

On the hill the fog became so thick and the air so quiet that there were moments when Isabel thought she was alone. At times, she was seized by a sudden temptation to scream as loud as she could, but she couldn't, like she couldn't scream in dreams. And what would people think, she asked, a girl alone, screaming at the fog?

She went down into the Center to look for her brother

almost every day now, except for the weekends, when she went to wave flags. She took Hugo, with a handkerchief to cover his head. His bottle dangled from her fingers in a plastic bag.

At first she walked without aim, a slow drifting path through neighborhoods of dry-goods shops and bustling street stalls. In the penny thrift stores, women burrowed through piles of colored clothing. Girls smoked beneath faded pink photos at the entrances to pornographic theaters. Unlit supermarkets advertised sales for boxes of rice and beans and ground manioc. The people seemed to move in whispers. When it rained, street children grabbed the bus fenders and slid on the soles of their sandals.

She walked for as many hours as her feet could bear. She descended on the shuddering buses with the day-shifters and returned with them, or waited until night fell and took emptier buses home. She recalled Manuela's warnings about the city at night, but she didn't care. She set out on long winding courses or circled the same blocks until the women at the thrift stores eyed her cautiously and the girls outside the theaters winked. She lowered her head and walked faster.

Her hands cramped with the weight of the baby. She brought the sling, but found she preferred holding him. She shifted him from arm to arm, rested him on her shoulder, crooked him in her elbow or canted her body to balance him on her waist. She knotted the handkerchief in the shape of a dog and gave it to him to play with. When he cried, she dipped the dog's head into the formula for him to suck.

She found a rhythm, slowly. The days washed over her as they did back home. At night, she sometimes went to watch the soap opera about the maid Cindy. She agreed with Josiane: there was no one so beautiful. She found herself floating into Cindy's world. On some nights, she stayed awake worrying for Cindy, whose mother was in the intensive care unit, after a heart attack. They were the only thoughts that could distract her from her brother. She remembered little from the walks or how she returned.

She surrendered to signs and suspicions.

In the city plazas, she watched the street pigeons and found significance in their flight, their numbers, how they watched her and when they took to the air. She noticed certain footprints shimmered on the wet streets; she took this to be a sign of Isaias's passage. Hugo's crying meant a path was mistaken, as did an ache in her shoulder. She rode a bus to its terminal because its numbers added to Isaias's age. On a misty afternoon, when a golden dog turned to look at her, she followed it for an hour, losing its trail in a back-alley tangle of greased crates and wet cardboard.

She heard a rumor that a statue of the Our Lady of Good Birth was found wet with amniotic fluid and was answering prayers of unmarried girls. It was on the western edge of the Settlements, but the story frightened her and she didn't go. The same woman told her of a magical baby who could find missing people. She imagined it on a wooden throne, attended by women in white gowns, a long line filing out through the door and down the hill. He was in Vila Marigold, said the woman, but when she asked, no one else had heard of a Vila Marigold.

A grasshopper appeared one morning in her room. Isabel knew this meant good luck, but the day unfolded like any other. She studied the swirls in the gravel outside the door for omens. She spent a day's wage on a street-corner prophetess. The prophetess rubbed her hands over a crystal and forecasted a man in her future and a new job. As the women spoke, Isabel wondered how she would explain the missing wages to her cousin.

She spent another day's salary on a magazine called *Woman's Life*. On the cover, in purple letters, it said NEW HOME? GUIDE FOR STARTING OUT. Inside there was a long article about decorating a kitchen. She returned to the man who sold it. 'There's a mistake,' she said, but he wouldn't give her money back.

At times she was seized by sudden waves of fear. She began to feel a pain in her stomach. She paused outside the white-tiled pharmacies and thought of going inside, but she didn't know how to explain what was wrong. In Cathedral Square, a man selling elixirs spoke through a megaphone about a new regimen for the liver. Perhaps it is my liver, she wondered.

She found a phone token. She clenched it in her fist until it grew wet and warm in her palm. Then she traded it for a coin, which she traded for a prayer card of Saint Anthony, saint of lost people and things. She tucked it into her dress, against her heart. At night, the print left ghostly images of the saint on her skin. She recited from the fading print until she had memorized the invocation.

Each day she wondered, When will I stop? The only answer seemed to be that she would stop when she was too tired to look more. She began to welcome the exhaustion that descended on her at night.

At the campaign office, Josiane asked, 'Why are you so sad now?' 'I'm not sad.' 'Did you go to the police?' 'Yes,' said

Isabel sharply. 'And?' 'And what? They told me that there were hundreds of Isaiases, thousands of Isaiases. That's the only thing they said.'

Josiane tried to cheer her with a story about the street carnival. 'The rides and machines are still there,' she said, taking Isabel's hand, 'I think someone forgot them. Maybe they will be there forever.' She said the couples went into a room filled with mirrors, so many mirrors that you didn't know which person was real and which was only a reflection. 'I went in there with a boy. I thought I would search forever and not be able to find him.'

Then she stopped, 'Oh,' she said. 'I didn't mean . . . I'm sorry, Isa. I didn't mean . . .'

On their way to the bus station, they passed a man with a sign that said NUMBER ONE SOLUTION TO POVERTY AND INJUSTICE 100% PROVEN FORMULA. WE MUST TAKE OUR FATE INTO OUR OWN HANDS 2 SAMUEL 6 (FATE OF UZZAH) PROVES IT IS THE WORKER THE OX-DRIVER WHO WILL ALWAYS BE PUNISHED GOD SAYS SAVE YOURSELF THE AGE OF JEREMIAH IS UPON US. Isabel heard him say, *They are cruel and have no mercy, their sound is like the roaring sea,* and she listened until Josiane pulled her away.

One night, at home, Manuela asked, 'What's wrong?' and Isabel told her about the police. Her cousin erupted, 'What are you trying to do to me, Isabel? What did I tell you about the police? You took my baby there? And now after what happened? What will people think if they know you went to the police days after a raid? They'll finish with us. I've seen it happen, I've seen them send families into the street. They'll do to us what they did to Junior.'

'I won't go again,' said Isabel. She didn't say she was going each day to the Center. She knew she couldn't tell Manuela about her dreams. They mean nothing, her cousin would say. They are just dreams, just the day passing through. Or she would mock her, Do they come with a map, these dreams? If he is eating an ice in a dream, do you follow the ice vendors? If he is swimming, would you look for him in the sea?

Isabel waited for her cousin to tell her not to worry about Isaias, but Manuela didn't say this.

She stopped sitting with the washerwomen, and didn't return to Junior's store, which had been reopened by his cousin. Twice, she saw the portrait seller lugging his bag of frames up the hill, his hair neatly combed, laughing with the children. She closed the door and motioned for Hugo to be quiet. Twice, she heard him clap and call to her.

In her dreams, she looked desperately for street signs or names, but there was only Isaias Street or Saint Michael Street or Street Isabel. She rode buses with aisles that stretched the length of city blocks; there were no fountains or towers to guide her. She had a vision, one afternoon, of Isaias in a graveyard, sitting on the crushed edge of a marble slab, swinging his feet. Around him, angels alighted on the headstones, curling up beneath their wings. Their faces were streaked with soot-black tears, their cheeks hollowed by the city rain. Candles wilted at his feet, and the pathways ran with wax. She stared at the photos entombed in glass on the headstones. Each showed his face, the fiddle in his hands, the backdrop of his orchestra. Gray men walked through the cemetery in ill-fitting pants that frayed about their ankles. She recognized the cemetery from her walks, but she refused to go back.

She went and sat with Hugo on the steps outside the subway stations. He played at her feet, but she ignored him unless he began to cry. She watched the rising waves of faces that came up the stairs, searching the thousands of eyes and mouths and hair, thinking *chance alone should bring him to me,* it is impossible that there can be so many of them and still he doesn't pass. Once, as she walked in a crowded street, she saw him staring out a window of a bank, until her eyes left his and saw the wild tangle of her own hair and the remainder of her reflection.

Sometimes when she walked she heard her name.

She learned after one or two times that there was no one there, but she always stopped. She did not understand why she took comfort in the crowds breaking and re-forming around her, the voices telling her to move, her importance.

One day, she passed a crowd outside a hospital. 'Isaias isn't sick,' she told herself aloud, and walked on. But at the end of the block she stopped and went back. She waited outside in the mist, watching the crowd.

At last she went to the window. 'I am here to look for someone,' she said. 'Then you are in the wrong place,' said a woman. 'These lines are for people who are sick, or who think they are sick. Visitors must go through the door.'

Inside, she found a desk with a sign that said INFORMA-TION. An old woman sat behind a thick black registry. She asked Isabel, 'Is he a patient?' 'I don't know. Maybe.' 'That isn't helpful,' said the woman. 'This is a very large hospital.' She ran a ruler down the pages of the register. 'Here's an Isaias with that name . . . Twenty-one years old. No hometown, no family listed, just *the Settlements.* Could that be him?' Isabel

stared at her. *'Young lady?'* 'Yes?' 'Could it be him?' Isabel
nodded slowly. 'Ward 27, Inpatient Psychiatry.' She wrote it
down. 'What does that mean, "Inpatient Psychiatry"?' asked
Isabel. 'Crazy,' said the woman. 'It means locked away.'

She had to sit again. It can't be, she thought. The inspector
told me: there must be thousands of Isaiases with our name,
twenty-one years old, from the Settlements. *Without a family.*
And if his family was recorded in the register? And if he was
Isaias, brother of an Isabel? How many hundreds of Isaiases
from the Settlements with a sister Isabel must there be?

I want to see this Isaias of another Isabel, she thought.
Maybe he is identical in every way—maybe his Isabel is just
like me.

She fed the baby from his bottle and pressed him to her
shoulder. He yawned and closed his eyes. He is good, she
thought, a backlands baby who learned long ago not to cry.

She went to a sign with arrows and ward numbers, and followed a large hallway to a bank of elevators. In an open lift, a
nurse stood behind a wheelchair-bound woman with a thin
tube in her nose. The woman sat crookedly against her chair.
Her hands trembled slightly in her lap, her fingers reminded
Isabel of bent fork prongs. The elevator groaned upward. The
old woman looked at Isabel. 'It's you, Lourdes!' She smiled
beatifically. 'Don't listen to her,' said the nurse. 'She's so
demented. She thinks she's still in the north.' 'Her family's in
the north?' asked Isabel. 'Who knows? They found her alone
in the Central Station, wandering by the track.'

The lift grated against the shaft. When it stopped, the light
from the elevator illuminated a sign that said VISITORS MUST
ANNOUNCE THEMSELVES. Isabel stepped tentatively out, and
then the door closed, shuttering the wall in darkness.

She followed the hallway to a rectangle of light cast on the floor by an intersecting corridor. She turned into it, not knowing where she was going. There were no signs; the rooms seemed empty. It smelled of bleach and urine, and something else—birth, maybe, she thought. In places, the paint was swollen in bubbles. She passed a discarded metal tray, and later, a stirrup and an archipelago of scattered pills. She could hear the echo of her own breathing. At the end of the corridor was a door with a glass window. It was a children's ward, and the floors were littered with discarded toys, but there were no children anywhere. She turned into another hallway, but it was also empty. As she went back, a child stepped in front of her. Its head was big and round, like the photo of the child in the magazine, and its arms were as thin as sticks. It looked like a little skeleton. It hobbled toward her, and she lifted Hugo away.

A nurse came from an open door and picked the child up. 'Come, now,' she scolded, softly. To Isabel, she said, 'This is Serafina. She's from New Grace, in the Settlements. Her mother left her and two brothers in a shack. She is named after the great actress Serafina, you know.' Isabel didn't know if the nurse was accusing the mother or the actress Serafina. She thought it was an odd thing to tell a stranger anyway, and so she didn't answer.

She showed the nurse the slip of paper. 'One flight down,' said the nurse.

She descended an empty stairwell and found herself in an identical hallway. At the end of it was a door with a small window, and the number 27. The handle was locked. She knocked. An old man passed, shuffling his feet.

A nurse appeared in the window, a fat woman with a white

paper cylinder for a cap. The nurse bent to speak through small holes in the glass. 'Yes?'

Isabel spoke loudly: 'I am here to see my brother Isaias.'

'This isn't visiting time,' said the nurse.

'Please, I've come a long way. I haven't seen him for months.'

'Not visiting time,' said the nurse, and went away.

Isabel watched the patients through the glass. They don't know how to take care of him here, she thought. If he were home, there would be a prayer or a candle to burn. He shouldn't be locked up like this, caged up with old men.

The nurse walked by again and stared. Isabel stared back. I am not going to move, she thought. If I go away, I am not going to have the courage to return. She saw the nurse talking to a second, wiry nurse. She returned to the window. 'Who do you think you are? We have two nurses for the entire ward. We can't let visitors in all day.'

'I will go when I see him.'

The nurse walked off. In the sling, the baby stirred. 'Don't cry,' she whispered, lifting him to her shoulder and stroking his head. 'Please, be good like you were good before.' He reached for her cap, and she tilted her head toward him and let her hair pass back and forth over his face. He laughed, and then clung to her again and soon went back to sleep.

She slouched against the wall. She waited an hour, and then the nurse returned to the door. 'Visiting hours are over for the day. You are making the patients upset. You have to go home.'

'I don't have a home,' she said. 'I don't have a place to go to. If you won't let me in, I'll stay here until visiting hours come.'

The woman looked behind her. 'It's not that I am against you. But there are policies.'

'He has been missing for over four months,' said Isabel. 'I'm not against you, either.'

After another hour, the second nurse appeared with a key. 'You can come quickly,' she said, 'but then you will leave.'

Two men sat on a battered couch, chewing their lips. Another lay on the floor. Isabel's stomach knotted. She feared she would pass out. She thought she should hand the baby to the nurse, but when she tried to lift him off her shoulder, she was shaking.

At the end of the hallway, the nurse said, 'He doesn't like being called Isaias, he wants to be called Arthur.'

In the room was an unfamiliar man. His head was shaved, and his arms were tied to the bed. 'Arthur,' said the nurse. 'See, your sister did come.' 'Yes,' said the man. 'He's heavily medicated,' said the nurse. 'If not, he screams. He thinks he is the Boy-King himself, that he has come to liberate the world.

'Is something wrong?' asked the nurse, but Isabel was crying. 'I need to go,' she said through the tears. The man watched her impassively. 'Goodbye, Arthur,' she said.

'I know it's hard,' said the nurse, outside. 'But at least you came. Maybe he is a special person, like he says. In another time, they would have called him a prophet. Back home in the north, where I'm from, we have many men who claim they are prophets or kings, who wander the backlands in great beards, preaching the end of days.'

'He's not my brother,' said Isabel.

'He has been speaking of his sister. Her name is Mary. That isn't you?'

'No,' said Isabel again, very slowly. 'Maybe he's also a brother, but he isn't mine. Maybe he means *that* Mary. It's a mistake, I'm sorry. I am Isabel.' 'I see,' said the nurse. She paused. 'You must be relieved, then. He's a very sick person.'

'Yes,' said Isabel, and walked out of the room, down the hallway and into an elevator, which carried her to the place where she began. She stood before the old lady at the register. 'It isn't my brother,' she said, and returned to the street, where the mist had given way to rain.

August became September. Hugo began to try pulling himself to standing at the side of the bed. Isabel fashioned him a rattle with stones and a plastic can, and he shook it by swinging his whole body. She found herself singing to him for hours. He was so transfixed by the songs that she wondered if he already knew them. But Manuela rarely sings, she thought. Can you be born remembering a song that your parents heard? She sang about a thrush whose call foresaw rain, and the laughing falcons that brought drought. She sang about traveling south on the parrot perches and about a blackbird whose eyes were gouged to make him sing more beautifully.

With the rain came flying ants, fragile creatures that were easily broken. They flew inside in lace-like clouds, pattering against the walls. They tangled themselves in the curtains and the sheets, shedding legs and wings in gossamer piles. They buzzed over the floor with the trajectories of skipped stones. Isabel spent hours watching them, holding them by their arcing brown abdomens. She found great solace in them, these delicate, carelessly made creatures that let themselves be captured and didn't resist.

When they died, she swept them into little mounds, set

them on the windowsill and watched the wind caress them into the air.

She didn't descend again to the city. Her world contracted to the hill.

When the loneliness of the room became too much, she went to Junior's store. His cousin let her sit and watch the afternoon soaps. Sometimes there was a program where a man granted wishes to poor people who wrote in asking for help. They came on the show, tears streaming down their cheeks as he gave them money for new houses, for private schools, for plane tickets to the north. He spoke to them like they were little children, and she despised him.

She didn't tell Josiane about the hospital, and when she waved her flag she lowered her cap over her eyes. Josiane didn't seem to notice any change. One Saturday, as they walked to the bus, she rested her pink fingernails on Isabel's arm and said, 'I never told you, but most Saturday nights I go dancing. I'm going tonight. Come. My friends will like you. They call you my backlander.' She laughed and then stopped. 'They don't mean it in a bad way—not that you are ignorant, just that you still have country ways. You should come.' Isabel shook her head. 'Just offering,' said her friend. 'Sometimes I don't understand you. Do you even think about what other girls think about? Sometimes I think you will always be so young.'

She returned to washing in the river.

With the rains, the water was high. She found comfort in the rocking, and in the river's new smell of roots and soil. She asked to help with the other women's clothes. She watched her hands disappear and twisted the shirts until her forearms ached.

'So,' said the women one afternoon. 'He came by yesterday.'
Isabel froze. 'My brother.'

'No, your brother, no, my love. The young man who makes
the portraits. Alin . . . you remember him, don't you? He has
been by at least three times now. He asks about you every
time. What is it, have you forgotten him already?'

For a moment, Isabel's rocking slowed. She watched the
ripples scallop her wrists and then began washing again.

A week later, in mid-September, the portrait seller appeared again in New Eden. He sang and swung his bag of portraits on his thigh as he climbed the hill, stopping before the
houses and clapping. Laughing, he growled at the children
who followed. Isabel watched him from behind the curtain.
He stopped before her house and called for her, but she didn't
move. As he walked away, she resisted the impulse to run after
him. She put the base of her thumbs against the cold, soft
soles of Hugo's feet. She kissed him on the forehead.

The next night, on the soap opera, a woman said of Cindy:
She is waiting for Alexandre to rescue her from her situation.
Alexandre was the heir to a coffee fortune who had fallen in
love with her when he came to dinner at her boss's house.

Outside Junior's store, Isabel watched quietly. That night,
she didn't sleep until the small hours. *Situation* was one of her
father's words, and one whose childhood definition she could
never fully escape. It's the situation that is against us, he
would say, both in moments of sobriety and desperation, and
she had grown up thinking it meant a special kind of enemy,
a landowner or a drought. Cindy's mother was still in the
hospital, and their family was deep in debt. But *I* do not need

rescue now, she told herself, her thoughts of Cindy melting confusingly into those of the portraitist, home and her brother. She wished Hugo would wake to stop the circling of her mind.

On the soap opera, Alexandre became a regular visitor. Cindy grew even more beautiful. Her cheeks glowed, and her eyes glistened with tears of joy. Her generous boss understood her love and bought her a satin shirt.

Isabel was mesmerized by the maid's transformation. In Manuela's cabinet she found lipstick and painted her mouth tentatively. She combed and tied her hair with a turquoise ribbon she had found beneath a seat on the bus. Then she wiped the lipstick off. Another time, she wore it to Junior's store. 'Young girls who wear lipstick look like whores,' said Junior's cousin, and handed her a napkin. She began to wish that the washerwomen would mention the portraitist again.

One morning she met him coming up the hill. He swung his bag from his shoulder and stopped. '*Isabel*. Finally, I found you.' He smiled broadly. He wore a T-shirt with a snow-capped peak and howling wolf, tucked neatly into his pants. 'I've been away,' she said, and added, 'My brother's not here yet.' She hoisted Hugo and busied herself wiping his cheeks.

Across the street, in an open doorway, an old woman watched them from a rocking chair.

Isabel saw he was out of breath. 'I have water,' she offered.

They sat on the step. Carefully, Isabel smoothed her dress over her knees and sat Hugo on her feet, against her shins. The young man asked for the baby's name. 'A good dignified name,' he said. 'You remember my name, right?' 'It's Alin.' She paused. 'Photo Alin.' She felt like giggling at her joke.

When he finished drinking, she thought he would leave. Instead, he began to tell her about his home in the north. He was the seventh of ten children. They lived near a river; his father was a fisherman, with a wooden head carved on the bow of his boat to scare off water spirits. When they went fishing, they tossed pinches of tobacco into the water as offerings. Plum-colored snails prowled the little creek where they swam.

'We used to go to the coast for Saint John's festival,' he said. 'They had a fair that went all night, with a rodeo and a mermaid played by the beauty queen from the agronomists' council. We used to throw stones at her tail. You should have heard her curse.' Isabel turned and smiled at him. 'It was the only time I left my village,' he said, and added, 'Until I came here.'

At her feet, Hugo lunged for something in the street. She pulled him back. 'Alone?'

'Alone. I had an uncle waiting, but I took that horrible ride down alone.'

Alin took a silver-colored wristwatch from his pocket. 'I'd better hurry,' he said. He kissed her once on each cheek.

Inside, she sat on the edge of the bed and rolled her toes. She touched her cheek where he had kissed her. It's just a goodbye! she cautioned herself. She tried to think of what Isaias would counsel. In Saint Michael and Prince Leopold, he'd watched over her at the dances. In Saint Michael she was a child.

Alin returned two days later. He clapped outside and called. She went to the door, then doubled back to the mirror. She put water on her hands and pressed her hair back, like a style she had seen in the magazines. She combed down the baby's cowlick.

At the door, her collar was wet. 'If you need to, I can wait for you to dry your hair,' Alin offered.

She walked beside him to the crest of the hill. They watched a boy run his kite on a half-finished roof, laughing as he hurdled tufts of bare rebars. The city stretched behind him. 'I bet he doesn't even notice the city,' said Alin. 'My cousin, who was born here, thinks that the world looks like the city.' He squinted.

'You forget,' he said.

You mean home, she thought, but he said, 'You forget how there's no end.'

She swung Hugo out of the way of a man pushing a wheelbarrow. A smaller boy climbed onto the rooftop and unfurled a second kite. It fluttered alongside the first. 'You know, they coat their kite strings with broken glass,' said Alin. 'Wood glue and broken glass, and they try to cut each other's strings. If I could write a song it would be about that, like a riddle, about which kite wins, the one that stays or the one that flies away.'

Isabel waited, expecting him to give her the answer. In the road, a group of children piled onto a bicycle, wobbling as they picked up speed.

He began to visit regularly. Slowly, she noticed changes in him, that after several visits he wore cleaner, ironed shirts, that he slipped into a northern accent. She settled easily into his presence. She found it calmed her, like movement calmed her. He asked many questions about Saint Michael, what the mountains were like and which festivals they celebrated. She waited for him to ask her about her brother, but he didn't. For the first time, when she talked about home, it was a joyous, beautiful place free of the desolation she remembered from the days before her departure.

He showed her his portraits. She could only look at them for a short time before they overwhelmed her. In the wooden frames, an old man in a cowboy hat stood before a photograph of steep mountains; a woman carried her baby before a vast marble square filled with statues; a man in a soccer uniform held the hand of a beautiful girl. At her side, Alin said: 'This old man scrapes wax from the altars at the cathedral. Once he was a miner—*the best,* he told me—he could find gold anywhere. The baby is a young man now, but he is so sick, he hears voices, he lives in the park, where his mother goes in the mornings to bring him food. I made this couple young again.' Isabel looked through them slowly. She began to feel that if she stared long enough she could know not only what had happened in their lives, but what would happen. Frightened, she put them away.

She began to borrow dresses from Manuela. Her favorite was lavender rayon, with bows on the cuffs of the short sleeves. It was loose and made her look very thin again, but she liked how it turned her eyes almost violet. At the beauty store, she looked at the magazine cutouts until the beautician wobbled to the door. She slunk shyly away. She studied the older girls and how they walked and laughed. In Manuela's room, she dragged the chair before the mirror and practiced sashaying. She stared at the magazines again. She wished for someone to explain whether there was anything wrong with putting so much hope in a single person.

She returned to the article she'd read when she first came: *Do you feel empty when he is gone?* She read it all. In one of the magazines, for younger girls, was a sweepstakes survey. She didn't have the stamp, but she filled it out anyway. *Best friend:* Josiane. *Favorite color:* pink. *Favorite television star:* Cindy. She left blank *favorite beach, favorite restaurant, teacher's name, favorite shampoo, favorite article in* Teen Style, *favorite department store.* Then, *favorite animal:* dog + cat. *Brothers and sisters:* Isaias, Daniel, Hector (dead), Flora. *Boyfriend:* Alin, she wrote, in recklessly flowering letters, and then tore the card to tiny pieces.

She thought of telling Josiane. On the bus, she stood on the tips of her toes and cupped her hand to her friend's ear. But the motor was too loud, and instead of repeating herself, she dropped back on her heels. She asked for the Thyago Firestorm book. Josiane said she wasn't finished, and Isabel didn't pursue it further.

Later, as they idled at a light, a girl passed carrying a baby. She stopped at a trash can and began to burrow through the garbage. Isabel leaned over to watch her as they drove away. 'Do I look like that girl?' she blurted out, and her friend eyed her strangely but didn't answer.

Alone, she recalled a story from Saint Michael. A boy from the sea was traveling in the backlands when he met a girl sleeping beneath a drinking-tree. That night, they fell in love, but in the morning, she had to leave him. He pleaded, *How will I find you again?* and she whispered, *Meet me beneath this tree.* Then they parted. He stayed by the tree, where he planted a little farm. He went hungry because the earth was so poor, but he could only think of his love for the girl. Each night he slept beneath the tree. In times of hunger, he lived on its fruit and leaves, and drank the water from its roots. He grew old, but still he waited. Then one night, his milk goat ran away. He thought, I have waited so long, one night won't matter. He went after his goat. That night the girl, now an old woman, visited. She found the tree empty and the farm abandoned. Weeping, she wandered away.

Often, in Saint Michael, when Isabel was alone in the white forest, she would hear crying like an old woman's voice. Now the story acquired the power of a fable. *It is the punishment for abandoning someone,* she knew. When Alin invited her to the municipal park south of the Center, she shook her head. She didn't explain.

The next week he asked again. She told herself it was only a children's story. Still she refused. The third time he asked, she wrote a note: *Isaias I am at the Park I will come back not too late.* She left it on the pillow. She hoped, secretly, that the washer-women would be at the river to see them pass together, but the banks were empty.

In the park, there was a large pond with dozens of white birds. When she squinted, they looked like slowly swaying S's. She told Alin. 'Swans,' he said. 'And those ones on the banks are egrets.' The egrets troubled her: their long threaded veils seemed too vain for an animal.

Alin offered to carry Hugo, but she shook her head. She wanted him to hold her hand. She let it swing, empty, near his left side, and for a long time she thought of nothing else.

He spoke as they walked. She liked how he didn't expect her to say much, that he didn't treat her silence as simplicity. He told her of home, of coming to the city, of selling candies on city buses and shining shoes. He told her about a library in the Center, where he met an old man who showed him a book in which the poor fled a great city and encamped in the hills, because *to remain there meant only to be slain.* 'The man was crazy, I think,' he said. 'He spent his days there, and would talk to anybody. But I wrote those words down.' When he saw that this frightened her, he said, 'There was another book— maybe one day I will show you. It was about this city, when it was all forest. It made me wonder if it is still the same beneath. Sometimes I imagine tearing the buildings off. It

would be like tearing bark from a log that's lain a long time
without being touched. With everything scurrying out: the
animals, the old ghosts, everyone that was here before.'

She smiled.

'You think I am crazy, too,' he said, but she shook her head.

They sat on a bench beneath a jacaranda, and she removed
her shoes and rested her feet on its roots. She took the blanket
away from the baby's face so he could see the trees, but he
seemed more interested in the bows on her dress. She plucked
some of the flowers from a low branch and absentmindedly
slipped them over his fingers. She watched out of the corner of
her eye to see if Alin was looking at her.

In the distance, they watched a pair of dueling singers performing for a crowd. Alin began a new story, about his great-
uncle, a poem singer in the north. He was senile now, an aunt
took care of him. 'The strange thing,' he said, 'is that even
though he makes no sense, he still rhymes. You should hear
him: he still remembers all the rhyme schemes, duets, simple
couplets, six-lines, roundabouts, even the harder ones, like the
seven-line rhymes with the six-line melodies, when the words
and the music drift apart. The words make no sense at all, but
the rhyme's still there.'

The story unsettled her. It made her think of the old people
in Saint Michael who refused to leave when their families
migrated away. They could forget everything, even their own
names, but they never seemed to forget which wells were still
alive or where to find food. She imagined their minds like
evaporating water retreating around the deepest part of a
pond. She wondered, What will be left of me when the rest of
me has gone?

By the pond, she saw a man wearing a checkered shirt similar to one Isaias owned back home, but it was new and brightly colored. Her eyes followed him until he was far away.

When the park closed, they filed along a thin sidewalk back to the bus. Alin asked, 'Now what will you do?'

'Cook for Hugo,' she said absently.

'No,' said Alin, 'not now. I mean, *now*—this month, this year.'

She shrugged.

'You haven't thought about it?'

I'm waiting, she thought. When he comes, I'll decide.

'You have to consider it,' he said. 'Or you will be stuck in the same place forever. I'm going to get a store, then expand, then maybe get two stores. Then I'll go to school. A technical school, so I can learn to repair cameras, electronics. My mother believed that wrapping a baby in newspaper would make him grow up to be a doctor. But everyone knows you can't just wait.'

'Maybe I will go back to school,' she said. 'My father never went to school. My mother went.'

'I don't mean *school*, like a school in the backlands, just for reading. Anyone can read. I could read a book a day if I wanted. But you need a skill. You have to want to be something, or you will end up a maid like your cousin.'

As he began to describe a famous technical school in the Center, her thoughts drifted again. She had never considered one could do better than Manuela. Is this the way it is? she wondered. All the way along: a world full of people who want to know what you will be, what is your skill and what is your purpose. In the north, if a man had come and said, *What will you be? What will you do?* I would have laughed at this kind of person that lives all the time in the future.

'You don't have enough ambition,' said Alin.

The wind was cool, and the park smelled strongly of fresh-cut grass. On a street corner, a little girl with wild yellow hair stretched out her arms and spun. Again Isabel was certain that most of her problems would be solved if Alin held her hand. It seemed as if it would rain, and she worried about getting home in time.

He came again. He took her on a train ride through the eastern settlements, to watch the shanties unwind over the hills; to the Center; to a skyscraper with views of the city.

She left the baby with one of the washerwomen, who promised not to tell Manuela, and Alin took her to a cinema, where there was a free screening sponsored by a bank. She had never seen a movie before. She was so overwhelmed by the seats, the high ceilings and the screen that when it started she began to laugh. 'Shhh,' said Alin. She was the only one laughing.

The movie was about a family of drought refugees in the backlands. The father worked a small plot of land on an abandoned homestead. The mother took care of the home; the children had never seen a town.

Halfway through the movie, the father was arrested and beaten. He had done nothing wrong, but he could not explain himself. The soldiers treated him as if he were a simpleton. 'Speak up!' they shouted, but he babbled incoherently. Watching, Isabel had two thoughts. The first was that he was hungry. The second unfurled slowly: It is not that he doesn't know how to explain, it is that they don't know how to understand his explanation. They are not watching his hands or his shoulders, they are not looking at his hat and where it's worn and where it's broken. They are not smelling, because if they smelled his breath, they would know he is starving. They do not notice how he keeps his water gourd close to him, and protects it before he protects his face. He doesn't have words because he has never needed words: his wife understands him without being told. At night, when they are silent, it is not because they are simple, but because he says what he needs to say in his posture, in how fast he eats, if he licks his fingers, if he sleeps early, if he cries. His wife knows just by watching his walk if he is proud or shamed. He can tell her everything by his walk. He in turn knows by how much broth she serves him what she thinks the days will bring. By the smell of her clothes, he knows if she is too exhausted to bathe. By the way she holds a child, he knows if the child is sick. Like him, her language, the language that has served since she was a little girl, is a language of gestures, postures and smells, and then speech, if speech is necessary.

The soldiers beat him with the flat edges of their knives. He moaned like an animal. Then one day he was released and began his walk home.

The lights came up. 'It's over?' she asked.

Following the free screening, there was a lecture and a discussion also sponsored by the bank. A poster read TELLING TRAGEDY: DROUGHT, MYTH AND REALITY IN THE BACKLANDS. A panel of well-dressed men and women settled around a podium lined with glasses of water. 'It is about the abuse of power,' they said. 'The domination of the strong over the weak. It is about a simple person in a world that is too complex for him.' For a long time, they argued with one another.

After half an hour, Alin made a yawning motion, and Isabel looked back toward the door. They slipped out, bought sodas and watched the people in the street.

On the television, she watched Alexandre kiss Cindy on the lips. She thought gleefully, If Alin kissed me, I would let him, at least for a little while.

Alone, she practiced the steps to the dances for couples. She collected petals from the coral tree and wreathed them with a loose thread from the curtain. She arranged the crown on Hugo, whose cheeks glowed as if he were blushing.

Then she waited a week, and Alin didn't return. She sat on the edge of her bed, her hands on her lap, ready to rise when he came. She tried to distract herself with the magazine or the baby. By the end of the week, she began to pace with worry. He learned who I really am, she thought, he learned I'm not the kind of person people visit, that I haven't seen the world, that before I came here, I hadn't even seen an apple. On television, she watched Cindy's kind boss, once abandoned by her husband, find new love on a moonlit shore. She remembered her mother's words: A man is like the rain, he's worth nothing unless he stays. She considered what she would say if he came back: You broke a promise, You said you'd come and you didn't, I waited for you, I thought I'd lost someone else, I could have been out looking for my brother, but I waited for you. I made a mistake, I trusted someone I didn't know.

When another week passed and he didn't come, she accepted Josiane's invitation to go dancing. 'The election is coming soon,' said her friend. 'After that it will be harder to see each other.'

Outside the banners of the campaign office, Isabel called

the pay phone by Junior's store. 'Do you want me to get Manuela?' asked his cousin. 'No, just give her a message. Tell her that I am with a friend tonight, a *girl*friend. Give a kiss to Hugo. I'll stay with my friend. I'll be home tomorrow.' Josiane took her hand and led her to the bus. From her stop, they walked down a long dirt street lined with container siding.

In Josiane's house, a man slept on a floor crowded with thin mattresses. On the wall were taped magazine photographs of a snowy mountain lake and a woman on a bicycle. A curled figure lay on a single bed with a baby.

'This is my little monster,' said Josiane, scooping up the baby. 'And that's my mother on the bed. She's sleeping. She has water on the heart so she always sleeps. When she doesn't sleep she coughs and scratches her legs. It drives me crazy. All night she coughs. The one on the floor is my uncle—he works a night shift as a guard, only now he's also sick. I sleep in the bed with my mother.' Isabel held the baby. Her head lolled. She slipped her finger into her hand, but her grip was weak. 'And the other mattresses?'

Josiane shrugged. 'Half the time I can't keep track. One cousin or another. People coming and going from the north.

'Come,' she said, and tucked the baby back into the shelter of her mother's arms. Her mother didn't wake. Stacked in the corner was a pile of brightly colored clothes. She pulled off the Candidate's shirt and chose an orange top that stopped above her waist and was open between her breasts. She wriggled into it. Isabel chose the most modest top she could find, a bright yellow shirt with a high collar. Josiane gave her a miniskirt and a pair of heels. The shoes were too large, so they stuffed the toes with toilet paper. Isabel tugged at the skirt as she walked.

Josiane led her by the hand to a house where a pair of twins in black skirts and matching tops of aquamarine was dancing to a blaring radio. Their bodies seemed to overflow from their clothing. Above them, torn kites fluttered from a line. They danced to another song. Then they slipped off their sandals and slid into black boots that stopped below their knees. They sprayed each other's hair until it hung in thick wet ringlets, and layered their mouths with maroon lipstick.

Isabel relented to their hands and sprays. Her curls swung heavily, the lipstick smelled faintly of perfume. She thought briefly of her brother. He would be angry, she knew. So would Alin. She looked for a mirror.

At midnight, they descended the hill. It had been raining and the ground was slick. They took a night bus, wobbling on their heels and tossing their hair as the bus shuddered through the streets. They got off on a block thick with discotheques. The traffic was slow, the lights of the clubs glittered in the street, the tires left prints like silvery tracks of snails. Isabel followed the girls' rank of swaying hips up a staircase, past a group of boys in sleeveless shirts who stood by the door.

Inside, music blasted from a pair of giant speakers. The beat was furious, an electrified version of music that Isabel knew from home. Couples swirled with their thighs interlaced, hips pressed together. The twins were already ahead, dancing across the dark floor. Other girls emerged from the mass of dancers to greet them. A heavy haze of cigarette smoke hung in the room. Josiane beckoned Isabel forward and danced on.

They sat at a table off the dance floor, and a pair of older men brought glasses of warm cane liquor. Isabel hesitated. 'Go!' said one of the twins, kissing her cheek, and threw the drink back in a single gulp. Isabel followed, grimacing as it burned her throat. Everyone laughed. One of the men leaned to Josiane and whispered something. His eyes didn't leave Isabel, and a bemused smile passed over his mouth. He passed her his drink. 'To the backlands!' he toasted, and with everyone's eyes on her, Isabel drank again. 'That's our girl!' they cheered.

The men escorted the twins off into the swirling crowds. Isabel stayed with Josiane until other men came. When they asked her to dance, she shook her head. She felt naked in Josiane's clothes and didn't want to stand.

The twins returned. Josiane left. Josiane returned. All three girls disappeared, dancing, into the crowd. A pair of shot glasses were left with a thick meniscus of liquor, which Isabel drank. She felt herself beginning to sway with the pounding of the music.

Josiane returned, leading a man in a white shirt. She introduced him, but his name was drowned by the noise. When he greeted Isabel, he kissed her cheek, close to her mouth. 'He was asking about you,' shouted Josiane into her ear. 'Other men, too, they all want to know who my new friend is.' She winked. She shouted something else, but it, too, was lost. 'I'll leave you two alone,' she said. The light shimmered on her lips.

The man pulled his chair next to Isabel. 'You're beautiful,' he whispered. She could feel the warmth of his breath on her neck. It smelled sweet, antiseptic. He passed her a glass of beer and she drank it quickly. He smiled. 'Do you dance?' 'A little . . . back home . . . not fast like this.' She moved away from him. He was silhouetted by the dance lights, and she couldn't see his eyes. He whispered again, but she couldn't hear him. He took her hand from her lap.

She danced with him. She could feel his fingers glide to the bare space of the small of her back. A chain around his chest pressed into her shoulder. Light glinted from the dancers' hair and the sweat on their shoulders. Her head spun. She felt his erection against her belly, said she wasn't feeling well and went to sit. Now the table held a dozen empty glasses. She couldn't remember how much she had drunk.

She excused herself and stumbled to the bathroom. A line of girls preened before a long mirror. She sought shelter in a stall and pressed her forehead against the door, trying to stop the spinning. She listened to fragments of conversation, *My God, girl, you've got gold feet . . . Girl yourself, you see who's here? You see that little whore he's with? . . . Shit, he is looking for trouble . . . He says Little Bird's coming . . . Little Bird scares me . . . Of course he scares you — Little Bird would scare the dead . . .* She had forgotten how much time had passed when there was banging on the door and a voice shouted, 'Hey, are you touching yourself?' and she slunk out. She briefly stopped before the mirror, wobbling, and pushed past the girls to the floor.

Now the room was packed. She looked for a familiar face, but it was as if she had entered a door to a different discotheque. She spied what she thought was her table and wove toward it, no longer bothering to excuse herself as she collided into dancers. She was at the edge of the tables when she sensed someone weaving through the spinning crowd.

She froze. Her eyes searched the dance floor. There was only light and movement now, but beyond it all she sensed a new presence. *Isaias. Like that day on the hill.* 'My God,' she said aloud. She closed her eyes and the sensation vanished. 'I'm drunk,' she mumbled. A man bumped against her, spilling his drink, which splashed on her knee and ran down her calf. She turned away. A girl spun past in a man's arms. Where is everyone? she thought frantically. The room seemed impossibly vast.

She felt a hand on her elbow and turned. The man with the white shirt trapped her fingers in his. Fearing she would fall, she clung to him. He led her smoothly, floating her with his hand. At the edge of the dance floor, she turned, trying to see. 'What's wrong?' he said, so close his forehead touched hers. 'Nothing,' she said, but she sensed it again, moving through the crowd.

She untangled her hand.

He grabbed her waist and pulled her closer. 'One more dance.' 'No . . . I have to go.' She twisted out of his grip with a force that surprised her. He lifted his hands. 'Take it easy,' he began, but she had turned away.

Retreating now. She shouldered her way toward the entrance, trying to steady herself. Halfway across the room, she felt another hand on her arm. She spun angrily. 'Hey, Isabel,' said Josiane, laughing. 'It's just me. I saw that you stopped dancing. I . . . Isabel, what's wrong? What are you looking at? What's going on?' *Moving along the far edge of the wall.* 'I have to go.' 'Now? Cool it. I want to dance some more.' 'No, it's not that—' *At the door now.* 'I have to go.' 'Isabel, you can't go by yourself. It's not safe. It's not . . . Hey!' Josiane caught her. 'You're acting crazy—what's happening?' She wasn't laughing now. 'My brother,' said Isabel. *'What?'* 'My brother, Isaias.' 'You saw him.' 'No, but he's here, outside now. I have to get to him. Wait for me.'

She broke free and pushed her way to the stairs. It was cold outside. Her ears rang with the sudden quiet of the street.

Above her the balcony was full of people, and the light of the bar blued the ceiling. A drunken girl leaned on a man as they descended behind her. Down the street she could see a pair of boys coming up the road. They were backlit by the colored neon of a distant club and the reflections in the wet sidewalk. She waited for the feeling to return, but now she doubted herself. 'I'm drunk,' she said. 'I'm going to be sick.' The heels were unsteady. She thought of the day on the hill and how she had lost him because she had hesitated.

The music dropped off swiftly behind her. The street bifurcated and then split again. Uncertainly, she bore right, her skin prickling in a sudden wind. The road was empty.

A pair of girls wobbled toward her. She ran to them. 'Did you see a man?' 'A man!' They laughed. 'We wish!' Isabel wavered uncertainly. 'No!' she said. '*Really*, did you see anyone?' One of the girls stared. 'You're serious . . . Yeah, sure, we passed a man just a second ago. He went into the tall building on the corner. Didn't get a good look at him, though—' 'Which building?' 'Gray one, that one there, with the metal fence.' 'He went inside?' 'Yes, but I didn't get a look at him. Maybe it's not your man . . .

'You alone?' she asked, and Isabel ran on.

The gate was topped with iron spades, and open. She pushed through and crossed a concrete yard, past an empty sentry box and a cracked fountain. The door handle was broken off, the lobby empty except for a fan of glass blown in from a window. A trail led through the debris to a rumbling elevator shaft. She watched the numbers rise until the 12 shimmered and the lift began to come down. It was on the second floor when she realized that someone might be inside. She pressed herself against the wall. The door opened. Empty. Without pausing, she slipped inside, squinted in the darkness and found the 12. As the lift rose, she waited for another sign of Isaias, but now she sensed nothing. It was dark in the elevator. Distant shouting began to get louder.

The door opened. For a moment, she hesitated. Go down, an instinct told her, get away, but blindly she stepped into the hallway. She had enough time to register two men, the glowing scribble of a lightbulb, chipped plaster and an open door, before she heard a hiss and rumbling, the elevator door scraping closed behind her. 'Who the hell?' she heard, and turned to hit the elevator button, but the carriage was gone. Without waiting, she turned from them and began to walk away down a long corridor, quickly, straining to hear footsteps following. She rounded a corner, and another, the hallway snaking past open doors until at the end she arrived at a stairwell. She didn't stop. As her foot touched the top step, she heard the distant ring of the lift.

She ran. She threw herself forward, almost falling, her legs breaking her descent in tiny, thudding steps. She descended through a strange gray light that seemed to emanate from nowhere, glinting on broken bottles, cigarettes, discarded clothes, a shoe, a dead pigeon, a corncob, twelve flights and then she reached the landing and slammed through the door.

A man was waiting in the lobby as the elevator door closed behind him. He followed her out into the street and walked calmly alongside her. 'Where you going, angel?' She glanced at him out of the corner of her eye. He had a narrow face like a goat's and he grinned.

His hand was suddenly on her shoulder. She lurched. For a second he held on, but then his fingers slipped and she pulled away. She ran, turned an ankle and shook off the heels. She sprinted across a street with a flashing yellow light, her arms pumping madly, her skirt riding up her thighs, her lungs burning. She could see a figure on a doorstep in the distance and ran toward it. As she came close, it stirred and sat up. 'Get her!' it shouted, falling over drunkenly, laughing. She turned a corner onto another empty street, this one longer. Behind, she heard the man gaining. She saw the mouth of an alleyway breaking a line of shuttered stores.

She dashed into it, stumbling over spilled trash to a jumble of garbage bins. Her hands felt their way through them to a chain-link fence, but it was too dark to see anything beyond. Something stirred. A dog backed away through a sliver of light, growling, the greasy hair of its haunches bristling. At the entrance she could see the man, staring into the dark, clenching and unclenching his fists, rocking lightly on his feet like a boxer warming up before a match. He began to speak, to taunt her. She pressed herself up against the wall and closed her eyes, terrified of the sound of her heart pounding. She began to mouth prayers, *Mother of God, Saint Michael, Saint George, Isaias, please.* She tried to remember the words of invocations, but her memory failed. *Isaias,* she whispered, *Isaias, now.* 'Come out,' said the man.

She felt around for a stick, a pipe, anything to fight with. Her hand found the splintered slatting of a broken fruit crate, and she lifted it, running her thumb over a cluster of nails at the broken end, letting it sway in her hand. More growling. In the street, the man hesitated at the edge of the darkness. His taunts trailed off. *'Angel,'* he said again, and for the first time she heard uncertainty in his voice. Her breathing slowed. She choked up on the crate, tears running down her cheeks, suddenly terrified less by her fear than by her own anger. 'If you're coming in, come now, coward,' she whispered. 'I'll crush your face, coward, I'll crush your head.' At her side, the shadows stirred. She saw the dog retreat and slip behind the trash bins.

Now that her eyes had accustomed themselves to the darkness, she could see a narrow gap along the wall at the edge of the fence. Then the man was beside her. He lifted his arm, and she hurled the crate into him, bolted, heard the wood break, a gasp of pain, but she didn't stop to turn. She squeezed through the gap, following the dog, the chain links catching on her shirt. The alley was long; at the end she could see a road, lights, the silhouette of the animal sprinting away.

In the street, a bus was leaving its stop. She banged on its door. It opened and she pulled herself in. It was empty. Wind whistled over a broken back window as it swung into the street.

'Where are you going?' asked the driver, staring at her as he upshifted. 'New Settlements,' she said, her shoulders heaving. 'This bus doesn't go there.' 'I don't care. It doesn't matter.' She began to cough. 'Just go. Just until dawn, I promise, then I'll go.' He stared at her again. She looked down at her bare feet. Her knee was bleeding.

The driver nodded. He was nearly the age of her grandfather. He rummaged in the space beside his seat. 'Here is my sweater,' he said.

'I can't. I'm dirty.'

He shook his head. 'You'll be cold.'

She took it, trembling. The wool scratched her bare arms, and it smelled of cigars. Still shivering, she looked at her hand, where she had torn through a finger with the edge of the crate.

'Sit close,' said the driver. 'It isn't a good hour for someone like you to be out.'

S he rode the bus until dawn. Somehow she slept. She lay on the seat with her hands together beneath her ear, her head pressed against the aluminum siding, the engine's vibration thrumming through her skull.

Sometimes she heard voices, but mostly the bus was empty. Once she sat up and saw a girl in a tight skirt standing in the center aisle. She sang and wobbled as if she were dancing. She wore a man's white shirt, the top buttons open. It fell unevenly on her shoulders, and Isabel could see the pale edge of one of her breasts. Mascara was smeared back past her temple. She filled the bus with the smell of cigarettes. 'The night is ours love ours love our love,' she sang. She pumped her fist at the air. 'What are you looking at?' she asked, laughing, when she saw Isabel stare.

The sky turned cobalt blue, and the bus began to fill slowly. Isabel went to the driver and handed him the sweater. He shook his head. 'You still need to get home,' he said. She got off at a bus station near the Settlements to wait until she knew Manuela would be at church. Curling up in a corner, she slept again and awoke with someone pressing a coin into her hand and a pair of feet walking away. There was a direct bus home, but she got off early and followed a backstreet up the hill.

Manuela's house was empty. In the washroom, Isabel sat on the cement floor and poured cold water over her body. She scrubbed her skin furiously. Still she smelled of cane liquor and cigarettes, and she washed her hair again. She buried herself into the sheets. When Manuela came home, she pretended to sleep. The following night, alone again, she took Hugo from his hammock and kept him at her side. He slept with his arms stretched above his head, as if relishing the space.

She returned to the river and beat the clothes angrily against a rock.

She was there when Alin arrived, two days later, on a cold afternoon that broke intermittently into rain. 'Look who's coming,' sang the women. Isabel pinched her lips. She could see him, with the portrait bag wrapped in plastic, treading the narrow edge of the road. When he called to her, she rose reluctantly from the water's embrace. She gathered the clothes in one arm and perched Hugo on her hip.

They walked up the hill. Alin reached over to stroke Hugo's head, and the baby smiled and leaned toward him. Angrily, Isabel shifted him away, realizing immediately that she was too rough. He began to cry. For a moment, she struggled with the balance of the baby and the clothes, then kissed his hair and walked on. Alin offered to carry him, but she shook her head. 'You said you would come sooner,' she said.

'There was a problem in the north. My brother had an accident in the cane fields.' He choked suddenly on the words.

'There was a novena.' Isabel turned to him. 'Not a novena of mourning,' he said. 'A novena of prayer, to obtain a grace, and on the tenth day he was well. I said it here, too, all nine days of prayer.'

Farther up the hill, he said, 'Something is wrong.'

'Nothing is wrong,' she answered quickly.

At her house, she said, 'I have work to do.' 'Of course . . . I understand. I'll go.' He rubbed the stubble of his cheeks with his palm. 'Listen, I was thinking, this weekend, if you want, we can go to the sea together.' 'I can't,' said Isabel coolly. 'It's too expensive.' 'I'll pay. It will be good, you'll see. We can get away from the city, just for a day.' She shook her head. 'Manuela won't let me.' 'Ask her. I will come Saturday. Unless there is another reason you are saying no.'

He left. She pinned the clothes deliberately and creased the wet fabric over the lines. She stood in their wet chamber, feeling the cold on her face.

For the rest of the week, she remained inside the room. When Manuela came home, she told her about Alin. 'I don't understand why you don't want to go,' said her cousin. 'Do you know that I've never even been to the sea?'

'I've been,' said Isabel. 'I went with Isaias. I went a long time ago.'

'I don't understand what is bothering you, then,' said her cousin. 'What if I came with you?'

Isabel bit her nails.

'Yes?' asked Manuela, and Isabel nodded.

In the middle of the night, Manuela took her hand. 'Can you swim?' she whispered. 'Yes.' 'How did you learn?' 'Isaias taught me. When the creek ran high.' 'I can't,' said Manuela, 'but I will go where the ocean touches my feet.'

Alin came in the morning. Isabel watched her cousin's face closely when he greeted her, but her expression revealed nothing. They took a bus to an empty stop, where they changed for a second bus bound for the coast. The traffic was light. After an hour, they passed an immense garbage dump, where carrion birds quivered in the sky and a row of shanties crested the hill like a coxcomb. Lone figures picked their way over the hillside, and children played.

The road was wide and wound through low hills. After another hour, the city ended and the plateau opened onto a view of the sea, the water vast and silver. Steep green forests draped the slopes. Manuela took Isabel's hand.

At the terminal, they boarded a bus with a sandy wooden floor. The shore was crowded with umbrellas. Alin led them to a cluster of seaside vendors, where they shared juice from a fresh coconut and scooped out slivers of soft meat with fragments of the husk. He bought them cubes of white cheese grilled on ceramic braziers, and skewers of dried shrimp. Oiled bodies glided along a mosaic promenade. 'Maybe we will see a movie star,' said Manuela as she tried to feed bits of cheese to the baby.

Isabel didn't have a swimsuit, so she folded up the cuffs of her pants and knotted the hem of her shirt. Alin took her down the beach, and they walked out into the water. Her stomach tightened with the cold spray. She rolled her shirtsleeves over her shoulders. Her arms were warm with the sun—it seemed as if she could feel every drop of spray that landed on them. The waves came and they dove. She felt herself tumbled by the swirling water, spinning, a weightless feeling of plummeting down.

Then they were out again, shouting as the wave retreated,

dragging at their ankles. She fell and came up laughing. Joyfully, she shook her hair and tasted the water as it dripped down her face. As they ran back toward the shore, Alin stumbled and his hand brushed hers. She held it, briefly. On shore, she took Manuela to the water's edge and laughed as her cousin held Hugo high above her and backed away distrustfully.

They lay in the sand. She felt sun-drunk and sleepy. The salt tickled her legs. Her eyes were warm. She could hear the waves crashing, laughter, and when she moved, she heard the sand squeak beneath her. She felt the heat dry her shirt.

In the shallows, children did backflips and somersaults and chased the shorebirds. Teenagers slouched and brooded behind dark glasses. The sand crawled with vendors extolling the pleasure of sugarcane juice and the most wonderful shrimp in the world. They sold sun oils and peroxide and pulled cold beers from styrofoam boxes slung from their shoulders. The tide rose, and she breathed in the salt water as it blew off the waves. She heard music in the distance. Manuela sat beside her with the baby between her legs and batted his hand as he tried to eat the sand.

Beside her, she sensed Alin sit up. 'Isabel,' he said.

'Yes?'

'Can I ask you something?'

'What?'

'I am going to the north to visit my family, to see my brother.'

'Yes?' she said, suspiciously. 'You are coming back, then?'

'Yes, yes, I'm coming back. But I was going to ask you. I was wondering if I should go to Saint Michael. It's not far, you know. A day by bus. To meet your parents.'

'I don't understand,' she said.

'I know you're only fourteen, and things are different in the city, so we would wait a couple of years. But my work is going well—maybe I can even open a store sooner than I thought. I was thinking, you could help me—we would be a good arrangement together. Like a team. You could go to school when I work and I could go to school when you work. That way both of us—'

She stood quickly and ran down to the water. She waded out to where it reached her waist. She stood there for a long time. She felt as if she could see herself from a distance, an unfamiliar girl against the backdrop of the sea. She heard her name, although she knew that the sound of the waves was enough to silence even the music blasting from the beach. She turned and stared out at the promenade. She closed her eyes, certain this time. She would open them and he would be there.

She looked at Manuela on the beach, the baby playing at her feet. She closed her eyes again. This time, she thought, he will be there, sitting with them.

She turned back to the sea. I will give him one more chance. One more. I will turn, and he will be here behind me, in the water. She felt a wet hand on her shoulder. 'Isabel,' said Alin. 'I was only thinking aloud. I shouldn't have said it. Back home, it worked that way, but here . . . It was the sun and the sea making me talk.'

Another wave broke over her knees. 'Please, Isabel,' he said. 'Please forget I said it. I don't want to ruin this day. It's such a good day.'

Back on the shore, she pressed her face into a wet towel and closed her eyes. She took Hugo and sat him in her lap, and Alin came and sat by her. She felt the sun warming her slowly.

Alin took them to a seaside bar, with plastic tables set out in the sand and walls covered with curling bikini posters. A stereo played loud music, and he invited Isabel to dance. She shook her head, embarrassed, but he persisted. They were barefoot. His back was warm and sandy. Later he asked Manuela. Her cousin danced well, Isabel thought, wondering where she learned.

At last Alin said he was tired. Manuela's cheeks were flushed. She laughed, 'No, please, it's wonderful!' She pulled Isabel from her chair and spun her away as the song began. Isabel felt the strength in her cousin's back, her heavy breasts, her warm belly, the muscles of her arms. Rough calluses covered her hands. It's still a sugar turner's body, Isabel thought.

The song stopped, but Manuela pulled her closer. Another began. She pressed her cheek into Isabel's hair and spun faster. Isabel held on, watching the shore spin past, then the shack and the tables and the sky, Alin staring into the sea, the baby reaching for his ear and Alin laughing, the shore and the shack and the tables and the sky. She felt her cheek was wet. 'Manuela,' she said. 'Please,' her cousin whispered, nuzzling into her hair. 'Please keep dancing.'

When the song finished, they took dizzy, weaving steps back to the table. Isabel slumped into a chair and wiped her cheeks. She didn't know whose tears they were.

A sea squall swept up the beach. Sunbathers rushed for shelter, crowding the bar with prickled, shivering bodies. The sky streaked with rain, they could barely discern the breakers. She found herself next to a taller girl with hoop earrings and a chatelaine on her ankle, who flirted with a tan, handsome boy in expensive sunglasses. They didn't seem to notice her, but the intimacy of their bare skin made Isabel feel as if she were with them. She laughed as he teased and tickled the girl. The sea squall retreated.

They made their way back to the bus station, where the next bus was scheduled in an hour. Alin led them to a canteen with a long glass counter filled with chicken croquettes and pastries with braided crusts. Three men sat at the counter. The display was warm, and Manuela rested Hugo on the top of the glass. He slept. Alin ordered them sweet coffee. The bartender dipped the rim of the cups in boiling water and filled them from a plain samovar. On the walls were beer posters. Prices were pegged to a black tag board with little plastic numbers.

Isabel watched the bartender stop by the men at the counter.

He lit a cigarette. 'I heard a good one today.'

He paused and leaned forward on the bar.

'Goes like this: A German, a Frenchman and a backlander are arguing about a photograph of Adam and Eve in Eden. The German says, It's obvious, Adam and Eve were German. Just look at him, with his strong jaw and his manly muscles. Not at all, said the Frenchman. They were French—look at her with her beautiful lips and her long, flowing hair. You are both wrong, said the backlander. They were from the backlands. They have no clothes, they are surrounded by snakes and they have nothing but an apple to eat. And still they think they are in Paradise.'

The men laughed. 'I've heard that one before,' said one of the men, 'except it was about a kid in the Settlements.' 'Who the hell in the Settlements thinks they are in Paradise?'

asked the bartender. 'You're right,' said the man. 'It's definitely better the way you told it.'

'You should have added that God sent them away,' said Manuela, beside them. 'Kicked them out and sent them walking down a long road. You should have added that, too.'

On the ride back, Isabel sat with Alin. 'You're sunburned,' he said, touching her cheek. Her face felt warm and tight. 'I can't be burned. I'm always in the sun.' 'You *used* to be in the sun,' he corrected. The skin on her arm was rose-brown, and it blanched when he pressed it with his thumb.

They passed the garbage dump again. 'Poor souls,' said Manuela.

Alin said, 'I once knew a man who worked on the mountain. That's what he called it. He would say, "I am going up the mountain," or "I found a good sheet of metal on the mountain." It's much more complicated than it looks, you know. It looks like people crawling randomly, like ants on an anthill, but really it's organized. There are glass scavengers and plastic scavengers and cardboard scavengers, and then there are those who are allowed to scavenge only things the others left behind.' He paused. '*Things without use.* That's what he said. People offered him help, and he always said no. He was the proudest person in the world. Once he said, "Every other man has something good to start with, the fisherman with the sea, the carpenter with his piece of wood, even a poet with his collection of pretty words. But I build houses with rubble, I eat food others think is foul, I find beauty in waste and uses for useless things." He said it like that, elegant like that. He said, "This is a holy place."'

The dump was long behind them when Alin finished. Manuela didn't answer, but held the baby close. Isabel felt strangely cold.

The bus took an off-ramp. 'This is my stop,' Alin said. He lowered his voice. 'Isabel, I'm sorry about what I said. I hope I can visit you again.' 'Yes,' she said. 'I want that . . .' She let the word drift. Ahead she could see a crowded pavilion.

'In Saint Michael,' she said suddenly, 'when the situation was against us, we gathered. People ate things most people don't think can be eaten. Like cacti, tree roots, ants. Things that other people don't have any use for. I did that once, too.'

He said nothing and descended without kissing her. Her eyes followed him until the bus pulled away.

That night, she dreamed she was in Saint Michael. The sun was very warm, the air smelled oddly of salt water. As she walked down the road, she felt another presence. She knew it was Isaias before she turned. He said nothing but let his hand rest on her shoulder, like a blind person being led, although somehow he was the one who was leading. They walked together for a long time. Finally she said, I am very tired, and he took her off the road to a field that was too green for Saint Michael, with little clumps of people sitting, scattered far into the distance.

Together they lay on the grass. She rested her head on his chest, as she used to do when she was little. His heartbeat was slow and strong. She could smell him—not the smell of backlands dust that she remembered but the simple smell of warmth, and in the dream she cried and felt his shirt grow wet. She heard music and he began to sing, comforting her with an unfamiliar song of words that had no meaning.

When she awoke, she rose quietly and went outside. The

hill was silent. The drunks slept, the night dogs slept, the birds were still in their cages, there were no airplanes and no wind.

She had dreamed of him many times since she arrived, but this time there were no clues to follow, only the comfort of his presence. But it isn't him, she told herself, it isn't the same. It is what her cousin would say, she thought, and for the first time she felt herself believing it, that *dreams are just dreams, just the day passing through.* She sensed suddenly that the convictions that had sustained her since Isaias left were no longer true: that being comforted in a dream wasn't the same as being comforted, that it didn't *count;* that talking to him when she was awake was different than dream-talking; that if he said something in a dream, he said it only in the dream and would not know it in his waking life; that if she held his hand, it was only a dream-hand; that if he sang to her in a dream, it was only her imagination and not him singing.

The city was silent while she had these thoughts and cried quietly, and then in the distance she heard footsteps. Then shouting, then the dogs started to howl, the birds stirred, the wind whipped up the road. A night bus switched gears and growled away, casting a light into the streets, a strange light that obeyed none of the rules of source and shadow.

She waited. After a long time, she went back to the room where Manuela still slept, and the baby was quiet.

As she tried to sleep, she thought, So this is what absence means. I never thought it was something that came so quietly. That you only really notice it later, when you go to look for someone and he isn't there.

Back when he left home, she had known he would return, so goodbyes were unnecessary. He would have told her this, he would have called them frivolous, *empty*. It was a word that appeared often in his songs. Just worries, he would say, just empty worries. Now she thought again of the word, but in a different way, like an empty place, this second meaning suddenly haunting the first. She wondered why she felt this now, if it had been the dream of him in that large field, with its strange quality of light and its distant people. Or just the day, the beautiful day without him.

Empty, she later thought, *empty,* not as a quality, but as a movement, *to empty,* to abandon, to go. To go away.

She called home.

'There is good news,' said her mother. 'There's rain. Can you believe? It's October and there's already rain. And not just once, but every day. Even if it doesn't come again, it doesn't matter—the stream is running, the cane will bloom.

'Isabel?' she said.

'Yes.'

'Isa, is something wrong?'

On the other end of the phone, she shook her head.

'Isabel. You haven't heard anything from him, have you?'

'No,' she managed.

'He will come back. I promise, Isa. With rain like this, he has to come back.'

Isabel tried to answer, but she couldn't. In her mother's voice, she heard the steadiness that she had come to know from times her mother was afraid. A way of speaking that reminded her of walking and trying not to fall.

'Isabel, are you there?'

'Yes—yes, I'm still here.'

'You sound so sad.'

The words caught in her throat. She waited for her mother to say she could come home, and she didn't know how she would answer. But her mother didn't say this.

'Isabel, I can't hear you.'

'I'm all right,' she said. 'I am happy. It will be a good year.'

She returned with Hugo to the park. This time she sat on the corner of a bench and watched the pond. The water rippled with feeding catfish, and then a light rain. The air was humid and heavy. The trees bloomed with tiny flowers that looked as if they had been painted with a brush that was running out of paint.

She bought a sweet cake of cornmeal and crumbled the softest pieces for Hugo. She mixed formula with water from a drinking fountain. They played together. She held his ankles and swung him upside down so his head brushed very lightly against the grass, and then put his feet on hers and held his hands, walking him in big, awkward steps. On a palm, a single frond began shimmering in the wind. It danced and swiveled on its stem. The other leaves were still.

She lay in the grass and watched a wasps' nest on the trunk of a bare tree. In Saint Michael, when it rained and the white forest bloomed, they were visited by plagues of thin black wasps. They appeared as if from nowhere, gathering in a single spot, first one fly, then others, growing swiftly into a violet-black ball of wings and oily abdomens, swelling to the size of a head, trembling, humming, dripping insects. From a distance, it looked like a decoration for a festival, or a stain.

The mass of wasps would grow like this until they flew

away, or until the weight of their bodies became too much for the single wasp that held them. Then the ball would break from its mooring and crash in a soft thump that strewed the insects over the ground in confusion, wandering in stunned circles until they beat their wings at the air and buzzed away.

Once, she was playing with Isaias in the sun-washed yard behind her aunt's house. She was chasing him in circles when suddenly he turned and swept her up. She hadn't seen the ball of wasps break loose and fall, the insects scattering like stirring pebbles. His feet were bare, so they waited. She began to laugh. 'Stop,' he said. 'Stop, you will make them angry.' She buried her face into his shoulder, waiting until he tiptoed her away.

When she thought of him now, she realized she couldn't remember his entire face, only fragments of it. He is ceasing to be, she thought, but then later she wondered: Maybe I am getting closer, to that place where a person breaks into pieces—a walk, a laugh, a smell, the strength in an arm. Isaias used to say this when they told stories of grandparents or aunts who were gone. Think, he said, of people you know, You don't know their faces, You know bits of them, their movement, their voice, The closer you are, the more broken they become.

She slept on the lawn, still moist from the light rain. She rested the baby on her chest, and awoke to find that he had slipped out of her arms and was pulling at a clump of grass and murmuring. In the late afternoon, she stopped by a crowd that had gathered around a magician. He had a boa constrictor and a corduroy sack, and bragged about the power of his spells. He said he was from the north, where such magic was common, and claimed the snake was a feared snake from the backlands. He talked about his hard life cutting cane, but he knew nothing about cane, or snakes, and she left.

She thought, October and there is already rain. The soil would be moist and warm, the green plants spilling their perfume into the air. Without her, her mother and father and aunts and uncles would be moving back into the hills in defiance, watching the road for approaching cars. They would stay away from the open slopes. They would find spaces to plant between the rocks, in the crevices that no one knew. If there was rain, all they needed was a tiny piece of earth, and they could grow anything: gourds, yams, heavy pieces of manioc. They were masters of the cracks between the lifeless places.

When dusk fell, Isabel followed the crowds to a bus stop, where passengers milled impatiently. Hugo twisted uneasily on her, beginning to whimper. She tried to stroke his hair and he pushed her hand away. 'It's okay,' she whispered, 'we're going home.'

'Has the 47 come yet?' she asked an old man, remembering the walk with Alin. 'The 47?' said the man. 'Where are you going?' 'New Eden—it's in the Settlements.' 'Take the 35 to Cathedral Square and go from there,' said the man.

They waited. The shadows on the ground lengthened, and more people gathered. The air was thick with the promise of more rain. She listened to a conversation behind her about Saint Jude. 'You don't know how many miracles he has performed,' said a woman. 'That's why he is saint of impossible causes. Cured my aunt of tuberculosis, found my son a job at the supermarkets, guided the surgeon's hand when he took out the tumor from my cousin and gave her twins the next year.'

It was Saint Jude's Day, Isabel remembered; he was revered in New Eden. She found DON'T GIVE UP HOPE! prayer cards of him taped to the walls or curled in the street. She heard neighbors planning visits for months. Even her parents and Isaias prayed to him in Saint Michael, but Isaias never told her why.

Still the bus didn't come. Isabel shifted Hugo on her hip, which had grown moist where she held him. He looked pale, and he sniffled. When she brushed the back of her fingers to his forehead, he arched away.

In the street, a little boy stood on the shoulders of two other boys and juggled before the rank of idling cars. The cement vibrated with the engines' rumbling. A motorcycle pulled up between the cars and then roared past the children. At last the boy dropped to the pavement with a light slap of his feet and took a bow. Isabel found herself clapping. The boys were joined by a little girl. They walked between the cars with their palms out. The traffic light changed and the children dashed onto the sidewalk.

The light turned red again. Cars pulled up at the crosswalk. Isabel could see the drivers' eyes shifting as they rolled up their windows and locked their doors.

Again the little boy climbed onto the others' shoulders. Before the grille of a massive truck, he wobbled, the movement of his juggling mesmeric. His hands seemed to brush the balls into their slow arc and fall. The girl stood between them. She wore a dirty, threadbare dress with an unraveling hem. She reminded Isabel of herself when she was young.

The two boys crouched and transferred the third to the

little girl's shoulders. She staggered and then began to turn slowly, the boy still juggling. She put out her arms.

In the car next to the truck, a teenager in the passenger seat reached over and honked the horn. The little juggler startled. The ball fell, bouncing at the girl's feet and rolling under the front wheel of the truck. The boy jumped down from her shoulders, the four took bows. They ran swiftly between the cars, begging. No windows came down. Ahead, Isabel could see the facing light turn to yellow. She wanted to shout to get the children out of the street. She saw the girl run and crouch beneath the wheel as the light turned green.

The truck lurched into gear. The girl leaped gracefully to the shadeless dry earth of the traffic island, the ball in her hand, triumphant.

The 35 didn't come. It grew darker. Her arm began to ache, and she repositioned Hugo on her waist. She asked a woman beside her about the 35. The woman frowned. 'I don't know. I think you actually have to take the microbus.' A man corrected her, 'You take two microbuses, one to Cathedral Square, and then another to the Settlements.' 'Two microbuses?' 'Actually, you take a normal bus from here, and then at Cathedral Square you get a microbus.' 'But I didn't think there are night micros.' 'There are,' said the man. Isabel said, 'I'm confused—is there anything direct from here?' 'No, go to the Center first. Maybe there is something that goes direct, but I don't know it.'

When they left, a boy took her elbow. 'None of them know what they are talking about. I used to live in the Settlements. You were right the first time. It's the 35. It comes every hour.'

She waited. As the buses approached, she stared at the placards with their litanies of destinations, the terminals she was always moving toward but never reaching, the mythological places at the distant ends of bus lines. At last a bus came, with the 3 painted on one window and 5 on the other. Isabel hoisted Hugo and pushed through the crowd. She asked the toll collector if it went to the Settlements, and he waved her through. A man gave her his seat at the back of the bus. She jigsawed around a pair of knees and sat. The bus joined a roundabout and followed an on-ramp to a highway. The traffic was heavy but moved swiftly. They were heading south. She shrugged; maybe they went south and *then* north, but her suspicion persisted. The traffic lightened and the bus picked up speed. She looked about. She wondered if anyone else was confused by the route. Hanging from the handrails, the passengers knocked and jostled against one another like bones on a wind chime.

The air grew heavier, sweet with rotting smells, the dusk blurry and saturated with a light that distinguished little between the city and sky. It was neither hot nor cold, just wet, and when she breathed she felt she was breathing in the street itself. Large raindrops splattered against the window. They gave a sudden, momentary warning, *pat-pat,* the sound so clear that they seemed like words themselves. She found herself mouthing them, *pa-pa,* and then the air exploded, the drops shattering against the glass. Outside, the rain shook the pebbles in the road, turned up mud in the barren spaces at the intersections, clipped leaves from the trees, *ting*ed against the skeletons of abandoned market stands and whipped the telephone lines. The brown puddles frothed and stained the walls. She held Hugo closer.

The bus sped up, sweeping around a taxi, and briefly—or so

it felt—losing traction on the wet road. It dashed into the turned-up spray between two rigs. One of the rigs lurched sideways, and Isabel gripped Hugo as it swung away. The driver must have seen them in the cloud, although she didn't know how—the cab was distant and vague.

They came off the highway; the traffic slowed at a light. The air stank of rot, of wet plaster and mold, dark and gray, like something sweet at the edge of turning.

She heard the slapping of sandals. A young man ran in the narrow passageway between the cars. He held a newspaper over his head, its wet pages cleaving to his neck. He wore shorts torn from blue jeans. Mud streaked his calves. His back was thin and muscular and his shirt was so worn that she could see the texture of a raised scar on his shoulder blade. *Not Isaias,* she thought: the reflex was still there, it still surfaced with every thin boy with a hidden face. She saw him disappear behind a truck. She searched for him as it passed and saw a girl pulling a child by the hand join the young man on the muddy divide. He swept the child up without stopping. The three leaped the barrier and crossed the street as the traffic bore down and the rain fell harder.

Again they picked up speed. Hugo grimaced. 'I know,' said Isabel. 'Be good. We'll be home soon.' She looked outside. They were riding a concrete tongue that wrapped through buildings she had never seen. Through the rain, Isabel could see the reflection of the bus in skyscrapers that rose on its flank. She turned to a woman sitting beside her, an older woman with tan-gray curls and a shopping bag on her lap. 'Excuse me, madam. Does the bus go to the Settlements?' 'I don't think so,' said the woman, turning to the man beside her. 'Does this bus go to the Settlements?' The man shook his head. 'The Settlements, no, that's in the other direction. Who told you this went to the Settlements?' 'Someone at the bus stop. I better get off, then. I thought this was the 35. The window . . .' 'Oh, that's old. You have to read the side,' said the man.

The bus swayed. Isabel closed her eyes and opened them again. 'You okay?' asked the woman. 'Yes—no, I need to get home—the baby . . .' She looked down at Hugo, who had begun to squirm. He would start crying now, she knew. 'Why don't you go ask the toll collector?' said the man. 'Up at the front?' 'Yes, good idea,' said the lady. 'I'll watch the baby.' 'I don't know. I asked him already . . .' but she had convinced herself he was listening. 'You don't mind?' 'No, I have kids. I miss them. I'll watch him.' The woman smiled kindly. Isabel nodded. 'Hugo, love, I have to go ask the man a question. You stay with this lady.' The baby clung to her, and she peeled him off, gently at first, but when he resisted, roughly. He started to scream. 'Stop it,' she said. 'Behave. I'll be right back.' He's just hungry,' she said to the woman. She fumbled with his bottle. 'Just give him this and he'll be quiet.' 'You better hurry,' said the man. 'He stops up there, it may be where you want to change.'

Outside, through the rain, she could see tall apartments. The sidewalks were full of people. The toll collector had left his seat and was talking to the driver. Isabel slipped sideways through the grate. 'I need to get to the Settlements,' she said.

The boy wore a black T-shirt with cutoff sleeves. 'You will have to change at least three times,' he answered. 'There isn't anything that goes direct?' '*Direct?* No. Take the 23 back to the park, go from there and vote for a new mayor, this bus is going south. But you need to move. Look how many people need to get on. It's Saint Jude's Day, and everyone wants to make a promise.'

He pointed toward a large crowd outside a church. The bus had slowed to a stop. She tried to push her way back, but the toll collector took her arm. 'Let those people off.' She protested, 'I need to get the baby.' 'I know, but you can't do it like this—these people need to get off. Do you think the whole city should wait for you? Let them out. I'll let you back on and you can get him.' She was pushed down the stairs. She tried to stay by the entrance, but the crowd shoved her back. Panicking, she ran toward the rear exit of the bus, where other passengers were descending. She fought her way through and pulled herself onto the bus. 'Hugo,' she said. The bus was half empty, filling with new passengers. She saw immediately that the woman's seat was empty. '*My God.*' She spun. She dropped to her knees and searched under the seats. She elbowed her way back to the toll collector. 'The baby—did you see my baby?' He shook his head. 'I told you to wait by the entrance.' 'He's missing.' 'He's not missing. A baby doesn't just vanish.' 'He is, he—' 'We have to go. Is he on the bus?' She stared at the seats again. 'No.' 'Then you better get off.' She raced down into the street, turned, shouting. The bus was full, the doors started to close. She circled it, dragging her hand on its wet siding as it swung forward, beating her fists against its side as it pulled away. She ran up the street. Through the rain, she saw a woman carrying a baby beneath an umbrella. She tugged the umbrella to the side, but it wasn't Hugo. Another woman with a baby, another umbrella. She grabbed for it with both hands. The woman moved away, her eyes wide with horror. Suddenly it seemed as if the street was filled with women and babies and umbrellas marching toward her like a nightmarish parade. She ran into the street. Cars honked, tires screeching. She stumbled again, ran her hands through her wet hair. She sensed the crowd make a cautious space around her. *Hugo,* she whispered, her voice failing. Her dress clung to her thighs but she did nothing to straighten it. She clenched her fists and pushed them against her forehead. She spun again, watching the umbrellas bloom and break around her.

She saw a street fair, a church, a crowd gathered and spilling into the road. She cursed at them. She wanted them to disappear, she wanted a great flood or wind to sweep the street clean of all the people. She ran along the sidewalk, frantically looking under the umbrellas, but she knew it was too late. 'No,' she said aloud. More umbrellas, more bundles of blankets streaming toward her. She stumbled and heard a voice behind her.

'We thought we lost you,' said the woman from the bus, handing her Hugo, smiling and disappearing into the crowd.

Isabel sought shelter beneath an awning, where for a long time she held the baby against her chest and didn't move. Then impulsively she lifted him, pressed her nose into his hair, his cheeks, his belly. She opened his blanket and smelled him and squeezed him against her again. He seemed, impossibly, to be sleeping, and he sighed and settled into his old place against her shoulder.

Gradually, the sounds of the street returned. The rain had relented. She looked out at the church. I must thank Saint Jude, she told herself.

She moved slowly, shaking, afraid she would fall.

It took her a long time to make it through the crowd. The church was massive, a complex of dozens of buildings without order. She found her way to the brightly lit blessing room, where she lifted Hugo to catch the sprinkling of holy water.

She put out her tongue when the drops touched her face. The room was packed. Behind her was a wide table where people left broken icons they couldn't bear to throw away. For a long time, she watched them: an armless Christ; an Our Lady of the Good Birth with a cape of torn crepe; a legless Saint Anthony like a ghost flying away in his robe; a Saint Lucy with a single marble eye on her plate; a Saint Rafael without wings; a Saint John the Baptist with a chipped coat of hairs.

'You can take one.' A woman in a worn wool sweater stroked Isabel's arm. Her skin was gray; her glasses magnified eyes filled with milky cataracts. She had a limp rose pinned to her sweater. She wrapped her fingers in Isabel's. Around her, other women cradled the saints gently in their hands. They were murmuring, 'Look at you, my little saint, you are beautiful. You aren't broken, my saint—how can someone be giving you away? I will help you stand, my little saint. I can take care of you, you are only missing a hand, a foot, a staff—the world is cruel, my love, to throw away a saint that's broken.'

Isabel turned from the table and closed her eyes. She untangled her fingers from the woman's and pushed her way outside. In the street, a line wrapped the city block before disappearing inside the church. She walked its length, past young girls with babies, old men and women supported by their children. Reeling, she accosted a woman with a palsied child in a plywood wheelchair, strapped with a pair of seat belts across his chest and legs. She grabbed her arm and said, 'Please, tell me: How many years have you been praying to Saint Jude?' 'Why, since the boy was born, seven years ago,' the woman answered. 'But this year I came to pay a promise, because Saint Jude cured him.' The boy was the size of an infant, his mouth was open, his hands were twisted over a

blanket. 'No!' shouted Isabel. 'He isn't cured! He is still sick!'
Stumbling, she turned and pushed her way into the chapel,
where she crouched at the feet of the saints in their naves.
She ran her hands through the piles of invocation cards and
scattered notes with handwritten prayers and promises. She
pulled out a note with a stapled photograph of a woman and
words in a child's pen. She put it down and reached in again,
again she pulled out a folded note, opened it and read, *Please,
Our Lady, Please watch over my son,* and then another, *Please make
my mother better,* and then in pencil on a little card, *Watch over
me, I am alone,* and then *Find him for me, Please find him for me—*
a young girl's handwriting, with a photograph stapled to a
lined piece of notebook paper: *Please find him for me Saint Jude
Thaddeus, he's lost and he can't be found.* She rose and cut the line
to pray to Saint Jude, pressing Hugo against the wall beneath
his icon, where a soft depression was worn into the marble.
She wondered, How many babies will it take before we break
through the wall? and a guard said, 'Young lady, you need to
move on.'

A woman took her arm and led her away. 'There are so
many people who want to pray,' said the woman. 'There are
too many people. The most desperate people come to the city
and the most desperate people in the city come to pray to
Saint Jude.' She caressed Isabel's hand. 'Why are you here?'
she asked. I took the wrong bus, Isabel thought, but she said,
'At home there is a drought.' 'Was,' said the woman. 'Not
anymore. You should be grateful. All over the backlands,
there is rain.'

The woman left her in the street.

A procession began, and she joined, falling in behind three
hooded members of a brotherhood. Saint Jude wobbled on

the back of a pickup. The crowds passed the flashing lights of bingo parlors, alcohol rehabilitation centers, evangelical churches, apartments filled with distant faces. They walked through rich neighborhoods, with high walls and electric fences. They sang hymns to Saint Jude and recited Hail Marys. They carried lit candles in the cut halves of bottles. The rims of the bottles puckered; the air smelled of incense and melting plastic. At times they merged onto larger roads, sharing them with buses that lumbered toward the shrouded light of downtown.

She felt carried along by the procession, which had swollen to impossible numbers, filling the road and overflowing into the side streets. As they walked, a vertigo seized her and the singing seemed to get louder until it filled her ears like a siren screeching. She wanted to go back and take a bus home, but each time she stopped the vertigo worsened, so she kept walking. What is this noise? she wondered, grimacing, putting her free hand to her ear. They turned up a long street, and she stared around her into the sea of bobbing candles. Is anyone else hearing this? She walked faster, and then suddenly it was quiet.

It was then that she saw Isaias. He was far ahead, where the procession climbed a soft rise in the road. She recognized his silhouette first, then the sway in his step. Frantically, she tried to push her way to him, but the procession had stopped, the truck carrying Saint Jude had stalled. 'Patience,' came the whispers, 'Don't push, Soon we will be moving again, we all will get there soon.' She called out, but another hymn had begun. Ahead the truck started again, the crowd surged, her brother disappeared behind the high cinder-block walls of a corner house. 'No!' she cried aloud, trying to push her way through the crowd. 'Stop!' She shoved between a couple holding hands. 'Let me through!' she said. 'I will lose him again!' She was blocked by a wall of shoulders. She tugged at their arms. 'Let me through! I will lose him!' A woman with a candle in her bare fist turned: 'You won't lose him. Your time will come. He can't go anywhere, he's only plaster.'

She rounded the corner. This time she saw Isaias walking at the edge of the crowd, singing. When he lifted his head, she saw he was thin, with dark sunken spaces around his eyes. She tried to shout again, but his name fell as a whisper. He walked on. He shouldn't be thin like that, she thought, and for a long time it was the only thought she had.

So she followed. Or, she let herself be carried along with him, and when at last the statue of Saint Jude returned to the altar, she watched Isaias cross himself, descend the steps of the church and head up the long road, his body red in the brake lights of the inching traffic. She waited. A siren wailed, a little boy pushed past her, an old woman limped up the steps. She expected a sign to tell her to follow: a light, a ripple in the air, a wind, a keening. None came. The red lights inched forward. Crossing herself, she descended.

On the steps, the wind ruffled piles of invocation cards, matted together like wet leaves.

The crowd fell away quickly. At the threshold of a dark stretch of broken lamps, she told herself to go back. 'It isn't him,' she said aloud. 'It's my mind, I'm imagining like I imagined I was following him before.' She pinched her hand and inhaled Hugo's faint scent of soap and talcum. She felt her arm burn with his weight. She thought of calling to Isaias, but the words eluded her. They passed an open canteen, where two old men played an accordion and a triangle. She breathed in the sudden warmth and heard a fragment of a melody. Then the street was cold again. There was a light mist, but she knew it wouldn't rain.

Isaias turned down an empty side street. She followed. She wanted to run to him, but something in his walk told her to wait until she understood what had happened and why he was there. So she remained a block behind and in the shadows. After a long time, she looked back. The lights of the church lit a distant halo in the mist. It seemed very small and very far away.

In her arms, Hugo cried.

Isaias stopped. Behind him, she waited. He didn't turn. Then he walked on.

She knew then that he knew she was following. No one from the backlands would allow themselves to be followed by a stranger.

After many blocks, she sensed him slowing. She walked closer until finally she was at his side. She waited for him to say something, fighting the need to touch him, to jump on him, to push him, to grab his hand. She wrapped her arms tighter around the baby. Once or twice, Isaias turned to her, but when she looked up at him, he turned away. So they walked in silence, like they had walked in silence before.

She ceased to be tired. The pain in her feet disappeared. The baby grew light, floating on her like a scrap of warmth.

Now, as she waited for an explanation, her mind wandered. She found herself remembering the first retreat, the darkness of the shelters, the charqui and the yellow dog. She felt the soft wind of the collapsing tents and heard the rain on the fallen canvas. She remembered, for the first time in her life, the trip home, the tired people waiting for a car and then setting out on the trail. She remembered clinging to her mother, and then, farther down the road, her father, then being passed from hand to hand until she reached her brother, where she became weightless and slept. She remembered this perfectly, the smell, the taste of dust and sweat on his shirt, his hand around her back, the trembling in his arm as the road stretched on.

It was then, in the midst of these memories, that the explanation came and once it came, she felt as if she had always known. By then the street seemed to have disappeared. There were no blackened lights, no shuttered houses with their barbed wire. It was like being in the cane when the cane was only emptiness: there was only a source and something that pulled her toward it. A gravity, she thought, she would spend the rest of her life trying to explain this, and the words would never be there. Just as he could never say: There is no music, there is no band, there is no beautiful girl in the square. There are no bars by the sea. There are no restaurants, no compliments from men who say that I have true talent. Those are words that I invented. In the world I must live in, I am just like everyone else, caught in the movement of those who have nothing. It has been this way since the beginning, since the day I saw you coming up the hill, since I saw you waving your flag in that valley of towers, when the streets were full but there was no one else there but you. I saw you looking for me, I saw you stop and break the crowds and drive the whole city to a halt, stop the flows of people through its streets, stop the fleets of perches hurtling south, stop the retreat of the clouds and send them swarming back into the backlands. I came to your door, but I did not have the courage to go in.

Is there any other answer? Any other explanation than my awe of you: a slope of cursive in a church register, a crackling of twigs beside me, a silent companion who cast me into the world by your belief that I was anything other than what I really am, a cane cutter like my father, wrapped in the same rags as the other cane cutters, beating the same burnt and crumbling path through an endless field that belongs to someone else. That you are the single person in the world who makes me more than what everyone else sees: that you created me, that in your mind lives the person I wish to be.

He could not say: There is no fiddle, I tried for a month and then I pawned it and sent the money home. The rest was a lie. That's all.

She could see the end of the road, where there was a bridge and the glint of train rails. She followed him down a crumbling stairwell, to the edge of the track, dark and littered with broken glass.

They walked for a long time along the rails. Then he entered a narrow alley that curled through the planked walls of a shantytown. He led her over a low rise, and they entered a field. There was a highway, empty save a rare car that appeared and disappeared like a fleeting thought.

He descended a short slope to a culvert and a corrugated drainage tunnel beneath the highway. She stayed back and watched him disappear inside. When he emerged, he was carrying something in his arms. He handed it to her. There was a blanket, a plastic bottle of water and an orange. She mixed the water with the little bit of formula that remained from the long day that had begun watching the egrets' veils and thinking of wasps. She wrapped the blanket around herself and the baby.

There was a wide stone on the bank. They crouched together and stared into the darkness. She peeled the orange with her teeth and split it in two. She offered it to him, but he shook his head.

Perhaps she slept, because dawn came soon. He rose. Still wearing the blanket, she followed him up the bank and to the edge of the road. The verge was narrow, and she walked behind him. He was a dark spot against the sun, and it hurt her eyes to look there.

In the distance, she could see the rise of the hill, the vultures circling in the air. Cars passed, the drivers leaning on their horns, but she didn't care. Her brother left the road and descended the embankment, hopped the thin stream that ran through the culvert and took long steps toward a cluster of ramshackle houses. It was then that she was aware of the other figures marching behind her on the highway, emerging from the shantics and climbing the slope toward the dump.

They came from all directions. They crossed the road and followed her down the shoulder, passing as she slowed. They walked in groups or they came alone. They were women and men of all ages and children who chased one another down the slope. They pulled carts and dragged burlap sacks behind them.

At the gate, she paused. He was already halfway up the hill, winding up a long and narrow path. She wanted to go on, but she couldn't. She remembered the story of the scavengers, who made beauty from things that others had discarded. She felt then that she was standing at the edge of a sacred place, like the silent shade of a cathedral or an offering in the middle of a backlands road. So she stopped, and watched the shadows of the people rise up the mountain. She remained below, stroking the baby's hair, and she waited for her brother to come down.

Theresa

Summer came and then another winter of rain. In Saint Michael, the cane blossomed again. When the harvest was over, her father found a job laying pavement at the edge of Prince Leopold. He spent the week there and came home on the weekends, to see her mother, who refused to leave their village.

In the city, families continued to arrive. The Settlements spread into the forest. Cinder-block houses went up in place of shacks, and a clinic was built on the hill. In the windows of the houses, hanging sheets changed like changing leaves. Manuela constructed a second story and rented it to a migrant family with four children and a brindled dog that came with them on the trip down south.

The evening he came down from the hill, Isaias returned with Isabel to New Eden. They walked in silence on the shoulder of the highway until they reached an empty bus pavilion. He held the baby until the bus came. When they reached the hill, a group of women was gathered in the road. They grew quiet when they saw the two of them coming, and parted to let them pass.

That night, he said, 'I've been working there almost since I arrived. Manuela doesn't know. I came here, to the door, but I couldn't—'

'I know,' she said. 'I know all of it.'

She knew he wouldn't say more. He called the north, but he turned from Isabel as he spoke, and she couldn't hear what he said. Two days later, when Manuela came home, he told her he had been working in a gold mine in the interior.

'There aren't any phones,' said Isabel. 'He sent letters, but they didn't arrive. It's very far.'

They strung a hammock for him to sleep. He began to go down to the highways to wait for pickups trolling for day laborers. Weeks passed without work, and he spoke about returning to the mountain. Then he found a job setting pylons for a bridge, and later as an assistant gardener with the city. He was promoted quickly. He laughed and told Isabel, 'Rich black soil and still these people can't grow anything.' In New Eden, he met a man with a fiddle, and at night, while the man worked as a watchman, he borrowed it and played with an accordionist who lived down the hill.

Elections came, and Isabel's candidate lost. New Eden filled with a victory celebration. Josiane told her about a factory in the East Zone making plush toys for fairground prizes. They sat together for an interview with a foreman who erased her questionnaire and rewrote her age as '18.'

In the mornings, she descended the hill alongside the day maids and the construction workers and the other day-shifters. The buses were full, and the fare collectors packed the aisles as tight as possible. They stood shoulder to shoulder and clung to the handrails. Sometimes the ride took two hours, but she didn't mind. She could watch the people and imagine their lives. She learned that because she was silent, they told her stories she couldn't imagine. In a barren industrial neighborhood she joined a long file that passed through the doors of the factory, punched in, donned a light pink bonnet and a mask with the black letters ISABEL and took up her spot on an assembly line, where she sewed and stuffed and snipped until the lunch bell rang. In the factory cafeteria, she sat with Josiane. Then the bell rang again and she sewed and stuffed and snipped until the end of her shift, punched out and took the bus home. Alin returned from the north. Some evenings she helped him with his work. Her job was to look through a pile of scavenged magazines and cut out images for his portraits. On Saturdays she walked with him to deliver them. On Sundays, after church, Isaias took her to the park. She remembered their old walks, and in those memories she was very young and small.

They left Hugo with the woman who used to watch him. It cost a quarter of a day's wage, so in the spring, Manuela's youngest sister came down from Saint Michael. She was thirteen. Her name was Theresa. When she opened her bag, Isabel could smell the dry earth from the north. The smell remained for a week, and then it was gone. They strung a second hammock next to Isaias, and Isabel explained how everything would be.